Victoria, Dept. of Agriculture

An Australian Colony

the government handbook of Victoria

Victoria, Dept. of Agriculture

An Australian Colony
the government handbook of Victoria

ISBN/EAN: 9783337313494

Printed in Europe, USA, Canada, Australia, Japan

Cover: Foto ©Andreas Hilbeck / pixelio.de

More available books at **www.hansebooks.com**

THE GOVERNMENT HANDBOOK

of

VICTORIA.

By Authority:
ROBT. S. BRAIN, GOVERNMENT PRINTER, MELBOURNE.

1359.

FERNS IN THE FOREST.

PREFACE.

The absence of knowledge by a large number of residents in Great Britain and Ireland of the Geographical Divisions of Australia, and of the Agricultural, Pastoral, and Mineral Resources of Victoria, is made apparent by numerous inquiries.

In order that information respecting the colony may be obtained by those seeking it, this brochure has been prepared.

Victoria, although the smallest of the five colonies of the Continent of Australia, is one of the most prosperous. It has an area of 87,884 square miles, and one of the finest climates in the world. The difference in temperature throughout the year is slight, the average being 49·2° in winter, and 65·3° in summer.

The average rainfall in the colony for a series of years was 26·81 inches. With such a genial climate, open-air work can be carried on throughout the year.

Compared with European countries, Victoria occupies a very favorable position as regards the health of its people, and is entirely free from epidemical disease, from which less favoured countries suffer.

The system of State Education is free, and schools are so situated as to be accessible for children in all parts of the colony. The standard of education is high, and many of our most successful men received their education in State schools.

The value of imports for 1897 was £15,454,482 and exports £16,739,670. Of the area of 87,884 square miles, only 3,242,600 acres are under cultivation, and as most of the area is capable of cultivation, there are possibilities of extending it considerably.

The value of the agricultural products for the past year, which was an unfavorable one, was £5,000,000, and the pastoral products, including butter and cheese, £7,500,000.

The mineral resources of the colony comprise most of the principal metals of economic value. The value of last year's production, principally gold, amounted to £3,500,000.

The present population is 590,755 males, and 580,179 females ; total, 1,170,934. Not counting the population of the metropolis and suburbs, which is 458,610, or any of the large towns and boroughs, it will be seen that the rural population is very limited, and there is ample scope for a considerable addition thereto.

In compiling this Handbook, the aim has been to supply the classes of information which have been found to be in greatest demand on the part of inquirers in the old country, and the result, therefore, is necessarily lacking in the completeness and symmetry that might be considered advisable from a local point of view. Having regard to the requirements of the readers for whom the book is specially intended, the endeavour has been, while presenting a general view of the colony, to deal more in detail with the Agricultural and Mining industries, in which the largest amount of interest is likely to be taken.

The work of editing was intrusted to Mr. T. K. Dow, and I am pleased to acknowledge the able manner in which he has carried out his task. I also recognise the valuable assistance given by officers of several of the Government Departments who have furnished information, also that of the able writers whose names are mentioned in connexion with the extracts.

For the photographs used in some of the illustrations my thanks are due to the proprietors of *The Australasian, The Leader*, and *The Weekly Times*, as well as to the artists connected with these journals.

J. W. TAVERNER,
Minister of Agriculture.

Melbourne, 1st June, 1898.

A MOUNTAIN STREAM.

CONTENTS.

AUSTRALIA.

The island continent of Australia was the last great
division of the world to claim the attention of the navigator
and the explorer. Nothing definite was known of this vast
and important section of the globe until about 300 years
after the discovery of the "New World," and it was not
until Britain had lost her American colonies that she turned
her eyes towards the lands which her brave navigators had
found in the southern seas. A little more than 100 years ago,
viz., in 1788, the first settlement of the continent was made
on the eastern shores ; and to-day Australia, with the adjacent
island of Tasmania, comprises six prosperous self-governing
colonies, whose agricultural and mineral wealth is a potent
factor in the commerce of the world. Situated in the south-
western portion of the Pacific Ocean, Australia lies between
the parallels of 10° 40′ and 39° 11′ of south latitude, and the
meridians of 113° and 153° 16′ east longitude. The length
from north to south is 1,970 miles, the width 2,400 miles, and
the area 2,944,628 square miles. The areas occupied by the
different Australian colonies are as follow :—

Queensland	...	...	668,224 square miles
New South Wales	...	309,175	.. ..
Victoria	...	...	87,884 .. ..
South Australia	...	903,425	.. ..
Western Australia	...	975,920	.. ..
Total—Australia	...	2,944,628	.. ..

AUSTRALIAN FEDERATION.

For many years a desire for federation has been growing
among the people of the Australian colonies. The federal
movement made slow progress at first, but recently
important steps have been taken in rapid succession, and at
present there are hopeful prospects of a speedy consumma-
tion. A Federal Convention, charged with the duty of
framing an Australian Constitution, has recently successfully completed its labours at Melbourne. The Bill has been
well received by prominent men representing all shades of
political opinion, and there are good grounds for expecting
it to be accepted by the people. If anything, however,

should occur to disappoint the present expectation, the result will delay, but not defeat, the formation of the Australian Commonwealth. It must be regarded as saying much for the peoples of these colonies that, without the stimulus of a common danger, they should have so far overcome the provincial spirit, and cherished the wider national sentiment expressed by William Gay in the following lines:—

> " From all division let our land be free,
> For God has made her one: complete she lies
> Within the unbroken circle of the skies,
> And round her indivisible the sea
> Breaks on her single shore: while only we,
> Her foster children, bound with sacred ties
> Of one dear blood, one storied enterprise,
> Are negligent of her integrity.—
> Her seamless garment, at great Mammon's nod,
> With hands unfilial we have basely rent,
> With petty variance our souls are spent,
> And ancient kinship under foot is trod :
> O let us rise, united, penitent,
> And be one people,—mighty, serving God ! "

Mr. Henry Heylyn Hayter, C.M.G., late Government Statist of Victoria, writes thus of the discovery of Australia :—

DISCOVERY OF AUSTRALIA.

From the period of the expedition into India of Alexander the Great (B.C. 330 to 325), allusions to a Great South Land begin to be met with in the contemporary writings, and later on Strabo (B.C. 50), Pliny (A.D. 77), and Ptolemy (A.D. 150) distinctly mention such a land, although the accounts they give of it and its inhabitants are wide of the truth. It seems clear at least that the existence of Australia was known to the Greeks and Romans, although its position and extent remained uncertain long after their times ; and it scarcely admits of a doubt that in the seven or eight centuries during which the Mahomedan power dominated in the Malay Peninsula and Indian Archipelago the northern coasts of Australia were often visited by their navigators, the results of these visits being plainly perceptible both in the persons and languages of the aborigines. The Chinese trepang fishery on the northern shores of Australia dates from very remote times, and traces of Chinese intercourse with the aboriginal inhabitants about Cape York and the Gulf of Carpentaria are said to be yet perceptible in the features of the latter. Marco Polo, the celebrated navigator (A.D. 1293),

NEAR THE SOURCE OF THE YARRA.

makes allusion to the Great South Land, and there is no doubt its existence was known to him, although it is not probable he ever visited its shores. The honour of being the first European to behold the Great South Land has been awarded with some confidence by Sir Robert Rawlinson to a Provencal navigator named Guillanme le Testu, a native of the city of Grasse. The evidence relied upon is furnished by certain French maps and relative documents found in the British Museum and the War Office of Paris, of dates respectively 1542 and 1555, and from these it would appear that the original discovery was made as early as 1531. Three-quarters of a century after this (about the end of 1605) Fernandez de Quiros, a Spanish navigator, started from Lima with three ships to try and discover the Great South Land, and on the 26th April of the following year he sighted land he believed to be the continent of which he was in search, which he named "Tierra Austral del Espiritu Santo." It is generally thought, however, that this was not Australia, but one of the islands of the New Hebrides. His crew shortly afterwards mutinied and would proceed no further, but two of the ships of the expedition, under the command of Torres, continued their course, and passed through the straits dividing Australia from New Guinea. In March, 1606, a few days before this, the Dutch landed on the shores of Australia in a small vessel called the *Dayffken*. She proceeded as far as Cape Turnagain (lat. $13\frac{3}{4}°$ S.), situated in the Gulf of Carpentaria, where some of the crew landed, and several were killed by the aborigines. The statements brought to Holland by the survivors awakened a desire for further information, and an expedition was sent out to found a colony. It is uncertain where the landing was effected, but the territory was soon abandoned in consequence of the hostility of the natives. On their return, the members of the expedition reported that the land was rich with gold, but this was not generally believed. After this, repeated attempts to obtain particulars of the land were made by the Dutch. Dirk Hartog, in 1616, fell in with the north-west coast, and examined it from lat. 19° to lat. 25° S. Jan Edels, in 1619, coasted along the shore as far as 29° S., and gave his name to portion of the present colony of Western Australia. In 1622 the south-western extremity of Australia was discovered by a Dutch ship named the *Leeuwin*; and in the same year Francis Pelsart, in a ship called the *Batavia*, was wrecked on a reef of rocks about 200 miles north of

Swan River. In 1642 Abel Jansen Tasman discovered Van Diemen's Land. now called Tasmania, which for a long time afterwards was believed to be part of the Australian main land. In 1688. and again in 1699, Dampier, a noted English buccaneer, visited and examined a considerable portion of the north-western coast of Australia : Dampier Bay. Roebuck Bay, and the Buccaneer Islands being named by him. Other English and Dutch navigators followed. They seem, however, to have confined their examinations to the western and northern coasts, and it was not until 1770 that the south-eastern and eastern shores were visited, the discoverer of these portions being the celebrated English navigator, Captain Cook. He made the land at that part of Australia now called Victoria. the point first sighted being apparently identical with the present Cape Everard, in Gippsland. situated between Cape Howe and the mouth of the Snowy River. He then sailed along the east coast, and carefully examined portions of it, especially Botany Bay, near which Sydney. the capital of the present colony of New South Wales, is situated. On his return to England Cook reported Botany Bay to be a suitable place for colonization, and in 1788 Captain R. Phillip, R.N.. on the shores of Port Jackson, a few miles to the north of Botany Bay, established a permanent settlement.

SCENE IN A COAST DISTRICT.

VICTORIA.

Victoria, so named after Her Most Gracious Majesty, although the smallest, is one of the richest and most prosperous of the various colonies situated on the Australian Continent, of which it occupies the south-eastern portion. It is bounded on the north and north-east by the colony of New South Wales, and on the west by the colony of South Australia. On the south and south-east its shores are washed by the ocean. It lies between the 34th and 39th parallels of south latitude, and the 141st and 150th meridians of east longitude. Its extreme length from east to west is about 420, its greatest breadth about 250, and its extent of coast-line nearly 600, geographical miles. Its area is 87,884 square miles, or 56,245,760 acres. The whole Continent of Australia is estimated to contain 2,944,628 square miles, and therefore Victoria occupies about a thirty-fourth part of its surface. Great Britain, exclusive of the islands in the British seas, contains 89,644 square miles, and is therefore somewhat larger than Victoria. The following notes upon the history of Victoria and descriptions of cities, towns, and institutions are by the late Mr. Julian Thomas :—

BASS'S DISCOVERIES.

The first known Europeans who trod what is now Victorian soil were Mr. Clarke, the supercargo, and some of the crew of the *Sydney Cove*, wrecked early in 1797, who reported, when they reached Port Jackson, that they were driven ashore south of Cape Howe. In December of the same year, Dr. George Bass, a surgeon in the Royal Navy, and also a skilful navigator, and Matthew Flinders, a midshipman, started in a whale-boat, manned by six seamen, and, passing Cape Howe, coasted along that part of Victoria now called Gippsland, and, rounding Wilson's Promontory —the southernmost point on the Australian Continent— entered Western Port on the 4th of June, 1798. He, however, returned to Sydney without discovering Port Phillip Bay. Up to this time, the southern portion of Australia was supposed to have been connected with Van Diemen's Land, and the wide passage now known as Bass Strait to be only a deep bight. Dr. Bass's discovery was of great value. His fate was an unhappy one. After having completed his survey of the Strait, he returned to England from Sydney, but came out again with Captain Bishop, in the brig *Venus*, intending to trade between Sydney and Spanish America. Bishop went mad, and Bass took command of the vessel, and sailed to Valparaiso, to open a trade. The Spaniards consented, and were at first amicable; but Bass and his sailors were taken prisoners their first day on shore. Dr. Bass was sent to work in the quicksilver mines, and was never heard of again.

FINDING PORT PHILLIP.

Lieutenant Commander James Grant, of H.M.S. *Lady Nelson*, was the first known white man who sighted the south-western district of Victoria. In 1800 this gallant sailor navigated the southern shores of Australia in his little vessel of only 60 tons, and emulated Captain Cook as a nomenclator. He named Capes Northumberland, Bridgewater, Nelson, Sir W. Grant, and Otway, and Mounts Schank and Gambier, Lawrence Road, and Julia Percy Island. Portland was called after the Duke, then one of the Secretaries of State. Lieutenant Grant was the first European after Bass to sail through the Straits. In 1801, Grant, in the *Lady Nelson*, surveyed the Victorian coast from Wilson's Promontory to Western Port. In the course of this voyage he landed on Phillip Island, in Western Port Bay, and cultivated a garden patch with a coal shovel, the only implement available! Lieutenant Grant returned to England, and was succeeded in command of the *Lady Nelson* by Lieutenant John Murray, who, on the 5th of January, 1802, first discovered Port Phillip Bay. The Heads were passed, the shores explored, the united colours of Great Britain and Ireland were hoisted on land and ship, and the port was taken possession of in the name of His Sacred Majesty King George III. In his report, Lieutenant Murray states that the country reminded him of Greenwich. The hill on the eastern side of the Bay, known to all Victorians as Arthur's Seat, was so named by the Scotch naval officer, after the eminence above Edinburgh. The next navigator in Victorian waters was Matthew Flinders, whose talent and services during the Bass expedition had been fully recognised by the English Government. In July, 1801, Flinders sailed from Spithead, in command of the sloop of war *Investigator*, with instructions to make a complete survey of the Australian coast. The Arctic explorer, Sir John Franklin, was a midshipman on board this vessel. On the 26th of April, 1802, Captain Flinders entered Port Phillip,

A ROAD THROUGH THE FOREST.

A FOREST ROAD.

and ascended both Arthur's Seat, on the eastern shore, and the You Yangs mountain, on the western. From the latter he viewed the fine plains of the interior, and the hills around the present city of Ballarat. Fifty years later, from the same height, one might see caravans of coaches, drays, and pedestrians by the thousand, bound to and from the fields of gold. Flinders afterwards sailed northwards from Sydney, through Torres Straits, and circumnavigated the continent for the first time, naming it Australia, and claiming possession of it for Great Britain. His after fate was an unhappy one. The first vessel in which he sailed from Sydney, on his return to England, was wrecked on the Barrier Reef. The record of that disaster, and of Flinders' voyage of 700 miles, in an open boat, is one of the most startling of the stories of the sea. Again starting from Sydney, the unlucky navigator was taken prisoner by the French, at the Mauritius, and detained for more than six years. When he was released, he passed four years at home, writing the account of his discoveries, and died in 1814, at the early age of 40. Posterity recognises Matthew Flinders to have been "the most generous, most learned, and yet most modest of Australian explorers." In the trio —Dampier, Cook, Flinders—British pluck and enterprise were worthily represented. They deserve honour from all Englishmen and all Australians.

Settlement of Melbourne.

In the early part of 1835 a syndicate was formed in Tasmania, then known as Van Diemen's Land, to colonize Port Phillip. John Batman, a native of Parramatta, New South Wales, was at the head of this. He sailed from Georgetown on the 12th of May, in the small schooner *Rebecca*. On the 29th he entered Port Phillip Heads, and, landing on the west side of the Bay, ascended Station Peak (the You Yangs), following in the track of Matthew Flinders, a copy of whose chart was in Batman's possession. He surveyed the beautiful downs, "called Iramoo by the natives," which Hume and Hovell had passed over. Then Batman ascended the Freshwater and Saltwater rivers, described by Surveyor-General Grimes. The former he called the Yarra Yarra, presumed to be the native term for "ever-flowing." He had several interviews with the natives, and entered into a simple arrangement with eight of the principal chiefs for the transfer "to him and to his

14

heirs for ever " of some 600,000 acres of land (which would now include Geelong and Melbourne, and all its suburbs) in consideration of receiving a certain quantity of apparel, and other miscellaneous wares, particularized as "20 pairs of blankets, 30 tomahawks, 100 knives, 50 pairs of scissors, 30 looking-glasses, 200 handkerchiefs, 100 lbs. of flour, and 6 shirts," a "deal" worthy of the Dutch captain who bought the island of Manhattan, the site of New York, from the Indians; or of the New Caledonian speculators of the present day in the New Hebrides. This " bargain " was, however, ignored and nullified by the Government : as was a similar one dealing with 100,000 acres of land beyond Geelong. Ultimately the Governor of New South Wales allowed the Batman Association £7,000 in the remission of the purchase of land at Port Phillip as compensation in respect of their claims, " recognising the services which the company had rendered, by assisting in the colonization of the new country." Batman was followed in the same year by Mr. John Pascoe Fawkner, who despatched the schooner *Enterprise* from Georgetown on the 27th of July, 1835, which sailed up the Yarra, and on the 28th or 30th of August was moored by its captain, John Lancey, to a tree standing on the present site of the Australian Wharf. Two horses, two pigs, three dogs, and a cat were landed with the provisions—the first imports into the new settlement, which Mr. Fawkner may fairly claim to have founded. Mr. Fawkner, when he landed on the banks of the Yarra on the second voyage of the *Enterprise*, formed a cultivation paddock of 80 acres on the south side of the river. " He turned the first sod, built the first house, opened the first church, and started the first newspaper in the settlement," and was, in fact, the father of Melbourne. To Batman, however, may be credited the fame of being the first colonizer of the shores of Port Phillip Bay. Mr. Fawkner died on the 4th of September, 1869. Mr. Batman died on the 6th of May, 1839, at his residence on the slope of Batman's Hill, and was buried in the Old Cemetery on Flagstaff Hill. In the early part of 1882, an obelisk of dressed bluestone, raised by public subscription, was placed over his grave. Mr. Batman's journal, and also the deed made with the natives, are now in the Melbourne Public Library.

Batman and Fawkner were soon followed by other pioneers from Van Diemen's Land. The " Wild White Man " Buckley, who had been 32 years among the blacks, became interpreter to one party of settlers. On the 10th of

A BULLOCK TEAM IN THE FOREST.

November, 1835, 50 pure Hereford cows and 500 sheep were landed. Stock was driven overland from New South Wales. The "downs of Iramoo" were soon covered with the flocks and herds of the white settlers. Officialdom in Sydney suddenly awoke to the fact that there was a southern part of Australia to govern and tax. The church, in the person of the Rev. Mr. Orton, a Wesleyan minister, had previously come to the fore. The first sermon was preached by him in April, 1836, under the shade of the *Casuarina* oaks on Batman's Hill. The State asserted itself five months later.

EARLY PROGRESS.

On the 29th of September, 1836, Captain William Lonsdale, of the 4th Regiment, arrived at Port Phillip, in H.M.S. *Rattlesnake*, Captain Hobson, after whom Hobson's Bay is named, and assumed the position of resident magistrate. He selected the present site of Melbourne for that of the future city, his selection being indorsed by Sir Richard Bourke, Governor of New South Wales, in his visit some six months after, in April, 1837. Captain Hunter, military secretary ; G. K. Holden, private secretary ; Captain P. P. King ; and the late Mr. Robert Hoddle, surveyor, accompanied Governor Bourke. Mr. Hoddle laid out the town of Melbourne, and the Governor gave it its name, after the then Prime Minister of Great Britain, and also named the principal streets. Prior to this time the settlement was variously known as Bearbrass, Bearpurt, Batmania, Doutigalla, Yarrow Yarrow, and Glenelg.

A few months later James Baker, the Quaker missionary, thus describes the settlement :—" The town of Melbourne, though scarcely more than fifteen months old, consists of about 100 houses, amongst which are stores, inns, a gaol, a barrack, and a school-house. Some of the dwelling-houses are tolerable structures of brick. A few of the inhabitants are living in tents or in hovels, resembling thatched roofs, till they can provide themselves with better accommodation. There is much bustle and traffic in the place, and gangs of prisoners are employed in levelling the streets. The town allotments (of half an acre each) were put up here a short time since at £5 each, the surveyor thinking £7 too much to ask for them; but the fineness of the country has excited such a mania for settling here that they sold for from £25 to £100 each." The Bank of Australasia was started in 1838.

Fawkner's first newspaper, the *Advertiser*, made its appearance the same year. Inland, pastoral man drove his flocks over the plains to the north and west. Far beyond Corio Bay most fertile land was discovered by the pioneers from Tasmania. The magnificent country around Lake Colac was taken up and afterwards purchased from the Crown by Mr. William Robertson, of Hobart, one of Batman's syndicate. The Colac pure-bred herds have since been renowned, even in Great Britain.

The city of Geelong, with its good harbor in Corio Bay, sprang into existence through the fertility of the western pastures. For a long time this was a formidable rival to Melbourne. The yearly exports of wool and tallow and hides from the province of Port Phillip went on increasing, immigration from Great Britain swelled the population, thousands of acres were under crop. Melbourne was made a city, and in 1850, the year previous to the gold discovery, Port Phillip, not fifteen years old, had a revenue of £230,000, its exports amounted to £760,000, and its population was over 76,000. Such figures show that the colony, even at that early day, had ample sources of prosperity quite irrespective of the golden wealth which shortly was to bring it so prominently before the civilized world, making Melbourne by name the best known of any city in the colonies of England. The year 1851 was notable in Victorian history. In February the great "bush" fires occurred. For hundreds of miles the whole country was wrapped in flames, the most fertile districts were utterly wasted, flocks and herds were abandoned by their keepers, the whole population fled for their lives, destitution and ruin spread over the whole colony. The ashes from the forests on fire at Macedon, 46 miles away, fell into the streets of Melbourne. The annals of the colony contain no more disastrous day than "Black Thursday."

THE COLONY OF VICTORIA.

On the 16th of July following, Mr. Charles Joseph Latrobe, who had been "Superintendent" of the district of Port Phillip since 1839, was sworn in as Lieutenant-Governor of the new "Colony of Victoria." "Responsible Government" was not, however, introduced until 1855. The present Constitution is moulded on those of the United Kingdom and the American States. The two Houses of Legislature make laws subject to the assent of the Crown, as represented generally

A FERNY GLEN

by the Governor of the colony, "advised" by Ministers having seats in Parliament. Both Houses are elective, members of the Legislative Council, or Upper House, being returned by voters possessing property qualifications. For the Legislative Assembly, or Lower House, an elector only needs residential qualification, practically manhood suffrage. In 1851, however, the Legislative Council, established by the Act of Separation from New South Wales, consisted of thirty members, ten Government nominees, the rest elected by the people. The early meetings of the Council were stormy, and Governor Latrobe was perhaps the best abused administrator the colonies have known.

DISCOVERY OF GOLD.

But shortly occurred an event which drove all ideas of politics from the minds of Victorian colonists—the discovery of payable gold diggings "uplifted Victoria in a night, as it were, to the position of a nation and a power in the world," and advanced her destinies hundreds of years at one bound. As early as January, 1849, a shepherd in the employ of Mr. J. Wood Beilby, who had a station on the South Australian border, discovered gold in a creek near the Pyrenees, a mountain range in the west of the colony so named by Major Mitchell, who was a Peninsular veteran. This shepherd sold his treasure to Mr. Charles Brentani, a jeweller in Melbourne, but carefully concealed the locality of the *trove*, until falling sick, and being nursed by his master, in gratitude he imparted to him the secret that he had discovered, worked, and sold gold. Mr. Beilby communicated this to Governor Latrobe, who, following the tactics of the Sydney authorities, would have hushed up the fact. But there were other than ignorant shepherds to deal with. At the time when people from all parts of the world hastened to the Californian goldfields, Australia suffered in losing hundreds of her people, who flocked thither. This in the end, however, proved a blessing, for when the gold-seekers returned they were struck with the similarity between the rock and soil of their adopted land and that they had just left. They sought for gold and found it. A man named Esmond discovered it in quartz rock at Clunes. Then it was found at Buninyong and at Ballarat. When the reports reached Melbourne, members of all classes were seized with the gold mania, and there was "a rush" to the gold-fields. Desks, offices, shops, ships were deserted. Closely following the Ballarat finds came those of Mount Alexander and Bendigo, which fanned the flames of excitement to a frenzy. The people were "drunk with the hope of gold." From every quarter of the globe ships sailed into the once peaceful harbor. Victoria was crowded with searchers for fortune: in one year nearly 80,000 immigrants being added to the population of the colony. From that time it has advanced with giant strides. Well may Victoria and its capital be termed marvellous! Well may old men who remember Collins-street as a broken forest shake their heads when they gaze upon the fashionable crowd on the "Block," and feel like Tulliver, that "the world is too much for them." Who would recognise in the Melbourne of 1885 the "bush town" of thirty years ago? Then the streets were full of gum-tree stumps and deep ruts. The principal thoroughfare, Elizabeth-street, was for months in the year a flooded quagmire, in which on one occasion a waggon and team of horses were absolutely swallowed up, and bullock drays were daily bogged. Iron buildings and bark "humpies" were seen on every hand, and what is now the important municipality of South Melbourne was a sea of tents known as Canvas Town. The old pioneers who have not "made their pile" tell strange tales of the doings in those early days when Gold was King, and each man did that which was right in his own eyes. Yet the records of crime are very slight. The rude rough hard life on the gold-fields, whilst it produced a few bushrangers, tempted by the enormous spoils within their grasp, was not productive of petty offences. With gold flowing from every man's hand and pocket, hunger and want were unknown here. Melbourne may not have been very moral in those days, but of "habitual" criminals it had few, and the vagrant and the pauper were unknown.

The City of Melbourne.

Melbourne is now one of the most beautiful capitals in the world, and it is also the most populous and important city in the Southern Hemisphere. Including its suburban municipalities, all lying within a radius of 10 miles from the Town Hall, it contains 458,610 inhabitants. Mr. Anthony Trollope well described it as "one of the most *successful* cities on the face of the earth." It is well laid out with wide and regular streets, with broad side-walks well paved and lighted. Tree planting in the streets has been extensively carried on, giving a pleasant shade as

well as refreshing the eye. The buildings are not only
handsome, but many are of great architectural merit.
The cathedrals and churches, schools, Parliament House,
Treasury, Town Hall, Post Office, Law Courts, Custom House,
University, Museum, Free Library, National Gallery, clubs,
theatres, and other public institutions are worthy of special
admiration. The banking corporations are settled in buildings which would adorn Threadneedle-street. The wharfs on
the banks of the Yarra now give accommodation to large
ocean-going steamers. The shops and warehouses are equal to
those of most cities in the Old World. Everything necessary
to make life content and easy can be procured in Melbourne.
And the mansions in the fashionable suburbs are only less
gratifying evidences of the prosperity of the people than the
thousands of pleasant cottages which one sees on every road
within a few miles of the city. Any visitor to the colony
must be struck with the perfect arrangements for water supply.
There is hardly the smallest cottage without its bath-room.
The most important reservoir is the Yan Yean, which is an
artificial lake at the foot of the Plenty Ranges, nearly
19 miles from Melbourne proper. The numerous parks
and reserves and public gardens in and around Melbourne
are heritages sacred to the health and enjoyment of the
people, which astonish the "new chum" from crowded European cities, where one is taxed for space to breathe. This is
above all a place for the people. In no large town of the
world has a working man so many enjoyments as in Melbourne, or so many privileges. There is no State Church
here, but free State schools give secular instruction to
children whose parents may be willing to accept it. Children
between the ages of six and fifteen who do not attend the
State schools must give evidence that they are educated at a
private school up to a given standard. The whole country,
as well as the metropolis, is dotted with State schools. The
Free Library, Museum, and Picture Galleries, and the
Botanic and Zoological Gardens afford free recreation and
instruction to the labourer and mechanic, as well as to the
clerk or shopman. Melbourne is plentifully furnished with
provident, charitable, literary, scientific, and social institutions to suit all classes and creeds. In the matter of amusement, the inhabitants of the metropolis are furnished with
four theatres and several music-halls. At the Exhibition
Building and at the Town Hall grand concerts are frequently
given. But theatre and concert loving as are the Victorians

generally, it is in outdoor sports that they chiefly relax. Cricket, lawn tennis, football, rowing, yachting, and bicycle riding are the most popular amusements. In cricket our native youth have made their mark against the Gentlemen and Players of England at Lord's. There are no more perfect arrangements of the kind in the world than those at the Melbourne Cricket Ground, where the members' pavilion is not only a "grand stand," but possesses dining, billiard, and bath rooms. Football is as popular here as in some parts of England. Next to cricket, horse-racing absorbs the affections of the Victorian people. In any new township a race-course is one of the first things laid out. Young Australian natives of both sexes are as much at home in the saddle as Arabs or Comanche Indians. Melbourne possesses two first-class race-courses within a few minutes' ride by rail from the city. At Flemington the greatest race in Australia, the "Melbourne Cup," is run early in November (our spring). From every part of the continent people of all classes then flock to Victoria's metropolis. The "Cup Week" is the Carnival of Australia. If Flemington is like Epsom, Caulfield course may be said to be the Ascot of Melbourne. The stranger at the Cup meeting will perhaps get a better sample of Victorian customs than anywhere else. There is an annual attendance of nearly 100,000 people on Cup Day, yet the "new chum" will be surprised to see that policemen are conspicuous by their rarity, that there is scarcely a trace of drunkenness, and that amongst the vast crowd, the members all well dressed, and with money in their pockets, nothing but good-humoured order prevails. Here, where every one's working hours are so much shorter than in other parts of the world, the toiler with hand or brain has no temptation to make a Saturnalia of his holiday. There is less drunkenness in Victoria and as little crime as anywhere in the world.

The City of Ballarat.

Victoria, however, should not be judged only by its metropolis. The inland townships deserve mention. Ballarat, the second city in the colony, is situated exactly 74 miles from Melbourne. It well bears the title of the "Golden City." In the early days, the gold-yielding powers of Ballarat were simply marvellous. No district in the world produced so much gold in such a short space of time. It has been stated that, in many instances, "claims" not more

SCENE AT THE FLEMINGTON RACE-COURSE.—MELBOURNE.

than 8 feet square, and about the same depth, yielded from £10,000 to £12,000 each. At the Prince Regent mine men made as much as £16,000 each for a few months' work. At one claim a tubful of dirt yielded £3,325. Those days have gone, but Ballarat, as it is now, is still more wonderful than when gold was, in very truth, "more plentiful than black-berries," when it was "scattered a thousand times like seeds upon the earth." Anthony Trollope, some 24 years ago, said with justice, of Ballarat, that it struck him with more surprise than any city in Australia, that "in point of archi-tectural excellence, and general civilized city comfort, it is certainly the metropolis of the Australian gold-fields." Sturt-street, the principal thoroughfare, is a mile and a half long, 200 feet wide, and has a fine double row of trees in the centre. The principal buildings on either side are the City Hall, Post Office, Mechanics' Institute, banks, theatre, hospital, and several large churches. The population is 46,158. The reservoirs from which the water supply is obtained have a storage capacity of 600,000,000 gallons. These works cost £300,000. Lake Wendouree now adds to the charming aspect of the city : hundreds of small yachts, miniature steamers, and rowing boats in numbers float on the lake, which is stocked with perch, trout, and carp. The Botanical Gardens, on the other side of the lake, are prettily laid out and well kept. The finest wool in the world is produced near Ballarat, and on the late Sir William Clarke's estate, a few miles from the town, and on the small farms in the Forest of Bungaree, splendid crops are grown. Ballarat is now not only "a city of gold," but is an important inland centre.

The City of Bendigo.

Bendigo is a little over 100 miles from Melbourne. It has a population of about 40,000. In 1851, shortly after the first gold discovery, Bendigo was found to con-tain that precious metal in such abundance that in a short time it became famous for the number of its immense nuggets, the best known of which was the "Victoria Nugget," which was bought by the Victorian Government and presented to Her Majesty. In 1872, Bendigo took rank as a principal Victorian city. It is certainly equal to any European city of the same size. The most prominent buildings are the Post Office, the Masonic Hall, the Town Hall, and hospital, together with a very fine theatre. The

streets of Bendigo are beautifully planted with English trees,
the cool shade of which is as pleasant to visitors as to the
residents. In the centre of the town is a public fernery
known as "Rosamond's Bower." Pall Mall is the principal
business thoroughfare. The streets have a total length of
about 100 miles. Bendigo is rich in other ways besides
gold. The district produces yearly more than 1,000,000
bushels of grain, 17,000 tons of hay, and some 60,000 gallons of good wine. Fruits of all kinds grow most luxuriantly
in the surrounding districts.

Schools of Mines have been established at Bendigo and
Ballarat, to which are attached museums, containing geological and technological specimens, models of mining
machinery and mining plant, sections of mines, and geological maps and plans. At these schools instruction is given
not only in the various branches of science connected with
mining operations, in the theory and practice of mining
and safe conduct of mining works, mining surveying and
mining engineering, but also in many other subjects not
necessarily connected with mining. Students at the Bendigo
school number about 380, and at the Ballarat school about
500. The annual income of the two institutions is about
£5,900, of which all but £1,900 is granted by Government.
Schools of Design have also been established at twenty-five
other places in Victoria, in connexion with a Royal Commission for promoting technological and industrial instruction. There are over 2,800 pupils on the rolls of these
schools. An exhibition of the works of pupils is held yearly
in Melbourne, and local exhibitions are held in other towns.

OTHER TOWNS.

Geelong, which takes rank as fourth in Victorian cities,
is picturesquely situated on Corio Bay. At one time it was
thought it would continue to rival Melbourne, and from its
fine harbor, position, and rich back country there was a
good foundation for the idea. But an idea it remains,
although Geelong is ever ready to come to the front. Some
important woollen factories are situated here, and "Geelong
tweeds" are celebrated in the colonies. In the Western
District of Victoria there are many important towns, Warrnambool being the chief centre as well as an important
shipping port. Belfast and Portland rank next to Warrnambool as sea-port towns. Hamilton, nearer to the South

LANCASHIRE LASS
VICTORY

MURRAY BRIDGE, ECHUCA.—MURRAY RIVER.

A BUSH HUT.

Australian border, is the capital of a fine pastoral district. In the east, Sale is the chief town in Gippsland, an extensive and prosperous division of the colony, which was discovered by Mr. Angus MacMillan in 1839. Echuca, on the Murray, is the principal city in the north of Victoria. In the old days this was a crossing-place for stock from New South Wales. From Echuca there is a vast river traffic.

The Murray River.

During the winter months, when the Murray's waters are swelled by the thousand tributaries from the Australian Alps, steamers ply to Albury on the one hand, and to South Australia, New South Wales, and far inland rivers on the other. Echuca, a river port, is only second to Melbourne in the amount of its shipping tonnage inwards and outwards. The most beautiful thing in Echuca is the park, chiefly because nature has been encouraged, educated in fact. Sitting here on the logs in careless happy indolence, watching the river in its ever-flowing passage to the sea, and listening to the sweet warbling of the birds overhead, every sense is pleased, "drinking delights from the murmur of streams and the flutter of wings." The railway bridge at Echuca is the finest thing of the kind in the Southern Hemisphere. Of iron (over 4,000 tons being used in its construction), it is 1,905 feet long, and cost £124,000, having been built at the joint expense of the two colonies. It was opened in March, 1879. The Murray is for nearly 1,000 miles the northern boundary of Victoria. It was discovered and crossed in 1824 by Hume and Hovell. But Captain Charles Sturt, in 1830, was the first to explore this splendid river. From New South Wales he traced the Lachlan to the Murrumbidgee, and the latter to its *débouchure* into a magnificent stream of 350 feet wide, and from 15 to 20 feet deep, which, in honour of the then Colonial Secretary, Sir George Murray, he gave its present name. Leaving the main body of the expedition in depôt on the Murrumbidgee, Captain Sturt started down the river in a whale-boat and a small skiff, built in seven days. Captain Sturt overcame all obstacles—dangers from snags as well as from the hostile natives on shore—and in 32 days arrived at a large but shallow lake, where, finding it impossible to force a passage through the dangerous navigation of Lake Alexandria to the sea, he turned back. The return journey was one of suffering, as the stock of provisions were all but exhausted. Brave Charles Sturt lost the use of his eyes through blight and lack of proper treatment on these journeys. He died in England, in 1869. Few men have done so much good work for Australia and received such a pittance of reward and honour. Until 1851 the mighty father of Australian waters, the Murray, was almost an *aqua incognita*. No sounds, save, perhaps, the "coo-ee" of some wandering blackfellow, or the screech of a wildfowl, flying startled from its nest among the reeds, awoke echoes in the quiet bends. The pelicans and the beautiful blue and white cranes lazily flapped their wings above the river's surface unmolested. The fish in its waters multiplied, unheeded by all except the natives and the hungry shags, whose descendants to this day haunt dead trees along the banks. The pant and thud of a river steamer, retarded by a heavily-laden barge, ne'er, as now, caused a "mob" of kangaroos to pause, curious for a moment, and then to scamper across an arm of land till lost to sight in the bush. In 1853, Captain Francis Cadell, in the little steamer *Lady Augusta*, navigated the Murray for a distance of over 1,300 miles from its mouth. A true Argonaut was Captain Cadell, for he exploited the land of the real Golden Fleece, opening up a vast extent of country for pastoral purposes. The Murray would be one of the most useful rivers in the world if the channels of its head-waters were locked, and a supply stored for navigation during the dry season.

Conclusion.

It is but 64 years since the first settlement was made in Victoria : now it possesses over a million of inhabitants. The country is traversed by a network of over 3,000 miles of railway, and dotted with prosperous townships. Victorians are proud of their colony, but they are also proud of being Australians of British blood. More than 95 per cent. of our Victorian population is British, or of British parentage. England and Great Britain are yet spoken of as "home" here. In spite of the establishment of the Melbourne University, which grants every degree except those in divinity, a large number of Victorian youths are yearly sent "home" to school and college. Yet there is room here for many of our race ; for although, by the side of the flocks and herds of the squatter, one sees the corn-fields and potato-patches of the small farmer, and the vineyards of the wine-maker, there is plenty of forest yet to be cleared and bush land to be cultivated.

A PICNIC ON THE MURRAY.

Those early pioneers! From Henty and Batman and Fawkner and Robertson to the men of the last decade, farmer or sailor, or trader or miner, they were all the very salt of the earth! During the gold fever, the brains and the blood, the mental courage, as well as the bone and muscle, of Europe flocked hither; and the fittest survived. Victoria has ever been essentially a pioneer colony. It owed nothing to Government aid; in fact, its early prosperity was retarded by Government interference. It was founded solely by individual energy; and its people have ever remained pioneers. It is in their blood. Victorians—Burke and Wills—were the first to cross the continent in 1860. They lost their lives, but made their names immortal. A massive monolith of granite was placed over their graves in Melbourne Cemetery, and a fine bronze statue of the two explorers, from a design by Charles Summers, was for years the chief sight of Collins-street—an object-lesson for our youth. It has now been removed to a more retired spot to make room for the cable tramway. The Burke and Wills expedition cost the people of Victoria £57,000. The end justified it, for within two years of the death of the leaders from starvation, "tierces of beef" were displayed in Melbourne, salted down from cattle pasturing on the spot where they perished." Far away in the "back blocks" in the centre of the continent, in the sugar lands of the North, on every new gold-field, Victorian muscle and energy and capital are to be found. In the South Sea Islands, in the pearl fisheries of Torres Straits and Western Australia, Victorian pioneers are foremost; and Victorian enterprise has done much towards the exploration of New Guinea. Although they claim Victoria to be the richest, the most populous, the most prosperous, and the most energetic of all the Australian colonies, yet Victorians were the first to raise their voices for the Federation of the Colonies, the Political Unity of Australia. Then the peoples of all the provinces, at present divided by absurd local prejudices and jealousies, will be joined together for defence, and, if need be, for defiance; and some day in the future, following out the manifest destiny of the British race, with the dear Old Mother Country, and her eldest-born the United States of America, will be linked together in a strong bond, ruling land and seas and giving laws to all the world.—*Julian Thomas.*

THE FINANCIAL POSITION OF VICTORIA.

The Colony of Victoria has no " National Debt." There have been no wars, earthquakes, or other wealth-destroying disasters to involve the community in national indebtedness. Victoria, however, has a " Public Debt," which is a very different matter. All progressive communities of limited population, occupying new countries, have adopted a system of making use of the public credit for the purpose of financing large national undertakings of a reproductive character. Under this system loans are raised from time to time by the Government, for the carrying out of public works, and a Public Debt is thus created. It is evident that in such cases a country's financial position is not to be judged so much by the amount of the Public Debt as by the character of the works upon which the borrowed money has been expended. The Public Debt of Victoria is small, and 94 per cent. of the entire amount represented has been expended in revenue-producing public works. The remaining 6 per cent. has been expended, for the most part, upon harbor improvements, bridges, public buildings, schools, and defence works, so that even this small balance may be considered as representing expenditure which is indirectly reproductive.

BALANCE-SHEET.

The Public Debt of the colony amounts in round figures to 45 millions sterling, and of this amount $35\frac{1}{2}$ millions have been expended on railways, and 5 millions on water supply and irrigation works. The balance is represented by expenditure upon docks, harbor improvements, public buildings, and other permanent works. If the railways be valued at the cost of their construction, the estimate will be a moderate one, for their earning power is destined to increase with the development of the country which they serve. The unsold Crown lands of the colony constitute a tangible asset, which, at the lowest valuation, is worth 30 millions sterling. When it is remembered that £1 per acre is the price received for the lands which are offered by the Government as a special inducement to homestead settlement, it will be admitted that for the remaining 30 million acres, which include the valuable State forests and the rich auriferous and other mining reserves, the valuation is well under the mark. A deficit of £2,600,000, which accumulated during the recent period of universal depression, has to be reckoned among the colony's liabilities. The following are the tabulated figures :—

ASSETS.

Railways	...	...	£38,294,191
Waterworks	...	...	4,909,707
Crown Lands	...	...	30,000,000
			£73,203,898

LIABILITIES.

Loans ...	...	...	£45,170,164
Deficit ...	...	...	2,604,346
Assets Balance	...	...	25,429,388
			£73,203,898

Upon these moderate estimates the public account shows a credit balance of over 25 millions sterling. No account has been taken of the remunerative investment represented by the Yan Yean Waterworks supplying the city of Melbourne, this being under the control of the Metropolitan Board of Works. If we accept the estimate of Mr. Hayter, late Government Statist, as to the private wealth of the colony, viz., £407,000,000, we have a total surplus of 432 millions.

DETAILS OF EXPENDITURE.

If the whole of the capital represented by our Public Debt had been lost in war it is evident, from the amount of our national wealth, that the colony could, by the ordinary methods of taxation, readily provide for the liability, but as 94 per cent. of the sum has been expended upon reproductive works, taxation is only required to make up the deficiency between the amount payable as interest and the income accruing from the railways and other State-conducted services. The loan moneys have been expended as follows :—

Railways	£35,490,451
Country Waterworks ...	4,909,707
Defences	98,299
Yan Yean (taken over by Metropolitan Board of Works)	3,142,578
Graving Dock	341,818
Law Courts	347,322
Schools	1,063,507
Parliament House	242,463
Yarra Bridge	106,258
Public Offices	162,430
Harbors	303,995
Country Tramways	60,000
Mining, &c.	14,658

It will be observed that in estimating the assets of the colony no account was taken of any of the above public works except railways and country waterworks, although they unquestionably possess a high value.

Revenue and Expenditure.

As expenditure upon the railways has absorbed by far the largest part of the capital borrowed by the colony, the revenue of the railway system is a matter of first importance in connexion with the public finances. The primary object of the State railways being rather to develop the resources of the country than to make profits, it is not surprising that many of the lines should at the outset be unremunerative, nor is it to be wondered at that during times of great general prosperity an expensive system of management should have been developed. The railways were certainly extended somewhat beyond the existing requirements of the population, and the character of the management suffered the consequences of a long period of unusual prosperity. The results were a serious annual deficiency when the colony was struck later on by the world's period of commercial depression. The railway deficit for a time seriously affected the general revenue of the colony, but among the several methods adopted by the Government of Sir George Turner for balancing the National Ledger was a new system of railway management, which

A STREAM IN THE MOUNTAINS.

A BIT OF FOREST COUNTRY.

has already made considerable progress towards placing the lines upon a satisfactory financial basis. The profits over expenses made by the railways for the year ending 30th June, 1897, amounted to £1,052,130, and, as the amount payable by way of interest on railway loans is £1,447,452, the deficiency to be made up from the general revenue of the colony is £395,322. Although the various methods of reducing the cost of working have not yet had time to produce their full effect, the position already reached is that the railways yielded for the year mentioned a net revenue of $2\frac{3}{4}$ per cent. on their total capital cost, or 3 per cent. on the debenture capital expended in their construction. Considering that a large expenditure would be necessary on roads and bridges if it were not for the railways, and that the lines have greatly increased the value of land and other property, the indirect profits of the system far outweigh the apparent temporary loss of £395,000 per annum. The railway traffic is showing a satisfactory increase, so that, with the working out of the economies in management which have been instituted, this first-class public asset, the indirect cause of so much wealth, may be expected at no distant date to cease being any charge upon the general revenue of the colony.

In considering the general revenue and expenditure of the colony, it is well to note how small a sum requires to be annually raised by taxation for the ordinary purposes of government. About 65 per cent. of the interest on the public debt is provided by the earnings derived from public works, while a large proportion of the annual expenditure represents the working expenses of these State undertakings. The total annual interest on loans is £1,823,343, of which £92,446 is provided by the Metropolitan Board of Works. The estimated income for the current year from railways and other reproductive works is £1,176,526, leaving £554,371, or a little over half-a-million, only to be derived from taxation and land revenue, on account of interest.

As only 50 per cent. of the general revenue for all purposes is raised by taxation, it would be easily possible for the Government to provide for much larger responsibilities than have yet been undertaken. So far, however, from undertaking larger responsibilities, the policy of the Government during recent years has been to considerably reduce the public expenditure. A lengthened period of national prosperity brought about a system of lavish Government expenditure, which in 1889-90 reached £9.535,151. When the succeeding depression in the commercial world touched the colony, retrenchment of the civil service, restricted expenditure on public works, and general economy of government were inaugurated, which, without resorting to severe taxation, brought the public expenditure within the amount of the revenue. The expenditure, which for the year 1896-7 was £6,564.843, may be considered as having come down to its normal and proper dimensions. In 1872 a 4 per cent. Victorian Government Stock was erected, redeemable in 25 years, and under this authority over £2,000,000 was raised locally. Last year Parliament determined upon its redemption, and at the same time created a new stock bearing interest at 3 per cent., holders of the first stock being given the right of conversion at par. This privilege was availed of in full, with the exception of about £120,000, and for this amount public tenders were recently called, with the result that it was locally disposed of most successfully, a premium of £3 8s. per cent. being obtained.

According to the Budget statement of the Treasurer and Premier, Sir George Turner, the Estimates of Revenue and Expenditure for the year 1897-8 show a surplus of £166,364, without taking into account the sum of £250,000 required for retiring Treasury-bonds ; the statement is as follows :—

	Revenue.		Expenditure.
Taxation	...	£3,453,239	...	£2,317,720
Public Estate ...	452,895	...	257,437
Railways and other			
Public Works	2,897,062	...	4,061,675
	£6.803,196		£6,636,832
Surplus	...	...	£166,364

As an evidence of the increasing prosperity of the colony, it may be noted that the number of depositors in the Government Savings Banks increased last year by 9,602, while there was an increase of £322.553 in deposits. Nearly 30 per cent. of the population (men, women, and children) are depositors in these banks. The Savings Banks fulfil another useful mission besides serving as a perfectly safe investment for the people's savings—under the Crédit Foncier system the Commissioners lend to farmers at 4½ per cent.

A SHEEP RUN.—NORTHERN DISTRICT.

Summary.

Of the public debt. 94 per cent. has been expended in directly reproductive works; the most of the remainder upon indirectly reproductive permanent improvements.

The public balance-sheet shows a credit of £25,000,000, making, with the private wealth of the colony, a credit of £432,000,000.

The earnings of the railway system are increasing, and already the profits over working expenses are equal to 3 per cent. interest upon the debenture capital expended.

A period of exceptional depression has been successfully passed through, and all financial engagements have been met. without resorting to severe measures of taxation.

The revenue of last year was more than sufficient to meet the expenditure, and a surplus is shown upon the Budget statement for the current year.

The yield of gold shows a steady increase, that for 1896 being 805,087 ounces. This quantity is considerably greater than that produced in any other Australian colony. The total yield to the 30th June, 1897, is 61,394,150 ounces.

Various other sources of national wealth are dealt with in the different chapters of this volume.

NOTES ON THE MINING INDUSTRY OF VICTORIA.

By James Stirling, Government Geologist.

Although territorially Victoria is the smallest State in Australasia, covering an area of 87,889 square miles, yet its variety of physical features, climatic conditions, soils, &c., and more especially the proved stability of its splendid auriferous resources, render it at once the premier colony of the continent. When it is stated that since the early gold discoveries in 1851-2 no less a sum than £246,400,000 has been won—the bulk of this from a relatively small portion of the proved auriferous area—and that the gold-mining industry is only approaching a condition of permanency, through a better knowledge of auriferous matrices, economic methods of mining and treating the ore, it will not be difficult to realize how important a factor the mineral wealth, both actual and potential, has been, and will continue to be, in stimulating all other forms of production. Not only in the highest altitudes, over 6,000 feet above sea-level; in the deep recesses of the valleys, only a few feet above sea-level; but at depths of over 3,000 feet from the surface—or 2,000 feet below sea-level—are mining operations being profitably carried on. New discoveries in the depth of the dense forest-clad mountainous areas, as tracks are being cut into their secluded recesses, are constantly being made. Deep leads, concealed beneath extensive basaltic flows, are being traced over hundreds of miles of territory by boring operations. And as the areas over which the metallic substances are extended, and the methods of production cheapened, together with a constantly increasing feeling of greater stability in the mineral resources as fields for investment, so will the progress and prosperity of the colony proceed *pari passu* with the development of its gold-mining industry.

PHYSICAL FEATURES.

Fully two-thirds of the colony consists of mountains and undulating ranges, traversed by perennial streams and covered by a vigorous arboreous vegetation. The Main Dividing Range, which traverses the colony from N.E. to

DISH WASHING OR PANNING.

CRADLING.

S.W., rises to altitudes of 6,100 feet, while lateral watershed lines, formed by high ridges and elevated plateaux, rise to still higher levels—as Mount Feathertop, 6,300 feet, and Mount Bogong, 6,507 feet. The elevated table-lands, which are formed as extensions of the lateral water-shed lines both to the north and south of the Main Divide, comprise the Snowy High Plains, covering an area of 400 square miles; Dargo High Plains, 200 square miles; Nunniyong and Gelantipy, 500 square miles; and the Bogong High Plains, about 160 square miles.

GOLD-BEARING FORMATIONS.

The principal gold-bearing formations, covering fully one-half of the entire area, consist of silurian slates and sandstones, which have been intruded upon by plutonic rocks, such as granite, porphyry, diorite, &c., and which are overlain in the western portion of the colony by extensive lava flows—the basalts of tertiary age. Roughly speaking, there are 29,000 square miles of exposed silurian rocks, which are almost everywhere intersected by auriferous quartz veins or covered in the valley by auriferous drifts, while there cannot be less than 15,000 miles of silurian sedimentary rocks concealed beneath the tertiary lava flows or tertiary sedimentary rocks. In short, the older gold-bearing palæozoic rocks extend from the western portion of the colony, in the Glenelg Valley, to the boundary of the colony on the east, a distance of over 500 miles. In the eastern part of the colony the silurian formations are in places overlain by massive Devonian rocks, and in the southern by Jurassic rocks; while in the west are remains of an extensive formation—the Grampians—whose age is still uncertain. With the exception of one locality in the Devonian area of limited extent, these formations are not known to be auriferous.

The relative areas covered by the different rock masses at the surface may be estimated as under:—

Sedimentary formations: Palæozoic Devonian, lower, middle, and upper, 8,500 square miles; carboniferous, 400 square miles. Cambrian, 100 square miles; silurian, upper and lower, 28,300 square miles.

Mesozoic: Triassic, 200 square miles; Jurassic, 3,684 square miles.

Tertiary : Eocene or oligocene. miocene. pliocene, pleisto-
cene. recent. 30,000 square miles.

Plutonic and Igneous rocks : Basalt. 11,000 square miles :
granite. 4,000 square miles : porphyries. diorites, 2,000
square miles.

BENDIGO GOLD-FIELD.

The principal reefs in this field occur in the fissures produced by the arches formed by a buckling of the strata into
a series of folds ; or, in other words. the prominent feature
of the field consists of numerous more or less parallel axial
lines. having a strike of N. 16 deg. W.. along the course
of which the great mass of slate and sandstone rocks are
bent over into a series of anticlinals. with corresponding
synclinals or troughs between. The dip of the beds to the
east and west is about 60 feet. These axial lines or centre
country do not continue horizontal for any distance, but
have an end-long dip or pitch. The reefs are called saddles,
and thicken and diminish in size as they are traced along
the axial lines. The eastern and western extensions are
called legs. The saddles are often from 20 to 50 feet across,
while the legs are from 1 to 4 feet. but frequently become
attenuated in depth.

A succession of such saddles occurs at different levels. not
generally immediately below the other, but listed to one
side, principally to the west. In a limited area of about 7
miles in length by 3 miles in width. there are no fewer than
twelve distinct lines of saddle reefs, known as centre country.
Mining operations have extended to a depth of over 3,000
feet with profitable results. No less a quantity than
£18,000,150 worth of gold has been won from this limited
area, and from the Bendigo district up to date £53,063,356.
The deepest shafts on the field include :—

				Feet.
Lansell's 180 Mine	...	...	...	3,350
New Chum Consolidated		...	...	3,267
Lazarus Co.	...	...		3,210
New Chum Railway	...	...	...	3,037
New Chum and Victoria		...	...	3,100
Shamrock	...	...	...	...	3,000

GOLD MINE.—BENDIGO.

The enormous wealth realized from a few of the Bendigo saddle reefs may be estimated from the following figures :—

The Carlisle Company (now amalgamated with North Garden Gully, Carlisle, and Pass By) has produced over 350,000 oz., value	£1,400,000
Garden Gully United, 346,000 oz., value	1,384,000
Johnson's Reef, 281,000 oz., value...	1,124,000
Great Extended Hustler's, 235,000 oz., value	940,000
Catherine Reef (on New Chum line, Eaglehawk), 162,000 oz., value ...	648,000

Although the reefs in the central area of Bendigo occur in the form of saddles, yet to the north-west, as at Marong ; north, at Sebastian, Raymond, &c.; or south, at Mandurang, they assume different forms. At Marong, where gold occurs in the slates near the surface, slightly inclined or even vertical veins occur, in places forming irregular seams of quartz in a band of sandstone. At Mandurang, towards the Crusoe reservoir, flat veins occur ; and where such veins intersect a particular band of strata which contains a thin, almost parallel band or seam, of slightly different mineral composition to the enclosing strata, the richest gold is found. I have no hesitation in affirming that there is work for centuries to come, not only in exploiting the saddle formations down to as great a depth as 4,000 feet,* but in tracing the auriferous belt to the north and south, or developing such parallel belts as Ellesmere to Axedale on the east, or Marong to Lockwood on the west. It is estimated that, making due allowance for the increased cost of haulage and deep sinking, quartz containing 5 dwt. of gold to the ton can be made to pay in the deep levels at Bendigo.

Auriferous Contact Zones.

The influence exerted on the silurian strata by the enormous masses of eruptive rocks, such as granites, porphyrites, diorites, felsites, &c., and which now appear as bosses and apophyses, known as dykes, &c.; and the structural and

* Recent temperature observations tend to show that at the rate of increase measured by 1 deg. Fahr. for every 137 feet, mining will be possible at 4,000 feet, so far as the heat of the rock is concerned.

chemical changes of the mineral components along the planes of the contacts has for some time been the subject of critical research; but it was not until the relation between the occurrence of auriferous quartz veins formed at or near the contacts, both in the eruptive rocks, and to a greater extent in the sediments they invaded, that the attention of practical miners was drawn to the value of following out the contacts in the field as a guide to prospecting operations. To Mr. A. W. Howitt, F.G.S., the Victorian mining community is indebted for first scientifically directing attention to the importance of such contact zones, by his classic petrological investigations of the rocks of the Australian Alps. For instance, it was shown that, at Swift's Creek, in the Tambo Valley, certain intrusive granites, diorites, porphyrites, &c., had invaded the silurian sediments at places where these rocks were both metamorphosed and unaltered, and had converted the sediments into hornfels rocks in one place and mica schists in another; and that the auriferous lode formations are found to be connected with the contact action of the intrusive rocks. Similarly in the Dargo Valley, auriferous contact lodes have been generated by the intrusion of diorite masses into the silurian sediments. Mr. Howitt's exact description of this contact phenomena has undoubtedly paved the way for mining exploration in many other districts where such features occur. In the north-eastern district, in an area hardly yet touched by systematic prospecting, it is estimated that there are fully 300 miles of contact rocks intersected by auriferous quartz veins. Two of the older goldfields where some phases of contact metamorphism of the sedimentary silurian rocks and their associated auriferous veins may be studied are Maldon and Stawell.

Maldon.

The Maldon gold-field is principally to the east of the granitic rocks at Mount Tarrengower. The alteration of the sediments has produced rocks of the hornfels type. A well-defined elvan dyke traverses the field, and in the case of the Derby mine is flanked on either side by auriferous veins. Fully 17 reefs have been described on this field, which strike N. 12° to N. 30° W. Several of the mines are now approaching a depth of 2,000 feet. Such examples of permanency as the South German, &c., may be referred to as illustrating the stability of mining on the field, which, within a small area, has already produced £2,306,620 worth of gold.

Stawell.

At Stawell the auriferous quartz veins intersect a belt of country margining the granite of the Black Range. The rocks are very much indurated or altered by contact metamorphism, and the sediments are penetrated by numerous dykes of porphyrite and diorite. The auriferous quartz veins strike from south-east to north-west, and generally underlie to westward at an angle of 45 degrees. In almost every instance, except the Magdala-cum-Moonlight, a flat reef has been found abutting against the vertical on the eastern side, with a northerly underlay, and the richest quartz has for the most part been found at no great distance eastward from the line of junction. The principal mines include the Magdala, Oriental, Sloane and Scotchman, Perthshire, Hampshire, New Chum, Cross, &c. From this group of mines no less a sum than £4,018,884 worth of gold has been won.

A considerable amount of boring has been carried on over this field, and auriferous quartz veins proved in advance of the actual workings. There is no reason why the reefs should not extend still further to the north-north-west of present workings.

At present the Magdala, Oriental, and North Magdala are working at a depth of 2,409, 1,832, and 1,640 feet respectively.

It would not be difficult to multiply instances in other parts of the colony in order to show that the granitic intrusions have largely affected the metalliferous character of the adjacent strata, but to elucidate all the gold-fields which impinge on the areas occupied by the plutonic rocks would be beyond the scope of this article. I must therefore pass on to another class of auriferous veins, viz., those directly connected with the dyke formations.

Diorite Dykes.

In this case the principal bed rock is of upper silurian age, and the dykes intersect the strata both with and across the line of strike. The quartz veins traverse the dyke in various ways, either vertically from wall to wall across the dyke parallel to it ; either along the wall or in the body of the stone, and horizontally or nearly so from wall to wall. In places where the dyke stone is absent, the space between the walls is filled with broken-up rubbly shale or slate with thin quartz leaders.

Typical examples of such dykes are **seen at Wood's**
Point, Walhalla, Foster, Tanjil, Raspberry **Creek, Coster-**
field, &c.

WALHALLA.

At the celebrated **Long Tunnel mine, Walhalla, the dyke**
trends parallel with **the strike of the strata west of north.**
It is impregnated **more or less with iron and arsenical**
pyrites.

Two quartz lodes meeting **in an apex or cap accompany**
the dyke along or near **to its walls on either side, while others**
intersect the body of **the dyke. The shoots of auriferous**
quartz dip northerly, **the underlie being westerly. This mine**
is a splendid **instance of the permanency of the auriferous**
veins associated with the dykes; **it has yielded over 631,344**
oz., or in value £2,525,376, **and has been carried to a depth**
of nearly 2,900 feet.

The whole of the belt of country **extending northerly**
from Walhalla through the heads of **the Jordan and over the**
Dividing Range at Matlock to **Wood's Point, and still further**
northerly to Jamieson, is auriferous and of similar **charac-**
ter, although on the Dividing Range, near Matlock, **there is**
probably a junction of the upper and lower silurian **beds,**
from the occurrence of fossil graptolites found there by **my**
colleague, Mr. Ferguson, 300 feet or more below **the saddles.**

BALLARAT.

At Ballarat there are at least four well-defined **lines of**
reef, such as the Guiding Star, Star of the East or **Consols,**
the Indicator on the Llanberris and Speedwell line, **and the**
Fire Brigade line. It is believed that the Indicator **belt of**
country on the eastern side of the field will be **found to**
extend past Creswick and Allandale towards the **Moolort**
Plains. Some idea of the enormous value of the **gold mines**
within a limited area in the Ballarat district **may be gleaned**
when it is stated that the yield of gold up to **the present has**
been £71,886,080. One mine alone, the **Star of the East,**
carried to a depth of 2,000 feet, has yielded over **£520,000**
worth of gold, declaring dividends of about **£220,000; while**
the Band and Albion, with which is now incorporated **several**
smaller mines, has produced £2,078,325, **and declared**
£900,000 in dividends. The silurian slates and sandstones
of the Ballarat field differ slightly in composition from
those at Bendigo, and are intruded **upon by granitic and**

TUB PUDDLING.

felsitic dykes in places. The folds in the strata are not so readily distinguished as at Bendigo, and there is a marked absence of the fossil graptolites which characterize the Bendigo slates.

Other Indicators.

A few of these " indicators " may be referred to :—

At Rokewood Junction it is a soft slaty band, somewhat ferruginous, frequently soft and clayey, varying from brown and grey to nearly black in colour, in contact with the hanging wall of the reef. The gold occurs in most abundance in an inch or two of friable stone in contact with the slaty band, and generally in masses up to several ounces in weight.

At Creswick, Nuggety Gully : The indicator consists of a yellowish-brown fine-grained soft earthy shale, of somewhat soapy texture, with thin brown ferruginous veins. At the intersection of the quartz with this band the richest deposit of gold occurs.

At Wedderburn the indicators consist of an orange-coloured streak about one-sixteenth of an inch in thickness, scarcely distinguishable from the slates in which it occurs. Again, it resembles a miniature reef, sometimes laminated. The principal one, which has been followed for over a mile, consists of three parallel veins of ironstone or grit, about one-eighth of an inch in thickness and 4 inches apart. On the Champion reef the indicator consists of a thinly laminated unctuous clay of dark-grey colour, about 5 to 7 inches thick. The quartz veins crossing this are very rich, the gold in coarse nuggety pieces.

At Korong Vale, Nil Desperandum : A band of nodular micaceous schist, from a few inches to 2 feet in width, between walls of hard sandstone, constitutes the indicator.

At Elaine it is a thin band of highly pyritous black shale. When the lode intersects it, the latter carries gold. In another place a band of yellowish-white concretionary nodules, with gold on the face of the concretions, is considered as an indicator.

At Welcome Gully, near Daylesford : Wherever the quartz veins come into contact with a small slate band of soapy texture, usually of an olive colour, but often grey to black, and more or less ferruginous, the former is highly auriferous.

At Glenpatrick Creek : The indicator is a soft pug, with a well-defined foot-wall, intersected with small flat veins of quartz.

At Reedy Creek, Nuggety Gully : A thin continuous seam of soft tough steatic mineral, coinciding with the bedding planes, forms the indicator.

At Campbelltown : A series of parallel faults, filled with an ironstone conglomerate, form the indicator. The faults are irregular, and intersect the quartz veins nearly at right angles. Where the quartz strikes the latter portion of the fault the veins are very rich.

At Gaffney's Creek : A sandstone band, crossed nearly at right angles by quartz leaders ; contain gold only when crossing the sandstone band.

My object in dwelling somewhat upon the different "indicators" is to direct the closer attention of practical miners to their value as an aid to prospecting operations in newly-discovered gold-bearing districts. The axiom, "Like produces like," is as true in geology and mining as it is in other activities.

In addition to such indicators, there are in many districts, especially in areas covered by the upper silurian shales and sandstones, various eruptive dykes having a special local significance. Those belonging to the diorite and diabase class may be referred to. It may be inferred from the fact of nuggety or lumps, slugs, &c., of gold occurring in association with these "indicator" bands, that in those districts where heavy alluvial is found indicators may be searched for. My colleague, Mr. E. Lidgey, has recommended such districts as from Beaufort, through Redbank and Stuart Mill, to St. Arnaud, the Scarsdale and Smythesdale district, Enfield, Ballarat, Creswick, and on to Wedderburn.

Wood's Point.

The Morning Star dyke, which trends on the surface 54 deg. west of north, is intersected by quartz veins, which are nearly horizontally disposed, inclining but slightly to north-west. They penetrate the adjacent slates, and are richest near the contact. Several bores were put down, which proved floors of quartz at lower levels, and show that the quartz veins occur to great depths in the dyke masses.

GROUND SLUICING.

Foster.

Auriferous quartz veins penetrate into the adjacent rocks beyond the porphyritic dyke which intersects the silurian rocks at this place. Other localities where the dykes have associated with them auriferous quartz veins are numerous in the country occupied by the upper silurian beds. as at Alexandra. heads of Big River, Tanjil. Cassilis. Ovens Valley, Queenstown, &c., &c.

Meridional Belts of Reefs.

A feature which is common both to the lower and upper silurian beds, no matter what the amount of local variation in the direction or formation of the quartz veins may be, is the meridional belts which come into view when the position of the quartz veins are plotted on the map—*i.e.*. there is a general meridional trend of the gold-bearing portions of strata. This significant fact was drawn attention to by Captain Panton, P.M., and C. W. Ligar, ex-Surveyor-General, during 1858—by the former in the *Mining Journal*, and by the latter in the *Transactions of the Mining Institute*. In the latter publication the following pregnant remarks were made :—" With reference to the great national importance of the quartz reefs of the colony, every circumstance tending to illustrate the general law under which they have been called into existence must be of interest. . . To the casual observer the relative position of the groups of what are termed paying quartz reefs . . appear to be scattered over the country in an indiscriminate manner. . . I consider there is reason for supposing that such is not the case, but that they exist in lines running north and south in the magnetic meridian, and that these lines have generally a very remarkable equal relative distance from each other in an east and west direction. If so. significant facts are established for future exploration, and it may be that remunerative reefs will be discovered by a careful examination of these meridional lines within certain limits of deviation to be determined on after future investigation. In this way reefs of great value may be brought to light which evade the eye."

Several of such lines were shown on a map accompanying the article to which I have referred.

Now, these remarks are suggestive. and my predecessor, Mr. R. A. F. Murray. was able to direct special attention to their importance by defining a number of auriferous belts or zones (*vid.* *Physical Geography and Geology of Victoria*).

Later discoveries go to confirm the prediction of Messrs. Panton and Ligar in a remarkable degree, so that now fully thirty of such auriferous belts may be mentioned. I can only refer to the localities intersected by them as an instance of the fact without attempting a description of the local details. Of course, in tracing these belts on the map their continuity will be found to be broken in places by the granite, basaltic, and upper palæozoic rocks.

Commencing from the western portion of the colony, the first belt extends south from Balmoral, where alluvial auriferous deposits occur, but as yet no reefs.

No. 2 is on the Upper Glenelg, on the east of the Black Range, where several reefs have been prospected.

No. 3. On the eastern side of the Grampians a belt may be traced from Moyston to Fryingpan, where both quartz and alluvial workings occur.

No. 4. From Ararat, through Great Western, to Stawell, comprising both alluvial leads and auriferous quartz veins. The Hopkins Valley lead originates within this belt.

No. 5. East of Stawell a belt extends from Navarre, in the Pyrenees, southward to Buangor. (There is good scope for leasing along the western slopes of the Pyrenees within the limits of this belt.)

No. 6. From St. Arnaud where there is a group of three well-defined lines of reef—one of these, the Lord Nelson, being mined to a depth of over 1,600 feet with highly payable results; an auriferous belt extends south through Stuart Mill to Redbank, Moonambel, Percydale, and from the Avoca Valley across the Dividing Range past Elmhurst to Beaufort, and still further south to Lillie Plains, where deep alluvial ground occurs right across to the Skipton diggings.

No. 7. Still further east a belt may be traced from north of Bealiba through Homebush and Avoca leads to Wansford, Cardigham, Scarsdale, and Pitfield Plains. (In the latter, recent borings suggest that a deep lead may be found to extend beneath the basaltic plains towards Lake Corangamite on the west.)

No. 8. From Ballarat a belt extends northerly through Creswick, Clunes, Maryborough, Carisbrook, Majorca, and Timor, Dunolly, Tarnagulla, Moliagul, to Wedderburn.

Referring to this belt, Mr. Murray remarks that within this great auriferous zone he would include the gold-fields of Inglewood, Tarnagulla, and Kay's diggings, north of the plains of the Loddon Valley, and to the south the gold-fields of Smeaton, Kingston, Creswick, Ballarat, Buninyong, and the Durham, the last-named localities being continuous with one another as regards auriferous character, there being no break from Durham to Smeaton, a distance of 25 miles north to south in the alluvial gold workings, over a width of about 4 miles from east to west. The belt of the Leigh River has been profitably worked 20 miles south from Durham, and auriferous gravels have been traced from its banks under the plains south of Mount Mercer, where the further continuation of the Durham lead is sure to exist. It is, therefore, Mr. Murray thinks, quite likely that the belt of silurian rocks extending southward from Ballarat may be found to have regained its auriferous character, and that the deep ground resting on it beneath the basalt may be as rich in gold as those to the northward. As regards the portion between Smeaton and Tarnagulla, there is every reason to believe that the belt retains its character from the Madame Berry line, a distance of 30 miles to Tarnagulla, and that all the alluvial leads in its course will prove profitable. On a smaller scale, the flat alluvial country along the Bul Bul Creek, between Tarnagulla and Inglewood, is likely to prove auriferous in the vicinity of a line between these two places.

No. 9. From Inglewood (where a number of reefs have been worked to shallow depths, four distinct lines being traceable for a distance of 4 miles) a belt of auriferous country certainly extends through Newbridge, Baringhup, Campbelltown, Bullarook, and east of Mount Buninyong to Elaine.

No. 10. From Maldon south through Muckleford, Daylesford, Ballan, and Steiglitz (several of the mines at Daylesford have been carried to a depth of 1,800 feet, and there are no geological reasons why a highly auriferous zone should not be met with at lower levels than the present lowest workings). Similarly, the Steiglitz gold-field, which has produced £763,316 worth of gold, should yield profitable returns as deep as that now worked at Ballarat. Two mines alone (the United Albion and New Mariner) gave the following returns :—United Albion, depth 1,050 feet, £54,000, declaring £15,000 in dividends, on a capital of

£9,000; New Mariner. £109.000, dividends £56,000, on a capital of £8,000.

No. 11. A very important belt extends southerly from Bendigo, through Castlemaine, Chewton. Elphinstone. and Blackwood, towards Bacchus Marsh. Castlemaine. which has produced £1,802,604 worth of gold. has long been known for its surface auriferous wealth ; and it is believed that deep mining will reveal, between the 1,000 feet and 3,000 feet levels, a payable auriferous zone, and that at these deep levels saddles, similar to the Bendigo field, may be met with. Of course, the structural feature of the reefs will depend on the direction and extent of the compressive forces acting on the strata. It is probable that the granite masses between Castlemaine and Bendigo have played an important part in the genesis of the reef formations.

No. 12. East of Bendigo recent mining developments are disclosing the existence of a belt extending from Goornong. through Ellesmere (Fosterville) to Axedale, and further south to Redesdale, and on towards Macedon. intersecting the basaltic leads to the east of Kyneton and Malmsbury.

No. 13. From Runnymede. through Heathcote—where gold has recently been found in quartz veins intersecting a diabase dyke. near the junction of lower and upper silurian formations, which rest upon still older Cambrian rocks—to Lancefield. Romsey. and Riddell's Creek.

No. 14. An important belt. characterized by the occurrence of antimony ore in association with the auriferous quartz veins passed from Redcastle. Costerfield, Pyalong, Kilmore (where scheelite has been found). on towards the Morang district. near Melbourne.

No. 15. Another similar antimony-bearing belt extends from Rushworth (where cross, i.e., east and west, lines of reef occur) through Whroo. Mitchelstown, Reedy Creek (Broadford), Whittlesea. west of Queenstown, east of Oakleigh. and on to Tabberabbera. on the Mornington Peninsula. where quite recently gold was found in granitic rocks.

No. 16. From Murchison south through Yea and on to Enwcabl, east of the Dandenong Ranges.

No. 17. From Merton to Alexandra. Marysville, and south to Noorim. intersected by dyke formations.

No. 18. An important belt extends from Dookie, where ironstone deposits occur, south through Maindample, Darlingford, Frenchman's Creek, on the Big River, through the heads of the Yarra, to the west of Mount Baw Baw, and on to the Tangil, extending also, in all probability, beneath the South Gippsland mesozoic beds to Foster's and Wilson's Promontory.

No. 19. Another, and perhaps the most interesting of all the belts, extends south from Benalla, through Toombullup, Jamieson, Lauraville, Wood's Point, Matlock, Jericho, and Walhalla.

This is, *par excellence*, the belt of dioritic dykes, extending uninterruptedly for over 70 miles. The dykes run at various angles, with the strike of the enclosing strata. When they are parallel, or nearly so, the reefs are more persistent, and the shoots of gold longer, than in those cases where the dyke cuts the strike of the strata nearly at right angles. At present, between Walhalla and Toombon, at least 50 leases are being worked. Such mines as Long Tunnel, Long Tunnel Extended, Great Long Tunnel South, Toombon, Loch Fyne, the Hope, &c., may be referred to.

In the east of the Walhalla auriferous belt there is a large area covered by Devonian rocks, which have not yet proved payably gold-bearing. Although two minor belts may be traced—one from Cameron's Creek on the Howqua River, south to the east of Mount Useful and on the Siaton, and the other from near Briagolong (Gladstone Creek) northerly through the Wonnangatta Valley to the heads of the Buffalo River.

No. 20. From Rutherglen, where deep alluvial leads occur, a belt may be traced in a S.S.E. direction through Everton, Myrtleford, Buffalo River, across the Dividing Range, to the Wongungarra Valley and Crooked River.

No. 21. From Barnawartha, through Woorragee to the east of Beechworth, on to Bright (the yield of gold for the Bright district being £2,294,556), Harrietville, west of Mount Hotham, to the head of the Dargo, over the Dargo High Plains to Grant and Lower Dargo. It is on this belt that the highest altitude at which auriferous veins have been found is attained, as on the western side of Feathertop ridge, at 6,000 feet above sea-level.

No. 22. Still further east a very extensive belt stretches from Bethanga. on the Murray, through Eskdale, Snowy Creek. and Mount Wills, Livingstone (the yield of gold for the Omeo district being £1,293,732), Cassilis, Haunted Stream, and to Monkey Creek, near Bruthen.

No. 23. From Granya, through the head of the Dark River. to the Gibbo River. and in all probability through the head of the Tambo. southerly towards Mount Tara.

No. 24. From Corryong through Wheeler's Creek and Buckwing, to the Limestone River. and heads of the Buchan River.

No. 25. On the eastern side of the Snowy River recent mining explorations suggest several auriferous belts. as under :—From McLachlan's Creek. on the border line between New South Wales and Victoria, through Deddick, Mount Bowen, and the heads of the Yalma, west of Mount Ellery. and on to Cabbage Tree Creek.

No. 26. From Bonaug. through Boulder Creek, to Club Terrace, Lower Bemm. and Pearl Mount, on the coast.

No. 27. From Mount Delegate, through Bendock, over the coast range. to the eastern heads of the Bemm and western heads of the Cann River valleys.

No. 28. On the extreme eastern portion of the colony. from Mallacoota Inlet, across the Genoa Valley, into New South Wales.

Enough has been stated to demonstrate beyond the possibility of doubt the enormous extent of the gold-bearing belts of strata, and that there is practically an inexhaustible supply of gold yet to be won : in not only following the downward prolongations of the reefs already discovered. but in renewed search for further surface outcrops along the extension of the belts I have indicated. No theoretical speculations respecting the genesis of gold-bearing veins need militate against successful mining enterprise in those districts where the downward prolongations of the auriferous reef formation is at present a matter of conjecture. The fact remains that from the highest surface altitudes to a depth of 3,000 feet below sea-level gold-bearing strata undoubtedly exists. The permanency of Victoria's gold-mining industry is an established fact so far as the quartz-bearing formations are concerned.

HAND DOLLYING.

ALLUVIAL DEPOSITS AND LEADS.

There is hardly a single river in Victoria which does not contain alluvial auriferous deposits along some portion of its course. These detrital deposits have been classed as "surfacing," comprising earth or thin layers of clay, rubble, and decomposed rock on the slopes or summits of hills composed of silurian rock. The gold is found free, or associated with fragmentary quartz, from the surface earth down to chinks and crevices of the bed-rock.

River, Creek, and Gully Workings.—Deposits of gravel, drift, &c., resting on the silurian bed-rock, or on the banks of water-courses : in some cases terraces are met with on the rocky slopes high up above the present river beds.

Leads.—Gravels, conglomerates, &c., deposited in the beds of ancient rivers, in some cases only covered by recent accumulations, and in others by several layers of basalt. The beds of these ancient rivers are in some localities above, and in others below, those of the existing streams, as the Dargo High Plains and Clunes or Ballarat districts respectively, and are worked by tunnels or shafts accordingly.

In addition to the above there are widespread deposits of gravels, conglomerates, &c., believed to be due to estuarine or marine action ; the gold is more patchy in its occurrence, though sometimes found in defined runs ; not necessarily in the deepest hollows of the bed-rock, but often on the ridge or slopes thereof. Some of these deposits cap hills of silurian rock ; others constitute reef washes, beneath the basalt, but at higher levels than the deep lead gutters.

LOCALITIES OF LEAD SYSTEMS.

Commencing at the western end of the colony, the first is that along Mather's Creek, south of Balmoral, although there is a limited extent of slightly auriferous gravel south-west of Harrow, on the Glenelg. The Stawell leads comprise the deep lead and its tributaries, situated from 3 to 5 miles north-west of the town ; and the Commercial-street lead and its tributaries, commencing at the reef and terminating at Seventy Foot Hill, about 2 miles west of the town. These leads may still be traced further afield. The Great Western lead, from which over £100,000 worth of gold has been obtained, has been worked for over 2 miles to a width which exceeds in places 1,200 feet. Gold occurs principally in fine scales. Ararat : A number of shallow leads trend towards the Hopkins Valley, where they combine into one main lead, which extends southerly beneath the basalt. The borings put down prove that this lead system extends in all probability for at least 8 miles, with a covering of from 230 to 500 feet of basalt. Landsborough: This extends northerly from Barkly, past Landsborough, to Navarre, and on towards the Wimmera Valley. The tributary leads at Navarre were very rich; the depth of sinking from 50 to over 100 feet.

Beaufort.—This lead, known as Fiery Creek, has been worked from the head of Fiery Creek, through the town of Beaufort, in an easterly direction, to its junction with the Waterloo lead. It is believed that from this point the lead will be found to extend easterly through Windermere, and probably junction with the extension of the Haddon lead.

Smythesdale.—Rising in the Hard Hills, the Linton lead trends southerly to its junction with the Standard lead, and beyond that it is called the Happy Valley lead, which, trending rapidly to the east, enters the main Smythesdale lead, which rises near Nintingbool, and trends southward through Piggoreet, Cape Clear, and on to the Pitfield Plains. Many of the tributary leads to this system have been very rich. The continuation of the deep ground of the Stanley, near Cape Clear, remains to be proved. It is thought that the Victoria Mint Company is near it. The Snake Valley lead falls northward from the Hard Hills, and junctions with the Preston Hill lead. It is probable that these two leads will eventually join with the Haddon lead, and the latter junction with the Midas leads. As an instance of the richness of portion of these leads, the Magnum Bonum claim, covering an area of 12 acres, yielded at a depth of 102 feet 6,639 oz. of gold, value £26,556.

Ballarat.—Here several lead systems trend southerly, westerly, and north-westerly, noted for their richness and for the occasional discovery of large nuggets in such tributary leads as Little Bendigo, Canadian and Hiscock's—such nuggets as The Welcome, found at Bakery Hill, which realized £9,325; the Lady Hotham, at Canadian Gully, £3,000; the Nil Desperandum, £1,050; and another at Canadian Gully of £5,532. During 1855-6 such leads as Inkerman, Red Streak, Frenchman, Esmonds, Malakoff, Milkmaids, and Redan were opened out and proved very rich. It is estimated that as much as 1,637 oz. of gold was obtained

from one day's washing at the Band of Hope. My colleague, Mr. Lidgey, who has made a detailed survey of the field, estimates that from twenty mines £5,902,050 has been won; that dividends to the extent of £2,500,000 have been paid : the total amount of calls only reaching £594,914. The tracing out of the Bailarat lead systems to the west, north-west, and south-west still offers a field for mining development.

Rokewood.—The extension of the Break o'Day lead, already worked through the township of Rokewood, still further south, remains to be proved.

Bet Bet Valley Leads.—This extends from Lexton, through to Caralulup, Lilicur, and Bung Bong to Rathscar, in the Avoca Valley. The course of this lead is unmistakably marked by a strip of basalt, from 1 to 2 miles in width, which follows the valley, and is bounded on the east and west by ledges of outcropping silurian rock. The course of the lead goes northward about $3\frac{1}{2}$ miles into Rathscar, where it turns westward, and in about 2 miles further is joined by the Homebush lead. Beyond here it passes into and down the Avoca Valley, where it is joined by the Avoca lead system. It probably extends past Archdale and beyond St. Arnaud.

There is thus an average length of over 40 miles of main trunk lead traversing auriferous rocks fed by rich tributary leads and with numerous rich shallow workings in the bordering country on either side. That portion extending from the southern line of a series of bores put down at boundary of Lexton to the Homebush leads, a distance of 20 miles, deserves special attention, being well defined by borings and being bordered by rich auriferous country.

Amherst and Maryborough Leads.—A series of leads from Amherst, Daisy Hill, Alma, and Maryborough nearly all trend towards Timor, where the course of the main lead is marked by the deep leads worked by the various Duke companies. The continuation of this lead either north-westerly towards the Avoca Valley, or north-easterly towards the Loddon, is now being tested by boring operations to the south-west of Bet Bet.

Sadowa Lead.—The Sadowa lead extends for several miles towards Talbot. Its course is apparently interrupted by a basaltic dyke.

Loddon Valley Lead.—This lead system, with its tributaries, is probably the most important yet worked in the colony, extending from the Midas and Dowling Forest group

of mines, a distance of 16 miles of unworked ground;
then the marvellous Berry group of mines, with 4 miles of
unworked ground.

Northerly from the junction of these two lead systems as
far as the parallel of Carisbrook, the Mount Greenock,
Majorca, and Carisbrook leads come in from the west, and
the Loddon leads from the east. The boring near Moolort
proved a large and well-defined trunk lead, which extends
close to Eddington where the Bet Bet system probably joins
it. In the total length of this system there are 60 miles of
unworked leads.

Dunolly and Burnt Creek Leads.—Leads trending down
the Bet Bet Valley, such as Chinaman's Flat and Four-mile
Creek, were very rich.

Daylesford Leads.—These leads are all above the level of
the present stream. The most noteworthy are the Wombat
Hill lead, Deadman's lead, Italian Hill lead, O'Hara Burke
lead, Fern Tree lead, and Jim Crow Creek lead.

Bendigo Leads.—The rich alluvial gullies fed by the
Bendigo reefs tend toward Bendigo Creek into a main lead
near the White Hills, which has been traced a length of
7 miles. Several tributaries enter below the White
Hills from the westward, trending northerly towards
Huntly. It is estimated that for a distance of 6 miles from
the White Hills the lead yielded £2,000,000 worth of gold.
Its course from Huntly has not yet been definitely ascertained, although it is believed to trend north-easterly through
Bagshot towards Goornong, and to be enriched by a tributary
lead system coming in from the east. A minor lead system
extends north-westerly along the Myers Creek Valley, receiving tributary leads from Eaglehawk on the east. Still
further north a lead system extends for several miles past
Neilborough.

Heathcote Leads.—McIvor Creek has been worked for a
number of leads : most of the gold occurs in nuggets—one
of these weighed 658 oz. Several of the tributary gullies
are still being worked.

Castlemaine Leads.—Extensive gullies have been worked
at Chewton, Maldon, Castlemaine, and down through Yandoit
to Newstead.

Malmsbury and Coliban Valley Leads.—This system of
leads extends from the Main Dividing Range between Trentham and Blackwood. It is fed by various tributaries from
Trentham, Lauriston, Taradale, and Malmsbury. A line of

bores near Carlsruhe proved deep ground at 348 feet from the surface. Four and a half miles northward, near Lauriston, a lead was proved, and 2 miles further north a third series of bores proved wash at a depth of 371 feet. Near Malmsbury, the Taradale lead junctions with the main lead. Following down the valley of the Coliban, borings at Redesdale proved the bed rock to be 223 feet from the surface, the fall of the surface from Kyneton to Redesdale being evidently greater than that of the lead. From Trentham to Axedale, on the general course of the lead system, the distance is fully 50 miles, and from near Carlsruhe to a little beyond Redesdale the distance is 25 miles.

Plenty River Leads.—Rising in the Plenty Ranges, where several creeks and gullies have been worked with satisfactory results, notably Jack's Creek and Deep Creek, the lead extends to Whittlesea, while at South Morang a tributary lead has been worked for some years by means of tunnels. Boring is now being carried on to prove the position of the lead, which it is thought might extend still further south towards Collingwood.

Tanjil Leads.—Here a lead has been traced for several miles along the valley of the Tangil to a higher level than the present stream. A number of tributary lead systems exist at higher levels in the valley.

Neerim Lead.—A sub-basaltic lead extends for a distance of about 20 miles along the water-shed between the Tarago River and the Latrobe.

Moondarra.—This lead system extends along the plateau between the Tyers and the Thompson Rivers for a distance of 16 miles.

Rutherglen Leads.—There are two main deep leads now being worked—the Great Southern, which is a continuation of the Chiltern Valley Lead, and the Great Northern. The principal companies now at work include the Great Southern, Southern and Chiltern Valley United, Great Southern No. 1, Prentice United, North Prentice, Great Northern Extended, and the Wahgunyah. The yield of gold for the Chiltern and Rutherglen districts has been £2,282,384.

Ovens River.—The Ovens River and nearly all its tributaries below Porepunkah have proved auriferous. In the higher levels terrace washes, and in the lower there is evidence of a very extensive deep lead system, now being proved near Palmerston by boring. Similarly, from the neighbourhood of Beechworth in the highly auriferous plateaux situate on the water-shed line between the Ovens and the Little or Kiewa runs, a number of lead systems radiate towards the main valleys on either side, as the Eldorado, Woolshed, and Staghorn Flat, and numerous others.

Dargo High Plains.—Round the edge of this basaltic plateau, at an altitude of between 4,000 and 5,000 feet, gold has been found and partially worked for many years. Recently tunnelling operations by Ryan and Co. have disclosed what appears to be a deep lead system extending for a distance of over 20 miles. Whether there is more than one lead remains to be proved by boring operations across the plateau. In the Kiewa Valley there are miles of terraces which should repay mining exploration. Similarly in the Mitta Valley and all its tributaries alluvial deposits and leads occur. Towards the head of the Murray, Buckwong Creek, and Limestone Creek, along the Tambo Valley, terrace washes occur in the Mitchell and all its tributaries, the Wongungarra, Dargo, Wentworth, Crooked River, Wonnangatta River, the Bemm River in East Gippsland, the heads of the Broadribb, the Mackenzie—in short, the heads of the Yarra, Goulburn, and all streams to the east rising in the Main Dividing Range—contain auriferous deposits, either as creek and gully alluvium or as terraces, the former being more readily worked, even with the most primitive appliances, while the latter require the expenditure of capital for the construction of high-level races to sluice the deposits.

Who will dare to venture the assertion that Victoria's alluvial deposits and leads are worked out in the face of such overwhelming evidence to the contrary? When we realize how small a portion of the proved auriferous ground has really been worked as compared with that awaiting development, there can be but one feeling, and that of unbounded confidence in the future mining prospects of the colony. In one square mile of ground in the Madame Berry area gold to the value of £1,586,755 has been raised, £848,700 paid in dividends, £433,000 in wages, and £130,000 in royalty. There is no special reason why other portions of the unworked leads should not yield similar returns. They intersect similar belts of known auriferous territory, and when the location of the known quartz-bearing auriferous belts are mapped out, and also the courses of the leads which intersect them, a new mining era will evolve, and science and practice go hand in hand towards a more rapid industrial progress and continuous prosperity.

FACTS AND FIGURES.

By James J. Fenton (Assistant Government Statist).

AREA AND POPULATION.

Area.

Victoria, although small as compared with the other Australian colonies, occupying no more than the thirty-fourth part of the whole Australian Continent, is nearly as large as Great Britain, about half the size of Spain, three-fourths of that of Italy, or equal to Denmark, Belgium, Holland, and Poland combined.

Population.

Notwithstanding its size, the colony now contains one-third of the inhabitants of the whole continent, and is more populous than any other colony except New South Wales (which is three and a half times the size), its density of population being 13·4 persons to a square mile as compared with 4¼ in New South Wales, and a little over 1 in Australia as a whole. The population at the last census, which was taken on the 5th April, 1891, was 1,140,405. Between that period and 31st December, 1897, the inhabitants are estimated to have increased to 1,176,238, consisting of 595,402 males and 580,836 females. These numbers show an average of about 97 females to 100 males. Inclusive of the suburbs, Melbourne, the capital of the colony, and the most populous city in Australasia, contained 458,610 inhabitants at the end of 1897.

Nationalities.

According to the census of 1891, 97 per cent. of the colonists are British subjects by birth, and only 3 per cent. are foreign born. The native Victorians numbered about 714,000, or 63 per cent. of the population; the natives of other Australian colonies numbered 80,000; the English, 163,000; Irish, 85,000; Scotch, 51,000; Germans, 11,000; Chinese, 8,000; Swedes and Norwegians, 3,200; Americans (U.S.), 2,900; Italians, 1,700; Danes, 1,400; French, 1,300; Swiss, 1,300; Russians, 1,200; and the natives of other countries, about 15,000.

Aborigines.

At the first colonization of the district now called Victoria, the Aborigines were officially estimated to number about 5,000 ; but according to other and apparently more reliable estimates they numbered at that time not less than 15,000. When the colony was separated from New South Wales in 1851 the number was officially stated to be 2,693. In 1891 the number had become reduced to 565, viz., 325 males and 240 females. The existence of the few that still remain alive has no political or social significance whatever. The race is rapidly becoming extinct.

Religions.

The religions of the people, as returned at the census of 1891, were as follow :—Protestants, 837,000 ; Roman Catholics, 248,000 ; Jews, 6,400 ; Buddhists, &c., 7,000 ; persons of other sects or of no denomination or religion, about 19,000 ; and unspecified, 23,000.

Occupations.

The occupations as returned at the census are first classified under two main divisions, viz.:—Breadwinners, numbering 494,000, including 114,200 females : and dependants, 629,800, including 425,500 females. The former were again subdivided into Professional classes, 29,600, including 9,700 females; Domestic, 57,000 (42,431 females); Commercial *(distributors)*, 98,500 (9,300 females); Industrial—including commercial and industrial combined *(modifiers)*, 167,100 (28,700 females); Primary Producers (grazing, agriculture, mining, &c.), 124,000 (10,900 females) ; and Indefinite (pensioners, &c.), 17,800 (13,300 females). These figures are exclusive of Chinese, Aborigines, and the unspecified.

Marriages, Births, and Deaths.

Marriages in Victoria numbered 7,454 in 1897, or 6·36 to every 1,000 of the population. Births in 1897 numbered 31,302, or 26·69 per 1,000 of the population. Both the marriage rate and the birth rate are at present below the average, chiefly in consequence of a temporary deficiency in the adult male population at marriageable ages. Deaths in 1897 numbered 15,128, or 12·90 per 1,000 of the population, which is an exceedingly low proportion as compared with

European countries. For instance, in Sweden and Norway the death rate averages about 17 per 1,000; in England and Wales and Denmark, 19 per 1,000; in Belgium and Holland about 20; in France, 22 per 1,000; and in Germany, Italy, and Austria-Hungary, from 24 to 30 per 1,000.

FINANCE.

Revenue and Expenditure.

The State revenue of Victoria, in the financial year ended with the 30th June, 1896, was £6,458,682, and the expenditure £6,540,182. The revenue per head was £5 9s. 3d., and the expenditure per head was £5 10s. 8d. The amount raised by taxation was £2,691,000, or nearly 42 per cent. of the whole revenue, the principal item under this head being Customs duties, which yielded £1,733,672; next to which came Excise duties £297,030, Income tax (with exemption up to £200) £168,088, Probate and Succession duties £148,432, and Land tax (on large pastoral estates) £127,178. The land revenue amounted to £410,143, of which £295,200 was from land sales; and the railway revenue to £2,394,475. Of the ordinary expenditure in 1895-6, £1,419,000 went to defray the cost of working the railways, and £503,000 the posts and telegraphs; whilst £1,893,000 was paid as interest on the public debt, incurred chiefly for the construction of railways and other reproductive works; £571,000 was for free public instruction, including contributions towards the maintenance of various educational institutions; £255,000 was granted towards the maintenance of public and private charitable institutions, &c., and £155,000 to assist and encourage the agricultural and mining industries; whilst the cost of general administration absorbed £1,157,000. For economic reasons the colony has of late years considerably restricted its loan expenditure, and only £219,000, derived from the proceeds of loans, was expended during the year on railways and waterworks. In 1896-7 the revenue amounted to £6,630,217, and the expenditure to £6,564,852. Omitting the receipts from the sale and occupation of land and from railways, in order to make the figures comparable with those of other countries, the balance of revenue in 1895-6 was £3,654,064, or a larger amount in proportion to population than is raised in any country in the world out of Australia, except Germany or France. The amount per head was £3 10s. as against £3 9s. 6d. in Germany (with States); £3 7s. in France; £2 13s. 7d. in the United Kingdom; £2 18s. in Italy; £2 7s. 7d. in Belgium; £2 6s. 3d. in Holland; £2 5s. in Switzerland; £2 2s. 3d. in Austria-Hungary; £1 13s. 7d. in Spain; and £1 10s. 9d. in the United States.

Local Revenue and Expenditure.

The whole colony is divided into 208 municipalities, whose revenue consists of amounts received from rates, licences, dues, &c., supplemented by a State subsidy. In 1896 their total revenue amounted to £1,157,838, of which £111,967 was from Government and £905,458 chiefly from local taxation; and their expenditure to £1,098,336 (exclusive of loans). The State subsidy, which is divided amongst the different municipalities, with certain exceptions, according to a scale based upon the amount they respectively levy from rates, is at present £100,000 per annum. There are also other local bodies, viz., a Harbor Trust (Melbourne), with a revenue of £125,000; a Water and Sewerage Board, with one of £167,000; besides several waterworks and irrigation trusts, two fire boards, &c.

Public Debt.

On the 30th June, 1897, the State debt of Victoria amounted to £47,029,321, which is equivalent to a proportionate indebtedness of £40 3s. 9d. to every man, woman, and child in the colony. In order to place the colony on a sound financial footing, the borrowing policy has been discontinued for the present, and no further loans will be contracted unless they can be economically utilized in developing the material resources of the colony. Of the existing debt, nearly four-fifths was borrowed for the construction of railways, three-fourths of the remainder for waterworks, and the balance for school buildings, defences, docks, and other public works. It will be observed that the debt, unlike the national debts of most of the countries of the Old World, was not incurred to defray the expense of war or for other unproductive objects, but for the prosecution of works of a permanent character, necessary for the development of the colony, from which amounts are already received sufficient to go a long way towards payment of the interest on the loans, and by which succeeding generations will be largely benefited.

The annual interest payable amounts to £1,832,837, equivalent to an average rate of 3·8s per cent., and the loans have an average currency still to run of 16 years; but as the loans mature and are replaced by 3 or 2½ per cents., there will eventually be an annual saving of at least £450,000 per annum. Even in the present depressed times the railways are returning an annual profit of 2¾ per cent.

Debts of Local Bodies.

Besides the State debts, loans have been contracted for the construction of public works from time to time by various local bodies throughout the colony. The following amounts were outstanding in 1896 :—Municipalities, £3,569,904 (exclusive of Government loans, £342,656); Melbourne Harbor Trust, £2,000,000; Metropolitan Board of Works (Sewerage and Water Supply), £3,084,065 (exclusive of £2,359,157 lent by the Government, and included in the public debt); Fire Boards, £130,000. The total of these is £8,783,969. As against the municipal debt, there is a sinking fund of nearly half-a-million sterling. The loan of £1,650,000 contracted by the Melbourne Tramway Trust is not taken into account, as the principal and interest are repayable to the trust by the Melbourne Tramway Company.

Monetary Institutions.

Royal Mint.

The Melbourne branch of the Royal Mint was established in 1872. From the time of its opening to the end of 1896, 17,998,016 ozs. of gold had been received thereat, valued at £71,713,761. Gold is issued from the Mint as coin or as bullion. The former, with the exception of 884,584 half-sovereigns, has consisted entirely of sovereigns, which have numbered 65,477,718. The bullion issued has amounted to 1,393,164 ozs., valued at £5,796,791.

Banks.

There is no State bank in Victoria, but there are eleven joint-stock banks of issue, of which six are Victorian institutions, with about 420 branches within the colony. According to the sworn returns of these banks, their note circulation during the last quarter of 1896 was £979,460, and the amount on deposit was £29,973,000 ; whilst on the other hand the advances amounted to £37,935,000, and the coin and bullion to £8,000,000. The paid-up capital of the eleven banks doing business in the colony was 19 millions ; but their business is not confined to Victoria. Although the banks have suffered considerably from the recent financial crisis, they are gradually regaining their former prestige.

Savings Banks.

Every facility is afforded in Victoria to persons desirous of investing their savings securely and profitably. Trustee savings banks were established in 1842, and post-office savings banks in 1865, but in 1897 these were merged into one institution, controlled by Commissioners, and guaranteed by the State. According to the returns for 1897, the number of depositors in the institution was about 360,000, or about 31 to every 100 of the population, who had to their credit £7,944,800, or an average of £22 to each depositor. Most of the depositors belong to the working classes. The rate of interest allowed to depositors in 1896 was $2\frac{1}{2}$ per cent. for the first £100, and 2 per cent. for any excess over that amount up to £250. No interest is allowed on amounts over £250.

State Advances to Farmers.

In order to aid and encourage the agricultural community, which has for years past been hampered by the high rates of interest charged on private loans, a special department under the Commissioners of Savings Banks was created, by an Act passed in 1896, for the purpose of making advances to farmers at the low rate of $4\frac{1}{2}$ per cent. interest, repayable, principal and interest, by annual instalments extending over a long series of years (maximum $31\frac{1}{2}$ years). In the first year of its operation (1897), £365,000 was so advanced, and applications for a further sum of £183,000 were approved. The maximum advance allowed is £2,000, but the average amount agreed to be advanced to each of the 1,100 successful applicants was not quite £500. By this measure it is anticipated that the rate of interest on private advances will also be greatly reduced.

Moneys on Deposit.

The moneys on deposit in banks, savings banks, and building societies, at the close of 1896, amounted to £39,711,043, of which £31,217,091 was in banks, £7,638,682 in savings banks, and £855,270 in building societies. Other institutions, such as deposit banks and some of the insurance companies, also receive deposits, but of these no returns are furnished.

LIFE INSURANCE AND FRIENDLY SOCIETIES.

Ample provision is made by the colonists against old age and sickness, as, in 1896, the number of life policies in force in the colony was 132,684, assuring £22,757,000. Thus 11 in every 100 of the population (men, women, and children), were assured for an average amount of £171 per policy. Moreover, the Friendly Societies, which provide against sickness and disablement, and also hand over, in the event of death, a funeral donation, have a membership of 80,694 members, equivalent to over one in every four males between the ages of 20 and 60; they have an annual revenue of about £310,000, whilst their present annual expenditure is £270,000; they have accumulated funds amounting to £1,155,400—equivalent to an average of £14 6s. 5d. per member.

TRADE AND COMMERCE.

Imports and Exports.

In 1897, the declared value of goods imported into Victoria was £15,454,482, and that of goods exported therefrom was £16,739,670. The excess of exports over imports was thus £1,285,188, and the total value of external trade was £32,194,152. Per head of population, the average value of the imports was £13 3s., and that of the exports £14 5s., or together £27 8s. These proportionate values are higher than corresponding amounts in most other countries in the world. In the latest year of which returns are at hand, the value per head of the external trade of Holland, which is larger than that of any other independent country, was £43, whilst that of Belgium was £35, that of Switzerland £22, the United Kingdom £19, Denmark £15, Uruguay £13, Chili £11, France £10, Argentine £10, Sweden and Norway £8, Germany £7, and the United States £6. About three-sevenths of the total trade is with the United Kingdom and two-fifths with the neighbouring colonies—principally New South Wales.

Principal Imports.

It is a matter of considerable difficulty except in the case of dutiable articles, to ascertain the imports for home consumption. The following, however, may be regarded as the values of the principal of such imports in 1897 :—

Imports for Consumption, 1897.

Cotton piece goods and manufactures	£847,420
Sugar and molasses	625,162
Iron and steel	562,794
Woollen piece goods	478,758
Coal { Official value	228,647
{ Actual ,, ...	304,000
Tea	238,415
Silk and silk manufactures	301,457
Paper (including bags)	250,657
Timber	243,214
Apparel and slops	171,586
Spirits	186,579
Tobacco	146,242
Hides	122,577
Beef and mutton*	113,762

Principal Exports.

The exports of Victorian staple products are largely dependent on mining, grazing, and agriculture. The following were the leading items in 1897 :—

Exports of Principal Home Products, 1897.

Wool { Quantity	43,678,294 lbs.
{ Value	£2,035,082
Gold	£4,379,264
Butter { Quantity	22,167,002 lbs.
{ Value	£884,976
Breadstuffs { Quantity as wheat	—22,471 bushels†
{ Value ...	£57,955
Leather	£327,029
Hay and chaff	£193,744
Skins	£190,922
Tallow	£116,163
Horses	£104,898

Shipping.

The vessels entered and cleared at Victorian ports in 1897 numbered 3,280, of an aggregate burden of 4,598,515 tons.

---

* Either in the form of sheep and cattle, or meat.
† Net import in quantity—a most exceptional circumstance. During the previous six years the average annual exportation was 5,000,000 bushels.

and carried about 168,000 men. About five-sixths of the vessels, embracing over eight-ninths of the tonnage, and carrying over ten-elevenths of the men, were steamers.

AGRICULTURE, GRAZING, AND MINING.

Settlement on Crown Lands.

Land suitable for agricultural purposes may be obtained from the Crown in Victoria under the following conditions :—

The best unsold portions of the public estate have been divided into "grazing areas" of various sizes up to 1,000 acres, each of which is available for the occupation of one individual, who is entitled to select, within the limits of his block, an extent not exceeding 320 acres for purchase in fee simple at £1 per acre, payment of which may extend over twenty years, without interest. The selected portion is termed an "agricultural allotment," and of it the selector is bound within the first six years to cultivate 1 acre in every 10 acres, and make other improvements amounting to a total value of at least £1 per acre. The unselected portion of the original area is intended for pastoral purposes, and for this the occupier obtains a lease at a rental of from 2d. to 4d. per acre, an allowance up to 10s. per acre being made the lessee for any improvements he may have effected calculated to improve the stock-carrying capabilities of the land. Residence is compulsory if an agricultural allotment has been selected, but not otherwise ; or by paying twice the amount of purchase money, and expending upon improvements £2 instead of £1 per acre, residence may be altogether dispensed with. The area at present available for selection is about 6,000,000 acres.

Private Land.

Persons desirous of purchasing farms already improved can always do so from private individuals at prices ranging from £2 per acre upwards, according to the quality of the soil and value of improvements effected. The area of all private lands is about 23,100,000 acres, equal to two-fifths of the area of the whole colony, of which 18,000,000 acres are held in fee simple, and 5,100,000 acres are in process of alienation under the system of deferred payments.

Land in Cultivation.

Only $5\frac{3}{4}$ per cent. of the whole area of the colony, or 14 per cent. of that of the private lands, has as yet been brought under cultivation. In the season 1897-8 the area under tillage was 3,242,600 acres, and the number of cultivators 34,000. The principal crops are: Wheat, which covered 1.638,000 acres; oats, 294,500 acres; barley, 36.500 acres; potatoes, 42,800 acres; and hay, 578,400 acres. There were also 120,000 acres under permanent artificial grass; 22,300 acres under green forage; 36,300 acres under gardens and orchards; 25,300 acres under vines; 12,700 acres under peas and beans; 10,800 acres under maize; 8,100 acres in market gardens; and 15,500 acres under rye, vegetables. hops, tobacco, sugar-beet, and a few other crops of minor importance: whilst 400,500 acres were lying fallow. The produce of wheat was 10,426,000 bushels. or an average of $6\frac{1}{2}$ per acre: that of oats, 4,844,000 bushels. or $16\frac{1}{2}$ per acre; that of barley, 756,000 bushels. or 13 per acre; maize, 516,000 bushels, or 48 per acre; potatoes. 61,700 tons. or $1\frac{1}{2}$ per acre: hay, 648,000 tons, or over 1 ton per acre. The yields of most of the crops, more especially wheat and potatoes, were adversely affected by drought. It should also be pointed out that the greater proportion of the wheat-growing area is in the dry northern districts, where the yield is restricted by the amount of rainfall: in ordinary seasons the yield of wheat is about 10 bushels per acre.

Wheat.

During the last twenty years, with but one exception, the colony has produced more than enough breadstuffs for its own consumption. Of the quantity produced in the season 1897-8. viz.. 10,426.000 bushels. about 3,000,000 bushels will be available for export in 1898.

Fruit.

Fruit of all kinds could be produced. if required, in almost unlimited quantities : but owing to its perishable nature, and the want of economical. as well as efficient, means of preservation and transport, but little has as yet found its way to European markets. In 1896-7 the number of orchardists was about 4,100 : and the quantity of large fruits gathered for sale was returned at 1,100,000 cases, consisting chiefly of apples. apricots. pears. and plums. The quantity of small fruits. such as raspberries. strawberries, gooseberries, currants, &c.. was 21,114 cwt.: and that of nuts—almonds, walnuts, filberts, &c.—52,226 lbs. Fruit-drying is carried on chiefly at Mildura—an irrigation settlement on the River Murray ; the quantity produced in orchards in 1896 was 226,750 lbs., consisting chiefly of apricots. peaches, and figs; and in vineyards 11,276 cwt. of raisins, and $762\frac{1}{2}$ cwt. of currants.

Wine.

The wine industry, which promises to be of great importance to the colony, has made rapid progress during the last eight years, the area under vines having increased from less than 13,000 acres in 1888-9 to nearly 28,000 acres in 1896-7, the wine made from 1,200,000 gallons to 2,822,000 gallons, and the quantity exported from about 200,000 gallons to 354,000 gallons. In 1896-7 the quantity of grapes gathered was 601,000 cwt., of which 434,000 cwt. was made into wine; and the number of vine-growers was 2,600. The State has given special attention and encouragement to the industry by the founding of a School of Viticulture; by the establishment of Wineries, three of which have already been started; and by offering special inducements for the opening up of foreign markets.

Sugar.

One of the latest industries started in the colony is the manufacture of sugar from beet, for the growth of which the soil and climate of certain parts of the colony are believed to be especially adapted. One factory, equipped with the most modern machinery, has already commenced operations under favorable auspices. The only encouragement given by the State is in the form of a loan, at 4 per cent. interest, of about two-thirds of the capital invested in buildings and machinery, but this has to be repaid by instalments extending over a period of 25 years. One of the conditions antecedent to granting the Government advance was that occupiers or owners of suitable land should undertake to cultivate for three years at least 1,500 acres of sugar beet in the vicinity of the factory. The best sites for factories are reported to be Maffra, in Gippsland, where the present factory is located, and Port Fairy (formerly named Belfast), in the western district. A further Government advance has been authorized, and is available, for the establishment of a second factory.

Special Products.

There is also unlimited scope for the cultivation of maize, tobacco, the opium poppy, the olive, and other oil plants, flax and hemp—for oil seed and fibre, grass and clover seeds, scent and essential oil plants; but these have as yet received but little attention.

Grazing and Live Stock.

The area of Crown lands occupied for pastoral purposes was 19,500,000 acres, or 35½ per cent. of the area of the whole colony, and there are besides freehold grazing lands to the extent of close on 20,000,000 acres. The Crown lands are held by about 22,000 lessees or licensees, who pay the State an annual rental of £73,000 for the use of the land. According to the latest returns, the live stock in the colony consisted of 431,547 horses; 1,826,435 horned cattle (including 457,924 milch cows); 13,180,943 sheep; and 337,588 pigs. The number of dairy farmers was 27,000, of whom all but about 1,400 are also cultivators.

Wool.

Wool is one of the staple products of the colony, and the quantity produced in 1897 was 54,567,742 lbs., of the value of £2,105,936. With the exception of a small proportion manufactured in the colony, the whole of this is exported—about three-fourths being sent to the United Kingdom, and most of the remainder to the Continent of Europe.

Butter.

The dairying industry, for which Victorian pastures are well adapted, has made rapid strides during the last few years, owing to the opening up of markets in the United Kingdom, rendered possible by the incorporation of freezing chambers in ocean-bound vessels, and stimulated in the first instance by bonuses granted by the State. As, however, the bonuses have for some time past been discontinued, the industry now stands on its own merits. The industry has so far been mainly confined to butter, the manufacture of cheese on a large scale having attracted but little attention. The following figures, showing an increase in the exports of butter from 1,000,000 lbs. in 1889 to over 22,000,000 lbs. in 1897, speak for themselves :—

Export of Victorian Butter.

		Lbs.		£
1889	...	1,019,220	...	37,447
1891	...	4,652,344	...	226,326
1893	...	13,975,633	...	573,107
1897	...	22,167,012	...	884,976

Frozen Meat.

A considerable trade has also been established by the export of frozen mutton. In 1897 over 19,000,000 lbs., valued at £178,227, was exported, of which, however, about one-third came from New South Wales.

Gold.

Nearly one-third of the world's annual production of gold is raised in the Australasian Colonies, and of these Victoria still holds the premier position, notwithstanding the recent rapid development of the gold-fields of Western Australia. The quantity raised in Victoria in 1897 was 812,765 ounces, valued at £3,251,060, which was by far the largest yield in any year since 1882; whilst the total quantity raised since the first discovery in the colony in 1851 was 61,773,000 ounces, valued at about 247 millions sterling. The number of gold miners is about 26,000, of whom 2,500 are Chinese.

Coal.

Coal deposits of commercial value have only recently been discovered, but they are being rapidly opened up, and in 1897 the quantity raised was 236,777 tons, or nearly one-third of the colony's total requirements. Besides coal there exist in various localities immense beds of black and brown peat and brown coal, the latter varying from 60 to 200 feet in thickness, which when freed from moisture and converted into briquettes forms an excellent fuel, as has been proved by experiment. This industry, however, still awaits development.

Value of Productions.

In Victoria the annual value of the principal products of agriculture is about 5 millions sterling; grazing (including butter and cheese), about $7\frac{1}{2}$ millions; mining, about $3\frac{1}{2}$ millions; manufacturing industry, 10 millions (exclusive of cost of raw material); and poultry farming, about $2\frac{1}{4}$ millions; making a grand total of $28\frac{1}{4}$ millions sterling.

MANUFACTURES.

Manufactories, Works, &c.

Manufacturing enterprise in Victoria has for years past been stimulated by protective duties. Great difference of opinion exists as to the wisdom of such a policy; but, whether in consequence or in spite of these imposts, there can be no doubt that Victoria, as a manufacturing country, now occupies a higher position than any other colony of the Australasian group. Statistics of manufactures and works in operation are collected annually. The collectors are instructed to obtain returns only from establishments employing four hands or upwards, or those with less than four hands when machinery worked by steam, gas, electric, wind, or horse-power is used. No attempt is made to enumerate mere shops, although some manufacturing industry may be carried on thereat; were this done, the manufactories of the colony might be multiplied to an almost indefinite extent.

In 1896, the total number of establishments returned was 2,810, employing 50,448 hands, viz., 37,779 males and 12,669 females, in which capital was invested to the amount of over 12¼ millions sterling—£4,983,000 in machinery and plant, £4,376,000 in building and improvements, and £2,921,000 in land. In 1,252 of the establishments steam was used, in 478 gas, in 5 electric, in 19 water, in 6 wind, in 86 horse-power, and in 964 manual labour only was employed; and the engines in use were worked to an aggregate horse-power of 29,000, and had a full capacity of 38,543; whilst over three-fourths of the hands were engaged in factories using machinery worked by steam, gas, electric, wind, or horse-power. The factories may be divided into two main classes, those occupied with the partial or crude treatment of raw materials, which numbered 459, and employed 4,547 hands; and those engaged in manufacturing finished articles of consumption, which numbered 2,351, and employed 45,901 hands. Of the total number of industries, 227, with 1,862 hands, were working in animal, and 124, with 3,262 hands, in vegetable and mineral foods; 237, with 3,097 hands, in drinks and narcotics; 474, with 15,768 hands, in dress and textile fabrics; 120, with 1,696 hands, in furniture; 124, with 1,598 hands, in building materials; 240, with 3,237 hands, in road, railway, and water vehicles, and other apparatus for transportation; 130, with 2,235 hands, in animal matters; 391, with 3,934 hands, in wood and other vegetable substances; 62, with 676 hands, in oils and fats (animal and vegetable); 334, with 6,263 hands, in metals and minerals; 34, with 428 hands, in gold, silver, and precious stones; 57, with 787 hands, in heat, light, and energy; 203, with 4,654 hands, in printing, account books, and stationery; and 53, with 1,011 hands, in other industries.

The principal products manufactured during the year were as follow :—Flour, 122,541 tons ; beer, 14¼ million gallons ; spirits, 410,000 gallons (proof) ; sugar and molasses refined, 783,162 cwt.; tobacco, 985,811 lbs.; butter, 29,676,097 lbs.; bacon and hams, 7,817,977 lbs.; soap, 140,792 cwt.; candles, 51,552 cwt.; woollen cloth, flannel, &c., 2,180,704 yards ; blankets, 9,519 ; hides, tanned, 439,291 ; skins, tanned, 2,147,169 ; boots and shoes, made, 2,598,387 pairs ; timber (Victorian), sawn, 31,973,743 super. feet ; gas, 1,477,130,510 cubic feet ; electric energy supplied, 4,916,171 Brit. units ; bricks, 55,682,110. In freezing works, moreover, 271,790 carcasses of sheep and 860,904 of rabbits were treated for export.

RAILWAYS.

The Railways in Victoria are exclusively the property of the State, whose policy has been not only to systematically open up the interior and keep pace with the development of the country, but also to anticipate settlement ; and although in the past they were not, nor were intended to be, worked on strict commercial principles, still the whole community has derived from them incalculable benefits, and it is believed that few railway systems in the world could show from their inception so favorable a record. Their success would have been still greater, but for the construction of a large number of political lines, the heavy cost of construction—due to the sudden rise in the price of land immediately it was known to be required for railway purposes, and the high rate of interest on public loans. All these things, however, are now changed. The railways have been removed from political control, and an attempt is being made to work them on commercial principles ; unreasonable prices are not now paid for land, which is indeed in many cases obtained free of cost ; whilst the current rate of interest on loans, formerly as high as 6, 5, and 4 per cent., has fallen to 3 per cent., which will result in a considerable saving as the loans mature.

On the 30th June, 1897, 3,112 miles were open for traffic, about 300 miles of which were laid with double lines. The cost of construction of lines open for traffic was, inclusive of rolling-stock, £38,325,517, or an average of about £12,315 per mile ; of this amount about £35,521,777 was raised by means of loans, and the remainder—or about 7 per cent.—was contributed from the general revenue. The train mileage during the year was 9,228,687. The total receipts amounted to £2,615,935, and the working expenses to £1,563,806. The net income was thus £1,052,129, which is equivalent to a return of 2¾ per cent. on the mean capital cost, or close on 3 per cent. on the debenture capital. This must be considered a satisfactory result, considering the adverse effect on the revenue of the failure of the harvest, and seeing that at the present time the average rate of interest payable upon the railway loans is between 3¾ and 4 per cent.

Posts and Telegraphs.

Post-offices.

A very efficient postal system exists in Victoria, and post-offices are established throughout the length and breadth of the colony; 1,572 of such institutions now exist, as against 1,342 twelve years since. In the year 1896 the letters passing through the post numbered 84,124,347, in addition to which there were large numbers of newspapers, packets, and parcels. The postage on letters to places in any of the Australasian colonies is twopence per ounce, and on newspapers one halfpenny each. The postage on letters to the United Kingdom is twopence halfpenny, and on newspapers one penny.

Money Orders.

Money-order offices in Victoria in connexion with the post-office have been established in 443 places, and the system is being rapidly extended by the opening of fresh offices. Besides the issue and payment of money orders at these places, such orders are issued in favour of Victoria, and Victorian orders are paid, not only at places in Great Britain and Ireland and in the various Australasian colonies, but also in the principal British possessions and foreign countries throughout the world. The number of money orders issued during the year 1896 was 217,878, of an aggregate value of £668,882. The commission on money orders for sums not exceeding £5 is 6d. to places in Victoria; and 6d. for sums under £2, and 1s. for those under £5, to places in the other Australasian colonies ; and so on proportionately for larger sums up to £20. To the United Kingdom and other countries, the charge is on a scale averaging about 1s. for every £2, with a further rate varying from 3d. to 9d. for orders passing through the London office. The limit for a single order is £20 to places in the Australasian colonies, China, Italy, Germany, and the United States, and £10 to other places. Money orders may be made payable in all the Australasian colonies *by telegraph* on payment of the minimum charge for a telegram in addition to the above rates, except in the case of New Zealand, in which instance the charge for a money-order telegram is 5s.

Postal Notes.

Postal notes are also issued, chiefly for use within the colony, for any amounts not exceeding £1, at charges ranging from ½d. to 3d. The number of such notes paid during 1896 was 944,028, having a total nominal value of £385,403.

Electric Telegraphs.

Telegraphs in Victoria are Government property, and are worked in connexion with the Post-office. Telegraphic communication exists between 791 stations within the colony, and the Victorian lines are connected besides with the lines of New South Wales, and by means of them with Queensland and New Zealand. They are also connected with the lines of South Australia, and by their means with Western Australia, and with the Eastern Archipelago, Asia, Europe, and America. They are likewise united with a submarine cable to Tasmania. In 1896 the miles of line along which poles extended numbered 6,977, of which 3,146 miles belonged to the Railway Department, and the miles of wire 14,389, including 5,018 miles used for railway purposes; the telegrams transmitted numbered 1,872,615, of which 64,281 were on Government business. To places within Victoria, telegrams containing not more than nine words are sent for 9d., 1d. extra being charged for each additional word. To New South Wales the charge is 1s. for ten words; to South Australia and Tasmania, 2s.; to Western Australia and Queensland, 3s.; and to New Zealand, 3s. 6d. For each additional word 6d. is charged to the last named, 3d. to Queensland, and 2d. to the other colonies. To England or the Continent of Europe, the rate is 4s. 10d. per word; to India it varies from 4s. 10d. to 5s. 1d.; and to the United

States, from 5s. 10d. to 6s. 6d. In the case of telegrams to places on the Australian Continent, names and addresses are not charged for ; to places in Tasmania they are not charged for unless they exceed ten words, but all words above that number are charged for as part of the message. In the case of telegrams to New Zealand, England, the Continent of Europe, India, and the United States, the names and addresses of both sender and receiver are charged for as part of the message.

Telephones.

During the last few years, telephonic has in a large measure superseded the less expeditious postal and tele-graphic communication in the chief centres of population, and the telephone system has been rapidly extended to meet public requirements. At the end of 1896, there were thirteen public exchanges, having 2,754 subscribers, whilst the length of wire used exceeded 10,000 miles. A few bureaux for the use of the public have already been established.

EDUCATION.

University.

The Melbourne University, which has been established since 1855, is empowered to grant in any faculty except divinity (no religious test being permissible) any degree, diploma, certificate, or licence which can be conferred in any university in the British dominions ; and by Royal letters patent, under the sign-manual of Her Majesty Queen Victoria, issued in 1859, it was declared that all degrees granted by the Melbourne University should be recognised as academic distinctions and rewards of merit, and should be entitled to rank, precedence, and consideration in the United Kingdom and in British colonies and possessions throughout the world just as fully as if they had been granted by any university in the United Kingdom. The institution at present receives an annual endowment of £12,250 from the general revenue. On the 22nd March, 1880, the University was thrown open to females, and they can now be admitted to all its corporate privileges. Affiliated to the University are three colleges in connexion with the Episcopalian, the Presbyterian, and the Wesleyan Church respectively, and named Trinity, Ormond, and Queen's. Ormond

College, named after the late Hon. Francis Ormond, M.L.C., who contributed nearly £82,000 towards its erection and endowment. The University Hall, built at a cost of about £40,000, is called the Wilson Hall, after the late Sir Samuel Wilson, who contributed the greater portion of the funds for its erection. Since the opening of the University, 4,040 students matriculated, and 2,452 degrees were granted—including about 100 to lady graduates, of which 2,066 were direct, and 386 *ad eundem*. The students who matriculated in 1896 numbered 129—of whom 16 were females ; and the graduates in the same year numbered 123 —of whom 31 were females.

State Education.

The State educational system of Victoria, the basis of which is that secular instruction shall be provided, without payment, for children whose parents may be willing to accept it, but that, whether accepted or not, satisfactory evidence must be produced that all children, up to the age of 13, are educated up to a given standard, has been most successful in its operation. In 1872, just before the present system came into operation, the number of children returned as on the rolls of State schools was 136,055, whilst in 1896, after the system had been in force for twenty-four years, the number had increased to 235,617, or by 73 per cent., the increase of population in the same period having been only 52 per cent. It has been estimated that the proportion of children attending school for not less than 40 days in each quarter amounts to about 47 per cent. of the numbers on the rolls.

Private Schools.

Besides the State schools, which are attended by five-sixths of the children under instruction in the colony, there are, according to the latest returns, 939 private schools, attended by 49,996 scholars. Some of these private schools are attached to religious denominations, as many as 220, with 23,562 scholars, being connected with the Roman Catholic Church. Six are called colleges or grammar schools, two of which are connected with the Church of England, two with the Roman Catholic, one with the Presbyterian, and one with the Wesleyan Church. In these, as well as in some of the other private schools, a very high class of education, almost if not quite equal to that obtained in the best public schools in England, is given.

Results of Victorian School System.

It has been officially estimated that of the children in Victoria between the ages of six and thirteen (the school age), all but a very small proportion receive education during some portion of each year. The results are shown in the very large proportion of educated children comprised in the population. According to the returns of the census of 1891, of every 10,000 children at the school age, 9,389 could read, 8,770 of whom could also write, and only 611 were unable to read. The proportion of instructed children indicated by these figures is far higher than the proportion prevailing in any of the other Australasian colonies, and is equalled in few, if in any, other countries.

CLERGY AND CHURCHES.

Clergy.—There being no State religion in Victoria, and no money voted for any religious object, the clergy are supported by the efforts of the denomination to which they are attached. The clergy, ministers, &c., number 1,615, of whom 236 belong to the Church of England, 198 to the Roman Catholic Church, 237 to the Presbyterian Church, 218 to the Methodist Churches, 59 to the Independent Church, 52 to the Baptist Church, 38 to the Bible Christian Church, 474 to the Salvation Army, 95 to other Christian churches, and 8 to the Jewish Church. Besides these there are other officials connected with some of the sects who, without being regularly ordained, perform the functions of clergymen, and are styled lay readers, lay assistants, local preachers, mission agents, &c. The number of these is not known, but it no doubt materially swells the ranks of religious instructors in the colony.

Churches and Chapels.—The buildings used for public worship throughout Victoria number at the present time about 4,809, of which 2,651 are regular churches and chapels, and 2,158 public or private buildings. Accommodation is provided for 650,000 persons, but the number attending the principal weekly services is said not to exceed 500,000. About 350,000 services are performed during the year. Of the whole number of buildings used for religious worship, 1,081 belong to the Church of England, 570 to the Roman Catholics, 947 to the Presbyterians, 1,386 to the Methodists, 819 to other Christians, and 6 to the Jews.

PRICES.

The following are the quoted prices of the principal articles of consumption, also of live stock, in Melbourne during the year 1896. In country districts the cost of groceries, tobacco, wines and spirits, &c., is naturally somewhat higher, and that of agricultural and grazing produce, firewood, &c., somewhat lower, than in Melbourne :—

PRICES IN MELBOURNE, 1896.

Articles.				Prices.
AGRICULTURAL PRODUCE.				
Wheat	...	...	... per bushel	4s. 2d. to 6s.
Barley { Malting	...	...	,,	3s. to 4s. 9d.
{ Cape	...	...	,,	2s. 8d. to 3s. 8d.
Oats ...	...	...	,,	2s. to 3s. 8d.
Maize	..	...	,,	3s. to 4s.
Bran ...	...		,,	8½d. to 1s. 2d.
Hay ...	..	... per ton	£2 10s. to £6 5s.
Flour, first quality		...	,,	£9 to £15
Bread	...		... per 4-lb. loaf	4½d. to 8d.
GRAZING PRODUCE.				
Horses—				
Medium to heavy draught		each		£17 to £23
Saddle and light harness		,,		£10 to £35
Butchers' meat—				
Beef	...	...	... per lb.	3d. to 6d.
Mutton	...	...	,,	1½d. to 4d.
Veal	...	..	... ,,	2d. to 6d.
Pork	...		... ,,	3d. to 6d.
Lamb	...	..	... per quarter	1s. to 1s. 9d.
DAIRY PRODUCE.				
Butter	...	...	... per lb.	8d. to 1s. 3d.
Cheese		...	... ,,	6d. to 10d.
Milk ...		...	... per quart	3d. to 5d.*
FARM-YARD PRODUCE.				
Geese	...	...	... per couple	4s. to 10s.
Ducks	...	...	... ,,	2s. 6d. to 6s.
Fowls	...	...	... ,,	3s. to 6s.
Rabbits	...	...	... ,,	6d. to 1s.
Pigeons	...	...	... ,,	1s. to 2s.

* In the country the price is only 3d. per gallon.

PRICES IN MELBOURNE. 1896—*continued*.

Articles.					Prices.

FARM-YARD PRODUCE—*continued*.

Turkeys	...	...	...	each	5s. to 20s.
Sucking pigs	...	...	...	,,	5s. to 10s.
Bacon	...	...	...	per lb.	7d. to 9d.
Ham ...	...	...	...	,,	9d. to 1s.
Eggs ...	...	...	...	per doz.	6d. to 1s. 9d.

GARDEN PRODUCE.

Potatoes	...	...	...	per cwt.	2s. to 8s.
Onions, dried	...	...	...	,,	3s. to 14s.
Carrots	...	...	per dozen bunches		3d. to 1s.
Turnips	...	...	,,		3d. to 9d.
Radishes	...	...	,,		3d. to 5d.
Cabbages	...	...	per doz.		6d. to 2s. 6d.
Cauliflowers	...	...	...	,,	1s. to 5s.
Lettuces	...	...	...	,,	3d. to 9d.
Green peas, retail		...	...	per lb.	1d. to 3d.

MISCELLANEOUS ARTICLES.

Tea	...	...	...	per lb.	1s. to 2s.
Coffee	...	...	...	,,	1s. 3d. to 2s.
Sugar, refined	...	...	...	,,	$2\frac{1}{2}$d.
Rice	...	...	...	...	,,	3d.
Tobacco	...	...	...	,,	3s. 6d. to 5s.
Soap, common		...	...	,,	$2\frac{3}{4}$d.
Candles—Sperm		...	...	,,	5d. to $8\frac{1}{2}$d.
Salt	...	...	...	...	,,	$\frac{3}{4}$d. to 1d.
Coal	...	...	...	per ton	16s. to 20s.
Firewood	...	...	...	,,	15s. to 20s.
Gas (in 1898)	...	...	...	per 1,000 ft.	5s.

WINES, SPIRITS. ETC.

Ale—English	...	...	...	per doz.	8s. to 10s. 6d.
,, Colonial			,,		5s. 6d.
			per quart		6d.
Porter—English		...	...	per doz.	8s. 9d. to 10s. 6d.
Brandy	...	...	...	per bottle	4s. 6d. to 6s.
Whisky	...	...	...	,,	4s. to 5s. 6d.
Wine (Colonial)		...	...	per doz.	12s. to 20s.
,, ...	...	...	...	per gall.	3s. to 7s. 6d.

WAGES.

The following table contains a statement of the average rates of wages paid in respect to engagements made in Melbourne in 1896. The quotations are without board and lodging. unless otherwise expressly stated. Throughout Victoria, the recognised working day for artisans and general labourers is eight hours :—

Description of Labour.	Rate.

1.—DOMESTIC SERVANTS (WITH BOARD AND LODGING).

Males.

		Rate
Coachmen, footmen, grooms, gardeners	per week	20s. to 30s.
Butlers ...	,,	20s. to 30s.

Females.

		Rate
Cooks ...	per annum	£40 to £75
Laundresses ...	,,	£40 to £52
Housemaids ...	,,	£30 to £40
Nursemaids ...	,,	£30 to £40
General servants	,,	£20 to £35
Girls ...	per week	8s. to 10s.

2.—HOTEL SERVANTS (WITH BOARD AND LODGING).

Males.

		Rate
Barmen ...	per week	20s. to 30s.
Waiters ...	,,	20s. to 30s.
Boots ...	,,	15s. to 25s.
Ostlers ...	,,	15s. to 20s.
Cooks ...	,,	20s. to 65s.

Females.

		Rate
Barmaids ...	per week	15s. to 25s.
Waitresses ...	,,	15s. to 20s.
Housemaids ...	per annum	£30 to £35
Cooks ...	,,	£50 to £100

3.—FARM SERVANTS.

Males.

		Rate
Ploughmen ...	per week, and found	15s. to 20s.
Farm labourers	,, ,,	12s. 6d. to 15s.
Milkmen for dairies	,, ,,	10s. to 15s.
Cheesemakers ...	,, ,,	25s. to 40s.
Reapers * ...	per acre, ,,	10s. to 15s.
Mowers * ...	,, ,,	4s. to 6s.
Threshers * ...	per bushel, ,,	5d. to 7d.
Cooks ...	per annum, ,,	£50 to £60

Females.

		Rate
Dairy milkmaids	per annum, with board and lodging	£30 to £35
Cooks ...	,, ,, ,,	£30 to £40
General servants	,, ,, ,,	£20 to £30
Married couples (generally useful)	,, ,, ,,	£50 to £60
Hop-pickers ...	per bushel ...	2d. to 3½d.
Maize-pickers ...	per bag ...	4d. to 6d.

---

* The greater part of the reaping, mowing, and threshing is being done by machinery.

WAGES IN MELBOURNE, 1896—*continued*.

Description of Labour.					Rate.

4.—STATION SERVANTS.

Males (with rations).

Boundary riders	per annum	...	...	...	£40 to £60
Shepherds	...	„	...	...	...	£36 to £52
Stockmen	...	„	...	...	...	£50 to £60
Cooks	...	„	...	...	..	£60 to £70
Labourers	...	per week	...	...	...	15s. to 20s.
Drovers	...	„	...	...	...	25s. to 40s.
Sheepwashers	...	„	...	...	...	15s. to 25s.
Shearers	...	per 100 sheep shorn	...	...	15s. to 16s.

Females.

Cooks	...	per annum, with board and lodging	£30 to £60
General servants	„	„ „ ...	£30 to £36
Married couples	per annum, with rations ...	...	£50 to £70

5.—WORKERS IN BOOKS, ETC.

Printers—

Compositors	...	per 1,000	...	...	1s.
Machinists	...	per week	...	...	£2 12s. to £3
Lithographers	...	„	...	...	£2 10s. to £3 10s.
Binders	...	„	...	..	£2 10s. to £4
Paper rulers	...	„	...	...	£2 10s. to £3 10s.
Sewers and folders (females)	„	...	...	12s. 6d. to 27s. 6d.

6.—IN WATCHES, JEWELLERY, AND PRECIOUS METALS

Watchmakers	...	per week	...	...	...	£2 to £3
Manufacturing jewellers	„	...			£1 10s. to £4

7.—IN METALS OTHER THAN GOLD AND SILVER.

Blacksmiths	...	per day	...	...	9s. to 11s.
Die-sinkers	...	per week	...	...	£2 10s. to £4 10s
Engravers	...	„	...	...	...	£1 15s. to £3
Farriers—Firemen	„	...	...	...	£2 to £2 5s.
„ Floormen	„	...	...	...	£1 15s. to £2 2s.
Hammermen	...	per day	..	...	...	6s. 6d. to 7s.
Fitters	...	„	...	...	...	9s. to 10s.
Turners	...	„	...	...	...	9s. to 10s.
Boilermakers and platers, per day	..	...	...	10s. to 11s.
Riveters	...	per day	...	...	...	10s. to 11s.
Lamp-makers	...	per week	...	...	£1 15s. to £3
Pattern-makers	...	per day	...	...	8s. to 10s.
Moulders	...	„	...	...	...	9s. to 10s. 4d.
Brass-finishers, coppersmiths, per day	..	...	...	8s. to 10s.
Tinsmiths	...	per week	...	..	...	£2 to £2 14s.
Japanners	...	„	...	...	...	£2 to £2 14s.
Ironworkers	...	„	...	...	...	£2 to £3 6s.
Galvanizers	...	„	...	...	...	£2 to £3 6s.
Plumbers, gasfitters	„	...	...	...	£1 10s. to £3

Wages in Melbourne, 1896—*continued.*

Description of Labour.					Rate.

8.—In Carriages and Harness.

Smiths	... per week	...	...	...	£2 to £3
Bodymakers	... ,,	...	...	...	£2 to £2 10s.
Wheelers	... ,,	...	...	...	£2 to £2 10s.
Painters	... per day	...	..	...	6s. to 8s. 4d.
Trimmers	... per week	...		...	£2 to £2 14s.
Vycemen	... ,,	...	...	...	£1 10s. to £2
Collar-makers	... ,,	...	...	...	£1 5s. to £3
Harness-makers	... ,,	...	...	...	£1 5s. to £3
Saddle-makers	... ,,	...	...	...	£1 5s. to £3
Saddle-tree makers	,,	...	...	...	£1 15s. to £2 10s.
Whip-makers	... ,,	...	...	...	£1 10s. to £3 10s.

9.—Ships and Boats.

Sailors—					
Sailing vessels	... per month, and found		...	...	£3 to £4
Steam-ships	,, ,,		...	...	£6
Ship carpenters, shipwrights (steam), per month, and found					£9
Stevedores' men, lumpers	} per day	...			8s. to 10s.

10.—In Houses and Buildings.

Masons	... per day	...	...	...	8s.
Plasterers	... ,,	...	...	...	6s. to 7s.
Bricklayers	... ,,	...	...	...	6s. to 8s.
Slaters	... ,,	...	...	...	7s. to 8s.
Carpenters	... ,,	...	...	...	6s. to 8s
Labourers	... ,,	...	...	...	5s. to 6s.
Painters and glaziers	,,	...	..	...	5s. to 8s.
Signwriters	... ,,	...	...	...	7s. to 8s.
Paperhangers	... ,,	...	...	...	5s. to 7s.

11.—In Furniture, etc.

Cabinetmakers	... per week	...	...	...	£1 5s. to £2 10s.
Carvers	... ,,	...	...	..	£2 5s.
Turners	... ,,	...	...	...	£2 5s.
Upholsterers	... ,,	...	...	...	£2 to £2 15s.
Polishers	... ,,	...	...	...	£2 to £2 10s.
Coopers	... per day	...	...	...	7s. to 9s.

12.—Workers in Dress.

Tailors	... per hour	...			10d. to 1s.
,,	... per week	...			£2 to £3 10s.
,, in factories	,,	...			£2 to £3
Mantlemakers	... ,,	...			10s. to 25s.
Milliners—					
First class	... ,,	...	...	...	£3 to £4
Second class	... ,,	...	...	...	15s. to £2 5s.

WAGES IN MELBOURNE. 1896—*continued.*

Description of Labour.	Rate.

12.—WORKERS IN DRESS—*continued.*

Dressmakers ... per week	12s. to 25s.
Needlewomen ... ,, ...	12s. to 25s.
Bootmakers ... riveting, per pair—	
children's	5d.
boys'	7½ to 9d.
women's	8d. to 1s. 1d.
men's	11d. to 1s. 9d.
,, ... machine sewing, per pair—	
children's and boys'	6d. to 9d.
women's	1s. 1d.
men's	1s. 5d.
,, ... making wellingtons to order, sewn.	13s. 6d.
,, ... ,, ,, pegged	8s. 6d.
,, ... making elastics to order, sewn ...	10s.
,, ... ,, ,, pegged .	7s. 6d.
,, Machinists, per week	10s. to 25s.
Hatters—	
Gossamer trade—	
Bodymakers—silk hats, per dozen ...	10s. to 22s.
Finishers ... per dozen	12s. to 24s.
Shapers ... ,, ...	4s. to 12s.
Crown sewers ,, ...	3s. 6d. to 4s.
Trimmers ... ,, ...	6s. to 9s.
Felt Hat Trade—	
Bodymakers per week	£3 5s.
Blockers ... ,, ...	£3
Finishers ... ,, ...	£3
Shapers ... ,, ...	£3
Binders (females) ,, ...	24s.
Trimmers ., ,, ...	20s.
Clothing Factories—	
Cutters ... ,, ...	£2 10s.
Pressers ... ,, ...	30s. to 40s.
Tailoresses ... ,, ...	12s. 6d. to 27s. 6d.
Machinists ... ,, ...	12s. 6d. to 25s.
Shirtmakers ... ,, ...	14s. to 40s.
Drapers' assistants, carpet salesmen, per week ...	£1 10s. to £5

13.—IN FOOD.

Bakers—	
Foremen ... per week	£2 5s. to £3 10s.
Second hands ... ,, ...	£2 to £2 10s.
Butchers—	
Shopmen ... ,, ...	£2 5s. to £2 10s.
Slaughtermen .. ,, ...	£2 10s. to £3 10s.
Boys ... ... ,, with board	£1 to £1 12s 6d.
Small-goods men ., ,, ...	£1 10s. to £2 10s.
Maltsters .. ,, ...	£2 2s. to £2 15s.

Wages in Melbourne, 1896—*continued.*

Description of Labour.					Rate.

14.—In Animal Matters.

Description of Labour.					Rate.
Brush-makers	... per week	...	...	...	£1 10s. to £3
,,	Female drawing hands, per week		...		15s. to 25s.
Curriers	... per week	...	...		£2 2s. to £3
Tanners	... ,,	...	...		30s. to 36s
Beamsmen	... ,,	...	...		40s. to 45s.
Shedsmen	... ,,	...	...		30s. to 40s.
Fellmongers	... ,,	...	...		28s. to 40s.
Portmanteau, Trunk-makers }	,,		...		£1 15s. to £2 5s.

15.—In Vegetable Matters.

Description of Labour.					Rate.
Basket-makers	... per week	...	...	...	£2 to £2 10s.
Broom-makers	... ,,	...	..	...	30s. to 40s.
Cigar-makers	... ,,	...	...	...	30s. to 40s.
Tobacco (plug) makers	,,	...	...	...	£2 to £4
Cork-cutters	... ,,	..	...	...	36s. to £2 15s.

16.—In Stone, Clay, etc.

Description of Labour.					Rate.
Brickmakers—					
Clay-hole men	... per 1,000	..	...	...	1s. 9d.
Setters	... ,,	...	...		8d.
Drawers	... ,,	...	...		8d.
Burners	... per week	...	...		£2
Potters	... per hour	...	...		10d. to 1s.
Quarrymen	... per day	...	...		6s. to 8s.
Labourers	... ,,	...	...		5s. to 6s. 6d.
Stonebreakers	... per cubic yard	...	...		1s. to 3s.
Tarpavers	... per day	...	...		6s. 6d.
Asphalters	... ,,	...	...		10s.

17.—In Mines.

Description of Labour.					Rate.
General managers	per week	...	...		£3 to £10
Legal ,,	,,	...	...		£5 to £6
Mining ,,	,,	...	...		£2 10s. to £9
Engineers	... ,,	...	...		£2 8s. to £5
Engine-drivers	... ,,	...	...	..	£2 5s. to £3
Pitmen ...	... ,,	...	...	...	£2 to £3 10s.
Blacksmiths	... ,,	...	...	...	£2 to £3 10s.
Carpenters	... ,,	...	...	...	£2 2s. to £3 18s.
Foremen of shift	,,	...	...	...	£2 5s. to £3 6d.
Miners	... ,,	...	...	...	£2 to £2 10s.
Surfacemen—Labourers	,,	...	...	...	£1 10s. to £2 10s.
Boys ...	... ,,	...	...		10s. to £2

AGRICULTURE.

The agricultural resources of the colony, although only yet developed to a comparatively limited extent, have contributed in a marked degree to place Victoria in its present proud position, and the best guarantee for its future progress is to be found in the agricultural expansion capable of resulting from its rich soil, genial climate, and various other advantages. What has already been accomplished is the best indication of what may be expected in the future.

PIONEERING WORK DONE.

In the past all the difficulties connected with carrying on agricultural operations in a new country have had to be overcome. The pioneer farmer had to learn the peculiarities of the soil and the special conditions of climate with which he had to cope in an unknown and untried country, and all this had to be done under special difficulties. Seeds, plants, tools, and implements had to be imported from distant countries : horses, cattle, sheep, swine, and poultry had also to be brought from abroad, while the breeds best suited to the new conditions, and the peculiar treatment necessary, had to be learned by experiments more or less expensive. In establishing agriculture amidst all these difficulties there were other obstacles which had to be overcome. There were but few large towns, so that the markets for produce were limited, and it frequently happened that when a successful harvest was obtained the farmer would find the port glutted with foreign products. Not only were markets limited, but they were difficult of access. There were no roads through the forests, over the hills, or across the plains. Rivers had to be bridged and roads had to be made before the farmers' produce could be taken to market. All this up-hill work had to be carried on by farmers who were far from schools, churches, and social institutions.

PROSPERITY ASSURED.

Those who commence farming now, either upon Crown lands or upon farms purchased from settlers, have none of these difficulties to overcome. The large cities provide markets for produce, and supply implements and machinery of the most approved kind, manufactured locally and in Europe and America; seeds and plants of every kind have

STRIPPING WHEAT

STRIPPING WHEAT

een brought from all parts of the world; all the best breeds of live stock are available: and the conditions of soil and climate have been so well ascertained that all branches of agriculture can be carried on with a complete knowledge of the most suitable treatment to be pursued. Roads have been made in every direction, the rivers have been bridged at all necessary points, and railways have been extended to all settled portions of the colony, with the certainty that they will follow the settlers to the districts not yet occupied. In addition to all this, schools have been established in the midst of every group of settlers, churches have been built in every village, and even the most distant portions of the colony enjoy social advantages not surpassed in any country in the world.

Early Progress.

Much has been done in a short time. It is only 64 years since the first white man settled upon Victorian soil, but a much shorter time has elapsed since the march of progress properly began with the inrush of population soon after the discovery of gold in 1851. The development of agriculture had a still more recent commencement, for at the time of the gold diggings the land was in the possession of Crown tenants, who leased it as sheep and cattle runs, and many years passed before the new colonists, attracted by the discovery of gold, could succeed in passing laws for the throwing open of the land to agricultural settlers. Up to the year 1860 land could only be obtained at auction, and it was difficult for men of small means to obtain farms; and although more liberal land laws were passed after that date it was not until 1869 that an Act was framed under which agricultural settlement was effectually encouraged. During the period intervening between the landing of the first white men and the passing of the Land Act of 1869 agricultural settlement made very slow progress, but much useful work was done, the beneficial effects of which are still experienced. Mr. Henty, the first settler, commenced to cultivate immediately after arriving, and the plough which he used is preserved in Melbourne as a valuable historical relic, being the plough which turned the first sod in Victoria. The farms afterwards established near Melbourne, Ballarat, Geelong, Lancefield, Kilmore, Warrnambool, Belfast, and other early towns tested the quality of soils, and made known the peculiar treatment required by different crops in the climate of the colony. Owing also to the enterprise of the early colonists, live stock of different breeds were imported, so that when the public lands were thrown open for selection in 1869 the colony was well supplied with trained farmers of local experience, stud herds of shorthorn, Hereford, Ayrshire, and Jersey cattle had been established, as well as studs of the best draught and thoroughbred horses, flocks of merino, Lincoln, and Leicester sheep, with well-bred representatives of other kinds of live stock.

LATER DEVELOPMENT.

It was under the above circumstances that the agriculture of the colony began a career of remarkable development some 25 years ago. It may be mentioned also that the mining industry had been for some time affording employment to a diminishing number of men, and that many of the miners settled upon land under the liberal provisions of the new Land Act. Under preceding Land Acts the greater portion of the best land in the coast districts had been alienated, many large estates used for grazing purposes having been formed, so that agricultural settlement under the more liberal provisions of the Act of 1869 had to extend mainly over the northern or inland portion of the colony. Settlements were rapidly formed in all parts of the northern areas, and wheat-growing, the most suitable industry for the pioneering stages of such districts, was quickly developed to larger proportions. Three years after the Act came into force—viz., in 1873—the land under cultivation amounted to only 964,996 acres, while ten years later, in 1883, the area had increased to 2,215,923, and in 1893 to 3,019,002 acres. The total extent of land under the wheat crop in 1873 was 349,976 acres, and in 1893 it was 1,469,359 acres. As the production of all other farm products also increased during the same period, while live stock multiplied, and marked improvement was made in the quality of the various breeds, the natural advantages possessed by the colony for carrying on the various branches of agricultural industry are clearly manifested by the rapid progress which has taken place. Between 1881 and 1895 the number of sheep in the colony increased from 10,360,285 to 13,180,945, and the number of cattle from 1,286,267 to 1,833,900. When it is taken into account that the population of Victoria is only at present a little over one million, and that important mining, manufacturing, pastoral, and other industries have

A WHEAT FIELD AT HARVEST.—IN A COAST DISTRICT.

een carried on, the development of agriculture which has
taken place proves conclusively that the soil and climate
of the colony afford special advantages for agricultural
pursuits. In a new country the people are eager for large
profits, and so much attention would not have been given to
agriculture had not the favorable conditions of climate and
soil made the industry remunerative.

Fertility of the Soil.

It was soon discovered that the soil of Victoria was
exceedingly fertile. It had all the experience of being rich,
and when tried it more than realized expectations. Only a
few years after the landing of the first settlers "Port Fairy"
potatoes won fame, on account of their superior quality, in
older-established parts of Australia, and other products were
soon afterwards grown with equal success. The potatoes
were grown at Belfast and Warrnambool, on the south-west
coast of the colony, districts still famed for the production
of root crops. The rich soil of this region is of volcanic
origin, being very friable and of a reddish or chocolate
colour, capable of growing all kinds of crops for many
years without manure. A yield of from 12 to 15 tons
per acre of potatoes is sometimes obtained, and 10 tons
per acre is a frequent yield. The Lancefield, Daylesford,
Kyneton, Ballarat, and Gippsland districts contain land of
the same kind, and all over the colony a large proportion of
the soil is exceedingly fertile. Even in those parts of the
colony where the yield of the crops is smaller the defect is
not so much in the soil as in the supply of moisture. There
are in the inland northern portions of the colony districts
which do not enjoy such a liberal rainfall as others. In
such localities the yield of the crops is generally comparatively light, but the soil is rich, a fact that is proved from
the large yield obtained in a moist season. Having extensive
areas of fertile soil in all parts of its territory, and consequently under different conditions of climate, the products
of the colony are both abundant and varied.

The Genial Climate.

"The finest climate in the world." Such is the verdict
of all observant colonists who have travelled enough to give
weight to their opinion. There is no winter, in the English
or American sense of the word. The time called winter is
merely the season in which there is more rain and less heat

than in summer. Very few Australians have ever seen snow. Upon the inland mountain ranges and the elevated land in their vicinity a little snow falls occasionally, but only sufficient to make the ground white for a few hours. The native trees are evergreen, not casting their leaves in the winter, although English trees and others indigenous to cold countries go through the form apparently out of respect to old-established family customs, and altogether the winter is only a modified summer. Stock are neither housed nor fed in the winter. The merino sheep, which produce the finest wool in the world, run out on the pastures all the winter, generally without even a hedge to shelter them ; cattle in the same way are not only able to live on the pastures through the winter, but to fatten fit for the butcher. The dairy cows also are kept milking without being housed or fed, and when horses are not at work they spend the whole winter in the open fields. Any farmer who knows what it is to provide for housing and feeding his live stock through the winter in England, Scotland, Ireland, or America will be able to understand what special advantages Victoria possesses in its winterless climate.

The Rainfall.

In order to obtain a clear idea of the rainfall of Victoria, it will be necessary to take note of the physical features of the colony. It will be observed, by looking at the map, that the eastern coast range of the Australian Continent terminates about 100 miles south of the northern boundary of Victoria, or in the Gippsland district. From the terminal point a spur called the Great Dividing Range strikes off to the westward and extends across the colony of Victoria. This Dividing Range divides the colony into two parts, viz., the northern and southern division, or, if we take the whole course of the mountain chain, including the portion of the eastern coast range of the continent which extends into Victoria, we have the colony divided into the inland and coast districts. On the coast side of the mountains the territory, which averages a little over 100 miles wide, enjoys a copious rainfall, while in the inland country, averaging roughly over 100 miles from the River Murray, the average rainfall is somewhat less. All over the coast districts the rainfall is sufficient for the requirements of cereal and some kinds of root crops. Wheat, oats, and barley are successfully cultivated, and permanent pastures of English grasses

STUDENTS HARVESTING.—DOOKIE AGRICULTURAL COLLEGE.

can also be laid down. Root crops also do well, good crops of potatoes being obtained in many districts; and, although but little success has been obtained with turnips, mangolds and beets yield satisfactorily. The rainfall of Melbourne, which may be taken as representing the coast districts of the colony, has averaged for 30 years 25·44 inches. This is more than the rainfall of London (24 inches), Nottingham (23·7 inches), and Paris (22·9 inches). In the northern or inland districts the average rainfall is generally below 20 inches, and some specially dry localities do not average more than 10 inches. In the less dry sections of the northern districts, where the annual rainfall varies from 15 inches to 20 inches, oats, barley, and wheat are cultivated, and satisfactory yields are obtained, but root crops are rarely cultivated with success, while in the drier portions of the inland districts, where the rainfall varies from 12 to 16 inches, the wheat crop is the only one that can be depended upon to yield a fair return in average seasons.

Cheap Methods of Production.

It is important to note that the largest number of Victorian farmers are settled in the northern or inland districts, and, if the climate may seem to be too dry, it must be remembered that there are special advantages which compensate in a great measure for a deficiency of moisture. The land is generally ready for the plough, and even when some clearing is necessary the work is light and inexpensive. Stock of all kinds thrive remarkably well in the warm climate, and the Australian system of harvesting, viz., "stripping," or reaping and threshing at one operation, by far the cheapest in the world, can be adopted. The climate is, no doubt, drier than might be desired in these districts, but, with the advantages referred to, the farmers are able to carry on their industry successfully. The wheat-growers of the colony of South Australia have to contend against a drier climate and a smaller yield of grain per acre. It is only in the driest sections of the inland districts that oats and barley cannot be successfully grown, so that only a comparatively small number of farmers are compelled to restrict their agricultural operations to the growing of wheat. If we examine the driest sections of Victoria, we find that the settlers are in a prosperous condition, arising from other advantages which tend to compensate for the deficiency of moisture. The cheap system of cultivation and harvesting which is carried on enables the farmer to make good profits from light crops. There is comparatively little timber in the dry districts. Trees enough grow in patches or belts to provide fencing timber, but every farm contains a large area of open plain land which is ready for the plough. This land is more fertile and as easy tilled as the prairies of Western America, while a cheaper system of harvesting is adopted. The peculiar dryness of the air enables the stripper, which is a combined reaping and threshing machine, to be used, while on the American prairies the grain has to be reaped, bound, stooked, carted, and threshed. In the colony of South Australia, where this cheap system of cultivating and harvesting is adopted, the wheat-growers have been able to make a living from crops averaging only 5 bushels the acre. In the dry parts of Victoria the system of farming is similar, and the average yields vary from 10 to 15 bushels per acre. In the dry districts, too, the natural pastures are excellent, and, as the climate is warm, stock thrives well. Farmers in these parts, therefore, make profits, both from cultivation and stock-keeping, and they are generally prosperous and well content with their prospects. The system of irrigation recently introduced will make some of the arid districts the most productive portions of the colony. (See article upon "Irrigation.") A tract of 11,000,000 acres of land lying in the northern portion of the colony called "the Mallee," owing to being covered with a scrub of that name, is now being extensively cultivated by means of the South Australian scrub roller and stump-jump plough. The wheat grown here is of the highest standard of quality, and this tract has become now the great wheat-producing belt of the colony.

Crops and Yields.

The rich soil and warm genial climate combine to render the colony's productions abundant and varied. In the coast districts, where all kinds of cereals and leguminous and root crops are cultivated, the yields obtained from the unmanured land are all that could be desired. The average of the whole colony is always lower than the results obtained by farmers who understand their business. The system of farming carried on stands much in need of improvement. The majority of those upon the land have had no training as

farmers, and the system, like that of all new countries, is not calculated to produce the best results. Farmers who understand their business, and give the land reasonable cultivation, obtain from 35 to 45 bushels of wheat, oats, and barley per acre in districts where the general average is not more than from 15 to 20 bushels per acre. Much heavier yields than those stated are frequently obtained, but from 35 to 45 bushels per acre are common when the land is well cultivated. With potatoes, mangolds, beets, and peas, the same difference is observed between the average obtained by a rough system of farming and upon land properly cultivated. About 5 tons of potatoes per acre is a payable crop, and from 12 to 15 tons per acre are frequently obtained. Hay, which is made from wheat or oats, yields from 2 tons to 4 tons per acre, and English grasses for pasture are successfully cultivated in all the coast and elevated districts. Maize is a crop which grows well in the more moist portions of the coast districts, and as much as 100 bushels per acre is frequently obtained. Owing to the defective system of farming, many of the crops for which the colony is suitable are much neglected, the tendency of settlers being to neglect rotation and confine their attention to growing a single description of grain. Thus wheat-growing is carried on more extensively than most other departments of farming. All over the northern or inland districts wheat can be profitably produced, while in some sections other cereals do not do so well, and this fact also tends to swell the proportion of the colony's wheat production. The statistics of the harvest of 1883-4 show that the colony produced 15,570,000 bushels of wheat, 4,717,624 bushels of oats, 1,069,000 bushels of barley, 117,294 bushels of maize, 791,093 bushels of peas, 161,088 tons of potatoes, 18,906 tons of mangolds, 139,540 tons of onions, 433,143 tons of hay, 15,717 cwt. of hops, 9,124 cwt. of tobacco, besides smaller quantities of carrots, turnips, chicory, grass seed, and other products. In 1893-4 the wheat yield was 15,255,200 bushels; oats, 4,951,371 bushels; barley, 1,033,861 bushels; maize, 180,442 bushels; peas and beans, 1,050,082 bushels; potatoes, 144,708 tons; mangolds, 19,340 tons; turnips, 3,465 tons; onions, 203,980 tons; hay, 503,385 tons; hops, 5,684 cwt.; tobacco, 8,952 cwt. The three last harvests have come short of these figures owing to exceptionally unfavorable seasons. The wheat production of the colony is capable of great expansion, but there are more numerous opportunities and larger profits to be made by developing the various branches of husbandry which are partially neglected by the farmers.

Wheat.

The wheat grown in Victoria is the finest in the world. It always brings the highest price in the London market, fetching considerably more than English, Indian, American, or New Zealand wheat. The wheat crop is generally the first sown by the new settler, as it quickly returns a profit, and brings in resources to keep the farmer going until stock-raising, dairying, or other branches of industry are established. Many settlers have found continuous wheat-growing upon the rich virgin soil of the colony a profitable business; but the rule is that the best farmers, after a year or two, add the growing of other crops in rotation, and establish herds of cattle, flocks of sheep, breeding also horses and swine upon the farms.

Oats.

Oats grow well in all the coast districts of the colony and in the more moist of the inland districts. Even in the driest sections of the inland districts good yields of oats are being obtained by adopting the Algerian variety, while the straw is also valuable for fodder. In the moist districts from 40 to 50 and up to 60 and 70 bushels per acre are obtained with good cultivation, and the crop is successfully grown in rotation with wheat, barley, and roots.

Barley.

As barley requires more moisture than wheat, there are dry districts inland from the coast ranges where it cannot be properly grown, but the area of its cultivation is more extensive than that of oats. It yields good returns all over the coast half of the colony, and upon about half of the inland area. English barley grows well, producing a fair malting sample and a good yield, the crop being a profitable one. Those farmers who grow barley in rotation with oat, wheat, and root crops are generally the most successful.

Maize.

The maize crop is one which is not understood by the majority of Victorian farmers. Although crops of 100 bushels per acre, or as heavy as in any part of America, are obtained, and those who engage in its cultivation make large profits, the majority of farmers do not yet pay as much

attention to the cultivation of this cereal as they should. In America it is much more extensively cultivated even than wheat, maize being, in fact, the staple crop of the country. It is grown as a general crop in those States where only from 30 to 40 bushels per acre are obtained, and there are but few of the coast districts of Victoria where better yields would not be produced. The cultivation of maize, if attended to by the farmers, would be as profitable in Victoria as in many parts of America.

Leguminous Crops.

Peas are largely grown with most satisfactory results. Good yields are obtained, and the crop is profitable in more ways than one, for it has been found highly valuable in a system of rotation. Lands which had been impoverished by continuous grain growing have been brought back to a state of fertility by sowing the pea crop, and in limited districts where the merits of the pea crop are understood it plays a leading part in the system of maintaining the productiveness of the soil. Beans and vetches are also found to do satisfactorily. It is by the cultivation of many of these neglected crops that the agriculture of the colony is now being greatly developed. The comparatively backward state of our farming system offers encouraging opportunities for an influx of farmers, whose skill would turn our various unused advantages to account.

Root Crops.

The potato crop has been cultivated in most of the coast districts of the colony, and it yields, as a rule, a much more profitable return than cereals. Farms upon which potato-growing is carried on usually command an exceptionally high value, a fact which bears the best testimony to the profitableness of the crop. Mangolds have also been successfully grown, very heavy crops being obtained, but, owing to the defective system of farming, the potato is the only root which has received much attention. Potatoes, being required for human food, find a ready market, and hence their comparatively extensive cultivation by the farmers; but as mangolds, beets, and carrots are required principally for feeding stock, they receive very little attention. Feeding stock is a system not properly understood in the colony. The rich pastures, and the absence of cold winters, enable farmers to keep their stock in the fields all the year round, and at the same time cause the business of feeding stock to be neglected. Notwithstanding the richness of the pastures and the mildness of the winters, much could be done in the way of increasing the profitableness of stock-keeping by producing food, and the neglect of taking advantage of such an opportunity is one of the principal defects of our farming system. Those farmers who grow food for dairy cows, pigs, and other stock find the system profitable, and they are generally more prosperous than their neighbours. Where heavy root crops can be grown, it is not the fault of the country if they are not cultivated. As the system of farming improves, the growing of mangolds and carrots may be expected to increase, and it is believed that the cultivation of beets for sugar-making will ere long become an important industry. Most of the onions used in the Australian colonies are grown in Victoria. The crop in the coast districts yield from 10 to 15 tons per acre, and the soil, which is never manured, shows no sign of exhaustion after more than 30 years' cultivation.

Hay and Grasses.

Hay, which is extensively grown in the colony, is made from oats or wheat, cut just before ripening. The yield is from 2 to 4 tons per acre, the last named being the return obtained in the coast districts, and the former in the inland districts. In moist localities, or where irrigation is practised, lucerne is grown for hay, and it is one of the most profitable of crops. From 4 to 6 tons per acre are obtained, the crop yielding from four to six cuttings of about 1 ton each. In all of the coast districts, rye-grass, clover, cocksfoot, fog, foxtail, fesques, and other grasses are successfully cultivated, and it is the practice to lay down fields in pasture after they have been growing grain for a number of years. Very little manure is used in the colony, letting out the land in cultivated pasture being the most common means of maintaining fertility. In the northern or inland districts the rainfall is not sufficient to render the cultivation of English grasses profitable, but in those localities the growth of the natural grass is so rapid, and the quality of the pasture is so rich, that no inconvenience is experienced from the absence of artificial grasses. After the cereal crop there is good pasture afforded by the self-sown grain, and in the second year the natural grass has established itself so well as to carry more stock than the unbroken pasture.

STUDENTS PRUNING.—LONGERENONG AGRICULTURAL COLLEGE

THE BLACKSMITH'S SHOP. DOOKIE AGRICULTURAL COLLEGE.

Hops.

Hop culture has been established in the colony for some years, and there are extensive districts along the coast and near the mountain ranges specially well suited for the industry. Although hop-growing was introduced at a comparatively recent date, and much had to be learned as to the cultivation of the plant and the treatment of the hops, the industry has already assumed an important position. The soil and climate are much better suited for hop-growing than those of England or the eastern states of America, as shown in the higher yields obtained. From 20 to 25 cwt. per acre are frequently obtained from unmanured virgin soil, and about 10 cwt. per acre is yielded by yearling hops. California is the only country in the world that can show results in hop-growing equal to those of Victoria.

Other Products.

The tobacco crop is one which may be expected to increase as time passes. The soil and climate have been proved to be well suited for tobacco culture, and the cultivation of such a valuable crop may be expected to show development with the increase of population and the progress of the country. Great advantage to this industry has resulted from the employment by the Government of an American expert to instruct growers in improved methods. It will have been gathered from what has already been said that the climate resembles that of the South of Europe, and it follows that the various products of France, Spain, and Italy can be cultivated in the colony. This is not a matter of theory only, for practical experiments have already been tried which prove that the various rural industries of Southern Europe can be introduced with an assurance of greater success than ever attended them in their native country. Fruits of all kinds—from apples, pears, plums, peaches, apricots, and cherries to grapes, oranges, lemons, and olives—have been tried and found to flourish in a manner which astonishes natives of the South of Europe. The mulberry grows luxuriantly, and the development of silk culture is only a matter of time. The only reason why the colony does not produce more fruits, olive oil, and silk is that it is too prosperous. Wages are so high that other industries involving less labour absorb the attention of the population. The state of California, however, the climate of which resembles that of

Victoria, is teaching us that, by adopting machinery and labour-saving methods of management, many of the industries of Southern Europe can be profitably carried on when the population is limited and the rate of wages high. The attention of colonists has been attracted to the fact that in California fruit-growing has developed marvellously on account of the system which is adopted of drying apples, apricots, prunes, raisins, and currants, and preserving fruit in cans, and some progress is already being made to introduce the same system into the colony. Vines and fruit trees of all kinds grow well both in the coast and inland districts of the colony, and those colonists who are engaged in the cultivation of vineyards and orchards are generally even more prosperous than the farmers who grow grain.

Dairy Farming.

That the colony is peculiarly well suited for dairy farming follows from what has already been said in regard to the soil and climate. Rich natural pastures covering a fertile soil are sources of wealth in any country, but where the climate is so mild that stock require no shelter even in winter, special value attaches to well-grassed land. Just as the sheep farmer or the settler, who fattens cattle for the market, allows his stock to graze all the year round in the open fields, so the dairy farmer will take no special care of his milking cows. There are here and there farmers who take their cows into sheds on winter nights, feeding them upon straw or green fodder, but they are exceptions, the dairy cows in general, as all other stock, finding all their food and what shelter they need in the open fields. Those who had some straw, hay, or green food in the winter are rewarded by extra returns, and larger profits would be made if farmers did more in the way of growing supplies of winter feed for dairy cows, but the natural advantages of the country are indicated by the fact that dairying is generally carried on without resorting to any system of artificial feeding. (See article under the heading of " The Dairying Industry.")

Irrigation.

The most productive portions of America are those in which the rainfall is so deficient that it has to be supplemented by means of irrigation. The Government and Press Commissions from this colony to America (see " Victoria

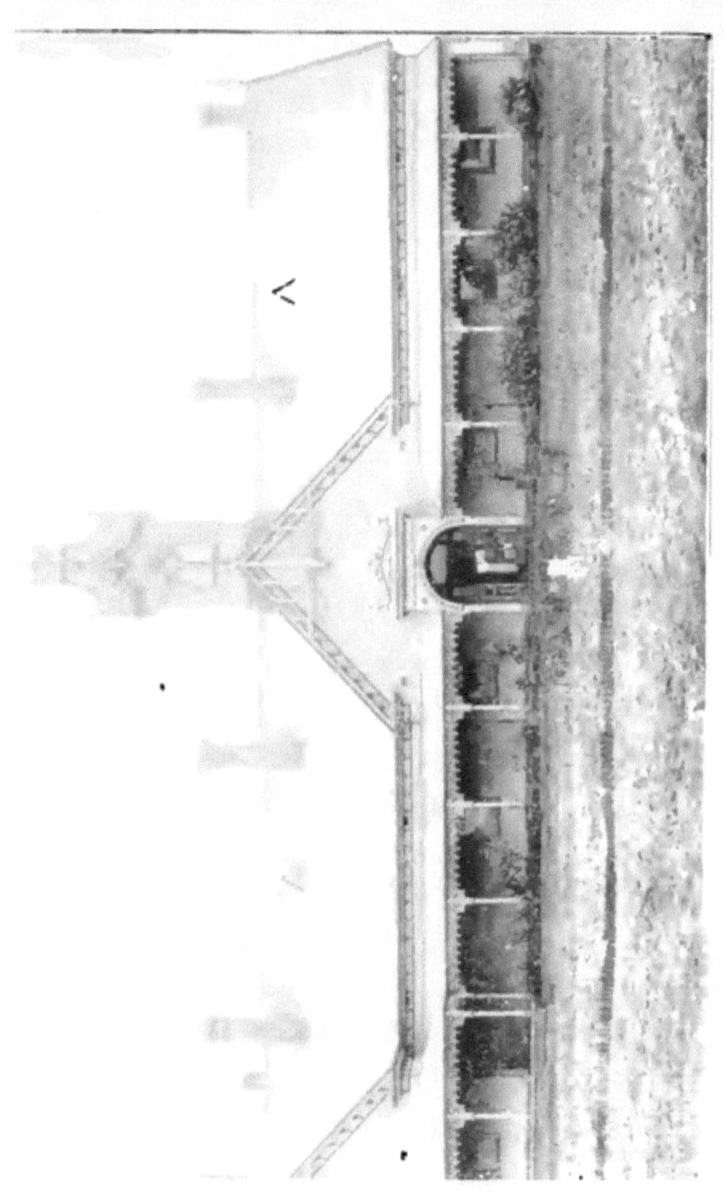

CHEMISTRY CLASS.—Longerenong Agricultural College

compared with America") saw no districts in their travels which were so productive, or which were so profitably cultivated or thickly populated, as the irrigated portions of California, Colorado, Utah, and New Mexico; and their reports established the fact that irrigation can be carried on with great success even in thinly-populated new countries. From this it is predicted that the inland districts of Victoria, in which the rainfall is lighter than on the coast side of the Dividing Range, will ultimately become the most productive and the most thickly populated. At present the land in the inland section is occupied in holdings of from 600 to 1,000 acres in extent, upon which a combined system of grain-growing and stock-keeping is carried on, but with irrigation the land will become so productive that subdivision into smaller holdings will take place. The Murray, the largest river in Australia, and the Goulburn and other Victorian rivers only require to be utilized in order to bring about such beneficial changes as have taken place in some of the driest tracts of Western America. Not only is the suitable-ness of irrigation founded upon American experience, but it has been fully proved by considerable practical experience within the colony itself. The Government, a few years ago, completed a scheme of irrigation which made the surplus water of all the principal rivers available for application to the land, and the results, wherever the water has been used for irrigation, have been highly satisfactory. Owing to the seasons having been less dry than usual since the completion of the water schemes, and the want of skill in the details of irrigation possessed by settlers, only slow progress has been made in turning such a valuable source of wealth to account, but those farmers who have watered their crops have been richly rewarded. The area under irrigation is now rapidly increasing, a fact which furnishes the best proof that farmers are finding the system profitable. The present farmers, who hold large areas of from 300 to 600 and 1,000 acres, will no doubt soon be glad to subdivide and sell their land in small and moderate-sized holdings, and such dense settlements as Ontario, Pomona, and Riverside, in Southern California, will come into existence, in place of the present extensive wheat farms. Those who buy farms before extensive irriga-tion shows the marvellous productiveness of the soil when supplied with water will have the best chance of obtaining cheap land. (See further remarks on this subject under the heading of "Irrigation Schemes.")

Fruits, Wine, Sugar-beet, and other Products.

Owing to different climatic conditions existing in various parts of the colony, from the coast districts to the elevated slopes of the Australian Alps and Dividing Range, to the dry warm plains of the north, the range of productions is wide. In addition to the branches of agriculture already dealt with, such subjects as Orchards, Vineyards. the Beet-sugar Industry, Tobacco. and Oil and Fibre Plants will be treated of in separate chapters.

Victoria compared with America.

North America receives a constant stream of population from the United Kingdom and Europe, and, in most cases, emigrants have bettered their condition by going to the newer country. Can Victoria offer equal inducements to the agriculturist who is seeking a new field of operation? Happily. an authoritative and satisfactory answer can be given to that question. In 1883, the two leading newspapers of Victoria sent special agricultural reporters to America to report upon the condition of farming in that country. The farmers of the colony wished to know what they had to fear from American competition in grain-growing, wool production, and other branches of agriculture, and to be instructed in the best and cheapest methods of carrying on farming operations. In order to supply this information. each of the two leading journals of Melbourne sent a special agricultural reporter to travel all over the United States in the year mentioned. The writer of these pages, who was one of the special reporters thus sent, reported that the colony had nothing to fear from American competition, and dwelt upon the many superior advantages possessed by Victoria. Upon these points the special reporter of the other journal fully agreed with the present writer, and thus the superiority of the colony was testified to by two independent experts. In 1885, a member of the Government. as chairman of a Royal Commission upon Irrigation. visited the United States, and he was accompanied by two reporters representing the same newspapers. The reports of the member of the Government referred to. and of press representatives who accompanied him, all agreed in testifying to the superior richness of the soil, and the more genial character of the climate. of this colony, as compared with those of the United States. The verdict of all those independent and well-qualified witnesses

STUDENTS PLOUGHING — LONGERENONG AGRICULTURAL COLLEGE.

was that, as far as climate, soil, and other natural conditions were concerned, the balance of advantages was on the side of Victoria. California was the only state in which the climate was anything like as favorable to agricultural and pastoral pursuits as that of the colony. The severe winter in the best parts of the Mississippi Valley, or out on the Western Prairies, is a great drawback to the progress of the farmer and stock-breeder. In America the farmer must house and feed his stock in winter, while in Victoria the custom is almost unknown. The fine-woolled merino sheep, the horse stock, the fattening cattle, and the dairy cows, all thrive throughout the year without shelter upon the open natural pasture lands. The lands in America available for settlement are from 1,000 to 2,000 miles from the sea-ports, while the compact colony of Victoria, with its extensive coast-line, lies near its shipping ports, the most distant districts being little more than 300 miles inland. The seasons are opposite to those of the Northern Hemisphere, giving the colony command of the great markets of the world, while those of India, China, and Japan are close at hand. What was worthy of imitation in American machinery, and methods of carrying on farming in a new country, was brought under notice, and the latest improvements are now being adopted. The farmer in Victoria can adopt the best American methods and labour-saving machinery ; he lives under institutions second to those of no other nation in freedom and liberality, and he carries on his industry upon a soil and in a climate unsurpassed in the whole world.

Agricultural Education.

The importance of instructing the youth of the colony in scientific and practical agriculture has long been recognised by thoughtful colonists, but little of importance was accomplished until 1885, when the Government set apart 150,000 acres of land as an endowment for agricultural colleges and experimental farms. The endowment lands were assigned to three trustees, and a Council of Agricultural Education, representing the Agricultural Societies of the colony and the Government, was appointed. Two colleges have been established, at which students receive a thoroughly liberal English education, combined with scientific agriculture, as well as practical experience of all branches of farming industry.

It is proposed to extend the scope of agricultural education by the establishment of a Dairy School; and a Viticultural School, which will shortly be organized, has already been erected by the Government. Students are also instructed in horticulture at the Government Horticultural Gardens at Burnley, near Melbourne: and a Government Scent Farm is also carried on to give instruction in scent flower farming. Experts are also employed by the Government to give instruction to settlers engaged in dairying, fruit-growing, viticulture, tobacco-growing, and the cultivation of fibre and oil producing plants. The absence, for many years, of any such schools, and the fact that the majority of the settlers have had no previous agricultural experience, accounts for the backward condition of many branches of colonial farming. While this state of things offers special advantages to new-comers with good agricultural training and experience, the new colleges will in time raise the standard of agriculture in the colony. The instruction is free at the agricultural schools, as it is in the ordinary State schools, and the charge for board and lodging, £26 per annum, is as low as the bare paying of expenses will admit of. The existence of such colleges should offer no small inducement to intending emigrants to make a home in Victoria, for a means of practically training one's family for a colonial career, while obtaining their education, is of no small importance. There are institutions in England which profess to give an agricultural education fitting young men for colonial life, but the training obtained under such circumstances must be very defective. The knowledge of colonial conditions must be wholly theoretical, and the time spent in such institutions is likely to be almost entirely lost. In the agricultural colleges and upon the experimental farms which are established in Victoria, students receive a practical and scientific education, which will fit them for a successful career in any of the Australasian colonies.

Wages.

The rate of wages must be studied in connexion with the peculiar condition of agriculture in the colony. The genial climate enables the farmer to dispense with the heavy staff of men needed in the old country. There is no hand feeding of stock, and thus a great deal of labour is saved. The rich virgin soil requires no manure for many years, and hence there is more saving of labour. Labour having always been

STUDENTS USING EARTH-SCOOP. Longerenong Agricultural College

high, all kinds of labour-saving machinery has been introduced, so that, from the double, three-furrow, and multi-furrow plough to the reaper and binder and Australian stripper, the system tends to keep down the expenditure upon wages. Farm labourers are generally provided with board and lodging, and the wages average as follow:— Ploughmen, per week, 16s. to 21s.; ordinary farm hands, 13s. to 19s.; married couples, 21s.; females, 8s. 6d. to 10s.; mowers, 24s. to 34s.; mowers, per acre, 4s. 11d. to 5s. 5d.; reapers, per week, 24s.; threshers, 6d. to 7d. per bushel; shepherds, £30 to £40 per annum; stock-keepers, £40 to £50 per annum; generally useful, 14s. to 20s. per week; sheepwashers, 15s. to 22s. per week; shearers, 14s. to 16s. per 100. The rate of machine labour is as follows:— Reaping, without binding, from 4s. 1d. to 5s. per acre; reaping and binding, about 6s. to 9s. per acre; mowing, 3s. 8d. to 4s. 7d. per acre; threshing, including winnowing, £1 2s. 10d. to £1 3s. 7d. per 100 bushels; threshing, with winnowing, 14s. 4d. to 20s. per 100 bushels. The cost of machine labour to the farmer who works his own machinery with his own teams is much less than the figures stated.

Prices of Products.

In studying the market prices of agricultural produce, it is necessary to remember the circumstances affecting the cost of production. In Victoria, while the rate of wages is high, the value of land or rent is low, advanced labour-saving implements and machines are employed in cultivating and harvesting, there is no expenditure for manures, and the taxes are low. In the city of Melbourne, which is connected by railway with all the important producing districts of the colony, wheat is at present (Oct., 1897) 5s. 7d. per bushel. Between 1885 and 1895 the prices varied from 1s. 10d. to 5s. 9d. per bushel. Prices for oats have ranged during the last eleven years from 1s. 1d. to 3s. 10d. per bushel; malting barley from 2s. 8¾d. to 4s. 2d. per bushel; maize from 1s. 8¼d. to 4s. 10d. per bushel; hay from £1 13s. to £5 2s. per ton; potatoes from £1 18s. to £4 per ton, and in one year reaching £8 3s. 2d.; mangels from 17s. 9d. to £1 10s. 7d. per ton; flour, £5 to £13 15s. per ton; butter (retail), 6d. to 2s. 6d. per lb., since 1892 8d. to 2s. per lb.; cheese (retail), 4d. to 1s. 6d. per lb., since 1892 6d. to 9d.

per lb. : beef (retail), 2d. to 10d. per lb., since 1892 2d. to
8d. per lb.: mutton (retail). 1½d. to 5d., since 1892 1½d. to
4d. per lb. : pork (retail), 3d. to 9d. per lb.

Prospects of Agriculture.

From what has already been said, it will be seen that the
scope for agricultural development in Victoria is almost
unlimited. With the exception of wheat-growing, all
branches of farming may be considered in their infancy.
There is great room for improvement in the system of
carrying on each branch of agriculture, and there are rural
industries capable of almost unlimited extension, which have
as yet made scarcely any progress. Cultivation has of late
years made satisfactory progress, and all the surroundings
of the case show that the rate of development will be much
more rapid in the future. The greatest increase has taken
place in the production of wheat, a result which may be
accounted for by the suitableness of the product for export
and the facilities offered by the crop in the way of giving
a quick return to the occupiers of new country. Dairying,
fruit-growing, vine-growing, hop culture, the cultivation of
tobacco, and other lucrative branches of industry require
some extra attention, and hence their progress has been less
rapid. These latter industries are now receiving increased
attention, and their progress opens up a very wide field for
future development. For many years the special industries
referred to were kept back through having to depend upon
the local markets. The American system of pushing exports
of butter, cheese, hams, and bacon, dried and canned fruits
and vegetables, out into the markets of the world had not
been yet adopted, and hence prices ruled low for what
should have been our most valuable products. Now, however, steps are being taken to organize an export trade in
the various products for which our soil and climate are
specially favorable. Now, fresh butter made here in our
luxuriant spring and summer reaches London to catch the
high winter market, and the dairying industry will soon far
surpass the production of grain. A few fruit-canning
factories have been established, and the increase of these
will enable our orchards to be extended in every direction,
supplying fruit to distant markets, and so on with the
various rural industries which at present are subordinate to
wheat-growing.

A Promising Outlook.

Those who are now engaging in agriculture will take part in the colony's new career of agricultural progress, and at the present time the colony offers special inducements to new-comers. It would be difficult to find a more promising field for the emigrant with capital, small means, or only his labour to depend upon. Wages are on a liberal scale, living is cheap, and capital commands a comparatively high rate of interest. The capitalist can find a profitable investment, be his resources extensive or limited, and the man who has no money can soon turn his labour into capital. Land being cheap, the freehold of a farm can easily be acquired, and the farmer carries on his industry upon rich soil, in a mild genial climate, under the security of the British flag, and in a country where the rough pioneering system has given place to the comfort and conveniences, as well as the educational and social advantages, of civilized life.

For further information apply to Mr. J. M. Sinclair, the Representative in London of the Victorian Department of Agriculture.

THE LANDS OF THE COLONY.

CHEAP LAND.

Free land is generally worthless, and is only obtainable in inaccessible or badly-governed countries, where it can be of little value to the settler. Even in the United States of America, where homestead farms are given to settlers, there are no available State lands near railways which can be taken up for nothing. Every alternate block is granted to the railway companies which have made the lines, and the remaining State lands within the area are raised to double the price of more distant areas. In a word, free land is not obtainable in any part of the world where railways, markets, and other advantages, without which land is valueless, are provided. As the colony of Victoria has been provided with railways, roads, bridges, schools, local government, and all the advantages of modern civilization, there is no free land. There is cheap land, however, and that is more to the purpose. In the United States, where free land is obtainable in distant places far from markets or railways, settlers prefer to purchase from railway companies or private owners near railways, and within reasonable distances of large towns. It is considered better to give £2 or £3 per acre near a railway town, £15 or £20 per acre near large cities, and from £20 to £40 per acre in fruit-growing districts supplied with water for irrigation, than to go out into the wilds and settle upon free land. In like manner there are distant portions of some of the Australian colonies where land is nominally much cheaper than in Victoria, but, when its inaccessibility and distance from market are taken into account, it is really dearer. Purchase money is paid once for all, but distance from market means paying annually a heavy tax in the shape of carriage, which would represent the annual interest upon an immense sum of money.

LAND A GOOD INVESTMENT.

In Victoria land is nominally and really cheap. It gives such a good return upon the market value that it is considered by capitalists one of the best investments. During the last 30 years the Government have been offering the public lands at a low price to promote settlement. Land

A BIG TREE IN THE FOREST.

worth from £2 to £3 per acre could be had from the Government for £1 per acre, with from ten to twenty years to pay the purchase money. This fact, together with the rough system of farming carried on, is sufficient to show that land could not rise to its natural value. Had an advanced system of farming been carried on, obtaining the best possible results from the soil, and if no land could be had without purchasing in the open market from holders who knew its worth, land values would have risen to their intrinsic standard. But land of the best quality could all along be obtained at the nominal rate of £1 per acre, with long terms, and the soil has not been developed to its full extent. At the present time purchasers get the advantages of these circumstances. They obtain land near markets, and upon railway lines, at a cheap rate.

Favorable Opportunities.

In the inland dry districts, where land is rising in value owing to its productiveness having been tested, good land is sold at from £1 10s. to £3 per acre. Farms with fencing and buildings upon them change hands at from £2 10s. to £4 10s. per acre. These may be taken as average prices. In positions specially convenient to large towns, first-class agricultural land is worth from £20 to £25 per acre, and land which is suitable for the potato crop fetches from £30 to £50 per acre, but these are exceptional values. It frequently happens that sheep farmers give from £2 to £3 per acre for unimproved grass land, to be used for grazing purposes alone, and the agriculturist can generally obtain a much larger return than the keeper of stock. It will be readily understood that the present value of land is low when compared with the returns obtainable from the soil, for the price is regulated by the circumstances of the country. Those circumstances which tend to keep down the price of land are the limited population, the quantity of Government land offered for the nominal sum of £1 per acre, with easy terms, and the absence of a system of high farming. When the Government lands are all taken up, and the growth of population increases, the demand bringing into existence also a system of high farming, land will command a much higher price than at present. The time is, therefore, a favorable one for obtaining cheap land. Farms are always to be had, as they change hands, and those who purchase within the next few years will not only make profits upon their agricultural operations, but at the same time gain advantage by the increasing value of the land.

Government Land.

The colony of Victoria is 56,245,760 acres in extent. Of this area about 23,000,000 acres have been alienated to private owners. Of the 30,000,000 acres available for settlement, 11,500,000 acres are what is known as the mallee country, which occupies the extreme north-western portion of the colony. The mallee country was some years ago set apart for occupation under a system of leases from the Crown. The mallee in its original condition being insufficiently supplied with water, and covered more or less with a scrub of small trees and shrubs, was unsuitable for being taken up in farms of the ordinary size. It was accordingly let in large areas for twenty years. At the end of the leases the land reverts to the Crown, and lessees are compensated for permanent improvements. At the expiration of the leases, the land, having being improved, will be suitable for occupation in smaller areas. About 2,000,000 acres of mallee land is now available for agricultural settlement.

The exact figures are as follows :—

Area of colony	56,245,760
Area alienated and in process of alienation	23,090,664
Area neither alienated nor in process of alienation	33,155,096
Area of mallee lands (exclusive of Mildura, 250,000 acres, and roads through mallee country 155,207 acres)	166,793
Area of mallee country available ...	2,195,380
Area of pastoral lands available 1,872,038	
Area of agricultural and grazing lands available 6,059,840	
	7,932,478

Pastoral Areas.

An area of about 7,000,000 acres of Crown lands, apart from the mallee, is now open for settlement under an Act

CARTING TIMBER.

of Parliament passed in 1890. This area is divided into "Pastoral lands" and "Agricultural and grazing lands." These pastoral holdings are leased till the end of 1898, the rent being 1s. per head for sheep and 5s. per head for cattle, the carrying capacity of the holding to be determined upon a basis of not less than 10 acres to a sheep.

Agricultural Allotments.

The agricultural and grazing lands are surveyed in blocks of not more than 1,000 acres each. These areas are leased for a term of fourteen years, expiring at the end of 1898, the rents being fixed at not less than 2d. per acre or more than 4d. per acre, the valuation, according to quality, being made by officers of the Government. The allotments are surveyed, and shown numbered upon a plan. The applicant makes application for a given block, and if there are more than one application, a land board decides which party is to obtain the land. The occupier of one of these allotments can obtain the ownership of 320 acres of it upon easy terms. Any person who has not previously taken up land in the colony can select 320 acres of his leased land as a freehold. If an occupier selects a freehold, he must pay for it at the rate of 1s. per acre annually for six years. At the end of the six years, he can either continue paying at the rate of 1s. per acre until a total amount of 20s. per acre has been paid, or he may pay the balance of 14s. per acre and obtain a Crown grant. The conditions are that the selector must reside upon his allotment or within 5 miles of it, for six years, and within that period put on improvements to the value of £1 per acre. All applications for agricultural and grazing lands, whether opposed or not, are heard by local land boards. Non-residence licensees, in addition to paying £2 per acre for their holdings, must also make improvements to the value of £2 per acre during the licence term—£1 per acre to be effected within the first three years, and the additional £1 per acre to be made before the expiry of the licence. Under the existing law, also, grazing licences are granted over auriferous lands and State forests. A limited extent of Crown land is sold at auction annually, and special leases are granted for swamp lands, but the great bulk of the remaining State territory is dealt with as "Pastoral lands" and "Agricultural and grazing lands."

Mallee Lands.

About 2,000,000 acres of mallee lands are now available for occupation, and areas will be thrown open from time to time as may be required. The agricultural settler upon these lands may take up a maximum area of 640 acres, either under a "licence" or a "perpetual lease." Under licence he pays at the rate of 1s. per acre per annum for twenty years, and at the end of that time the land becomes his private property; or, if he wishes to secure the freehold sooner, he can do so at the end of the sixth year by paying 14s. an acre, which is the balance of the purchase money. If the settler elects to occupy under perpetual lease, he pays at the rate of 1d. per acre per annum up to 1903, when the first revision of rent takes place. At the end of every subsequent ten years the rental is re-adjusted upon the natural unimproved value of the land. A licence for a mallee agricultural allotment is for a term of six years, and contains conditions in regard to residence, cultivation, and improvements. The issue of a lease or a Crown grant is dependent on compliance with such conditions. Holders of perpetual leases only pay 1d. per acre up to 1903, when the first revision of rent takes place. Subsequent revisions of rent are at intervals of ten years. The mallee settlement has been very successful, and the land has been rapidly taken up as it has been made available. A larger quantity of wheat has been produced in the mallee than in any other division of the colony, and as railway communication is being extended, and the water supply being improved, there is vast scope for the further development of successful settlement. The suitableness of the mallee district for dairying, the keeping of sheep, the growing of vines, fruit trees, and other special crops is being practically demonstrated, so that there is a promising field for a large accession of population.

Openings for Settlers.

It will be observed that the only means of obtaining the fee-simple of Government land in the colony is by taking up a 1,000-acre agricultural and grazing block, and selecting 320 acres out of it. In a few years the whole of the land will be taken up under the existing Act. The fact that the land is so quickly taken up is the best proof persons at a distance can have of the value of the land. Where there are large areas of free land awaiting settlement there must

SCENE IN A MALLEE TOWN.

A MALLEE RAILWAY STATION.

A PUBLIC WATER TANK IN THE MALLEE.

MALLEE ROLLER.

SCENE ON THE MALLEE FRINGE

ON A MALLEE FARM.

SCRUB-CUTTERS' CAMP IN THE MALLEE.

A WATER-COURSE IN THE MALLEE

THE LOWAN OR "MALLEE HEN" AND NEST.

be adverse circumstances which render it unsuitable for profitable occupation. In the colony of Victoria, land has always been eagerly sought after, and as it has been thrown open for occupation from time to time, under the different Land Acts, it has been quickly taken up. To the new-comer land ought to be worth as much, if not more than to the existing settlers, for, while colonial farmers are rather prone to follow an old-time system of management, the new arrival brings with him improved methods of procedure, acquired amid the keener competition of older and more thickly-populated countries.

Village Settlements.

To meet the necessities of persons and families without means who wish to settle upon land, an Act was passed in 1893 under which 2,339 settlers, comprising, with their families, some 8,928 persons, have been provided with agricultural homesteads in village settlements. Under this system 20-acre allotments are made available, and settlers are provided with sums of money, by way of loans, to enable them to meet the preliminary expenses of settlement. Sums of from £15 up to £50 each have been thus advanced ; the total for the past four years has amounted to £63,999 17s. 4d. Under this system 48,611 acres have been occupied, 10,390 acres cultivated, and improvements effected by settlers to the value of £141,128.

For further information apply to Mr. J. M. Sinclair, the Representative in London of the Victorian Department of Agriculture.

DAIRY FARMING.

RICH NATURAL PASTURES.

The fact that Victorian butter is made from cows fed upon natural pastures gives to the product a special value in the London market. The attractive flavour of our butter, its firm grain and small proportion of moisture, results of our natural pastures, have been specially noted by buyers, while our geographical position confers upon us another special advantage.

A UNIQUE GEOGRAPHICAL ADVANTAGE.

This geographical advantage consists in our situation at the Antipodes. As our summer is at the time of the English winter the produce of our spring and summer, cheaply produced by the bounty of nature, finds an open market during the winter of the Northern Hemisphere. This special advantage is not shared in by any European country, Canada, or the United States. Any farmer in the Northern Hemisphere knows the difference between producing butter in winter and in spring. It is surely unfortunate for the British farmer in his struggle against the competition of cheaply-produced imports that nature should have armed a competing country with this unique advantage. While the long rigorous winter is placing all kinds of natural difficulties in the way of the British producer, the farmers of Europe, Canada, and the United States are being met by similar climatic disadvantages, but at this particular period of adverse conditions nature is lavishing her richest gifts of sunny skies, genial warmth, and luxuriant pastures upon the favoured dairymen of the Antipodes. It is the possession of these incalculably valuable natural facilities that has enabled Victoria to so rapidly, and with such comparatively little effort, secure a respectable place in the British markets for a product which is destined to figure with increasing magnitude among her leading exports.

GOVERNMENT ASSISTANCE.

Notwithstanding the exceptional natural advantages possessed by the colony, the development of dairying was for a time beset with difficulties. Supplying the local

A DAIRY FARM.

markets was easy enough, but after that point was reached progress was suspended for many years. Making arrangements for placing a first-class article upon the British market presented many obstacles, and there is no saying how long the dairying industry would have languished had not an administrator come into power who knew what was required, and who had the courage to carry it out. The Hon. J. L. Dow, as Minister of Agriculture, commenced in 1888 a system of improving the dairying industry, which, in a few years, was abundantly justified by results. For three years bonuses were paid upon exports of butter, and by other means the modern factory system was brought into existence. A travelling dairy was employed in instructing the farmers; a model dairy was conducted at the Centennial Exhibition; Mr. David Wilson, the Dairying Expert, was appointed; refrigerating cars were put upon the railway lines, cool stores were provided at country railway stations, refrigerating chambers were built in Melbourne, and a system of inspecting and branding approved butter for export was organized. Satisfactory results were immediately realized, and succeeding Ministers of Agriculture continued to encourage the new export trade—the present Minister, the Hon. J. W. Taverner, having been conspicuous in his efforts to extend and improve the rapidly developing dairying industry.

Inspection of Dairies and Exports.

The Hon. J. W. Taverner's administration has been largely concerned in improving the cool storage arrangements in Melbourne, making better terms as to freights with steam-ship companies, and securing more effective inspection of exports, as well as providing for improved methods of examining herds and dairies in order to insure the soundness and wholesomeness of the produce. The exports of butter, which in 1890 amounted to only 409 tons, increased under the new system to 1,000 tons in 1891. In 1892 they were 2,140 tons, in 1893 3,611 tons, and they increased rapidly till 11,584 tons were reached in 1895, the value of butter and cheese exported in that year being over a million pounds sterling. Owing to an exceptional drought, there was a considerable falling-off in exports during 1896 and 1897, but the Dairy Expert has reported that reasonable precautions in the way of providing for the carrying forward of the surplus fodder of good years, to meet the needs of less favorable seasons, would easily enable the existing dairies to double the exports of 1895.

THE BUTTER FACTORIES.

Butter factories have now been established in all parts of the colony, from the cool coast districts to the drier and warmer inland and the far north-western " mallee." So effective is the factory system, with its modern methods of securing by artificial means the required conditions of success, that butter of the finest quality has been produced in the driest and hottest districts of the colony, even within the boundaries of the mallee division. The returns for 1895 show a total of 174 butter factories, and it is to be noted that, while these represent all portions of the colony, they are as yet spread only sparsely over the various districts. While progress has been satisfactory, the scope for development is so large that many years will elapse before the limits of the industry's profitable expansion will be reached. The factories are carried on upon the co-operative principle, the most of the shareholders being milk suppliers, who receive for their milk prices fixed from time to time by the directors, according to the butter market, and also their proportion of the profits made by the factory company. The milk supplied is tested and paid for according to its proportion of butter fat. The prices paid for the milk have generally been satisfactory, and, as a rule, dividends have also been paid by the companies.

THE CHEESE FACTORIES.

The cheese-making industry became prominent in the colony before the butter factories came into existence. Until it became possible to place first-class butter on the British market, dairying was practically restricted to supplying the limited local demands. As cheese could be exported, the production of that commodity received a good deal of attention, and the industry would no doubt have continued to make progress had not a more profitable one become available to the dairy farmer. The high price of butter, however, as compared with the price of cheese, has, so far, prevented any recent development in the production of the latter. There are at present twenty butter factories which also make cheese, and seventeen cheese factories. The development

A DAIRY HERD.

of cheese-making would rapidly take place if a serious drop occurred in the value of butter. The dairying industry has thus two strings to its bow. Cheese-making has paid well. and would pay now : but, for the present. butter-making pays better.

Veterinary Inspection.

Mr. David Wilson, the Government Dairy Expert, says— "Another effort has been recently made in England to raise a scare against Australian perishable produce. This time it is against our mutton. The charges, however, will be as easily disproved as were the charges of adulteration made about our butter. A committee of the House of Commons now sitting has recommended that all our beef and mutton for export, and all dairy herds, should undergo veterinary inspection. It cannot be made too widely known that many of our butter factories have had this system in operation for over twelve months, and that a veterinary surgeon's certificate as to the health of the cows from which the milk was produced accompanies every box of butter these factories export. No doubt all the factories will gradually adopt a similar system, even although their milk suppliers' herds may be in perfect health. As for the beef. mutton, rabbits, hares, and poultry that Victoria exports, I am pleased to be able to report that a system of veterinary inspection has been rigidly carried out during the past two shipping seasons. a veterinary certificate accompanying every carcass of mutton and beef. and every package of poultry, hares. and rabbits. certifying that same has been inspected, and is fit for human consumption. To a very large extent, therefore, we have anticipated the recommendation of the committee of the House of Commons."

Room for New-comers.

There are openings for large numbers of dairy farmers in all the districts containing factories as well as in many localities where factories could be profitably established. Dairy farms can be purchased at low prices or leased for reasonable rentals, so that only a small capital is required by freehold or tenant farmers. The "share system" of farming has lately been adopted in connexion with dairying, and the results have been so satisfactory that there is now a demand for dairymen to take land and cattle on shares in different parts of the colony. In some cases the farms alone are taken under this system, but the most common method is for the owner of the land to supply land, cattle, and other requisites, the tenant providing only the labour. Large estates formerly devoted to the keeping of sheep or the fattening of cattle are, in suitable dairying districts, now being turned to more profitable use in supplying milk to the butter factories under this form of the share system. The plan is one which suits the land-owner where workers of a suitable kind are scarce, and it opens up a profitable field for the employment of families whose only capital is their labour. The successful establishment of the dairying industry has thus done much to start the colony on a new career of prosperity by opening up a fresh avenue of employ- ment for land, capital, and labour.

AN AYRSHIRE HERD.

PIGS, PORK, AND BACON.

The keeping of pigs, while receiving some attention on many farms, has not been developed in the colony to the extent which the prospects seem to warrant. The fact that an export trade has not yet been established upon a permanent basis may be taken as accounting for the slow progress of an industry calculated under the peculiarly favorable local conditions of yielding handsome profits. Excellent specimens of the best breeds were introduced in early times, and careful breeding has been carried out for many years, so that the stock of the colony is generally of good quality. The Berkshire breed has met with the most favour, but recently Hampshires have been introduced, so that, with these and Yorkshires previously imported, the Berkshires are in some cases being crossed, in order to produce a type fulfilling the requirements of the modern market.

Favorable Local Conditions.

Cold weather is the condition which the fattener of pigs, as of other stock, finds it most difficult to cope with. Keeping up the heat of the animal body being an imperative first duty of food, a cold climate places a severe tax upon the fattening ration. In Victoria, the mild climate renders the work of the stockfeeder peculiarly profitable. Not only is the cost of expensive housing saved, but a large proportion of the food consumed is relieved from the duty of protecting against the cold and devoted to the making of flesh and fat. The pig-feeding experiments conducted at the Longerenong Agricultural College had the effect of demonstrating the favorableness of the climatic conditions under which pig-feeding is carried out in this colony.

Feeding on Grain and Milk.

In 1895, when grain was abnormally cheap, the writer, then Principal of the Longerenong Agricultural College, in the Wimmera district, carried out a series of experiments to test the question as to the return obtainable from feeding pigs with wheat, oats, and a mixture of both these cereals, with and without skim milk. The experiments were commenced on the 14th June, and continued for 92 days, the pigs being weighed at the commencement and the conclusion. Nine thrifty young pigs were selected as nearly as possible of the same size and quality, and divided into three pens, each containing three pigs. Pen No. 1 was fed with wheat and separated milk : pen No. 2 with a half-and-half mixture of wheat and oats, along with separated milk ; and pen No. 3 with wheat and water. The grain was crushed and soaked in water for twelve hours. In the case of pens 1 and 2 separated milk was given at the rate of 2 gallons per pig per day, and the same quantity of water in pen 3. Grain was fed at the rate of 6 lbs. per pig per day in two meals. The results were :—

Weight, 14th June.	After 92 days.	Gain.	Gain per day.	Gain per pig per day.
	lbs.	lbs.	lbs.	lbs.
Pen 1, 195 lbs.	608	413	4·489	1·496
Pen 2, 204 lbs.	595	391	4·25	1·416
Pen 3, 208 lbs.	552	344	3·739	1·246

Reckoning the live weight at 2d. per lb., the pigs in pen 1 returned a sum equal to 2s. 6d. per bushel for the wheat consumed. In pen 2 half the food was oats. Making an allowance of 10d. per bushel for the oats, the 825 lbs. of wheat returned 3s. 5½d. per bushel for the wheat consumed. The most striking features of the experiments are the profitable results of the wheat and oats mixture, and the beneficial effects of separated milk. The difference in the treatment of pens 1 and 3 was that one had separated milk and the other water, and the difference in the results were 69 lbs., or 23 lbs. per pig, a daily difference of ¼ lb. This gives a value of 0½d. per gallon to the separated milk. As the pigs fed with the milk were quite as fat, though lighter than those fed with water, the effect of the milk seemed to have been to produce a rapid growth. In pens 1 and 2 the difference in weight was only 22 lbs. Thus the selling price of the pigs would be only about 15d. per head less than if fed on all wheat, whilst the saving through the use of half oats amounted to 5s. 9d. per head, or a clear gain of 4s. 6d. per head. In pen No. 1 the increase in live weight for the whole period amounted to 1½ lbs. per day per pig, and 4 lbs. of wheat made 1 lb. of live weight or 15 lbs. of pork for each bushel of wheat. In estimating the value obtained for the grain used in feeding, it should be remembered that in the above calculations the gain or increased live weight had only been taken into account, whilst the feeding had also resulted in the whole animal becoming saleable at fat pig rates. Thus in pen 3 the 344 lbs. gain gives a return of 2s. 1d. per bushel for the wheat consumed, but the quantity of fat live weight for sale was 552 lbs. If the pigs had been sold in store condition the original 208 lbs. would not have fetched the same price as fat pigs. If 0½d. per pound were allowed as the difference in value between fat and store pigs, there was a gain of 8s. 8d. on the pen, or 2s. 10½d. per pig from that source, making the return on the wheat about 2s. 5¾d. per bushel. I consider a good deal of the success is due to the mild climatic conditions of the country.

A Promising Industry.

Pig-keeping in this colony is one of the most profitable branches of agriculture, the genial climate being specially favorable, and it is likely that in the immediate future the industry will be largely extended. Like all departments of production confined to supplying local markets, the raising of swine has been seriously kept back by the periodical occurrence of over-production and low prices. The attention which is now being paid, however, to opening up markets for more or less perishable products in London and elsewhere is likely to result in an outlet being found for our surplus of pork, bacon, and hams, so that an industry which is so profitable to such countries as America and Denmark will probably show a rate of expansion akin to that of the butter trade.

POULTRY AND EGGS.

The keeping of poultry, like several other minor branches of rural industry, is at the present time undergoing a change, which is likely to result in a great expansion of the business. Until recently local markets were relied upon, and these frequently became over-supplied, with the result that prices for both eggs and table birds fell to very discouraging rates. Under such circumstances poultry-keeping was kept within defined limits, and progress was impracticable. The opening up of an export trade, however, has entirely changed the prospects of this industry, and it is almost certain that the progressive movement which has now been commenced will be continuous. Local conditions, and especially the exceptionally favorable climate, have long been recognised as offering special advantages to poultry-keeping, but continuous progress could not be expected until an outlet for the produce had been assured.

SPECIAL ADVANTAGES.

The wonderfully mild climate of Victoria, with absence of cold winters, is exceptionally favorable to poultry-keeping, as it is to so many other rural pursuits. Very few native-born Victorians have ever seen snow, and it is rare to find ice as thick as a penny on shallow pools in the coldest parts of the colony. Under these conditions poultry thrive, with the minimum of food and attention, and there is another natural condition which is of immense importance, viz., the geographical position of the colony. Situated at the Antipodes, the time of the various seasons is opposite to that of the Northern Hemisphere. When England, Russia, Belgium, France, as well as Canada and the United States, are enduring the severity of the northern winter, Victoria is enjoying the warm summer. It would seem as if the colonies at the Antipodes had been intended by nature to compensate northern countries for the losses of the rigorous winter. However this may be, it is certain that a beginning has been made by this colony in a system under which the cheaply produced abundance of our spring and summer months will find a profitable market during the winter scarcity of the Northern Hemisphere. Our exports of eggs and poultry have not yet reached any considerable dimension, for the

RABBITS FOR EXPORT. COLD STORAGE DEPÔT. MELBOURNE.

practicability of exporting has too recently been demonstrated, but the market having been found remunerative, and the transport practicable, the expansion of this business has been fully assured.

Profitable for Families.

The interest of the poultry fancier in the colony is an important one. All the best breeds are represented by birds of the highest quality, and through the importing and stud-breeding operations of the fanciers, those carrying on the ordinary poultry business of the colony are able to obtain the stock most suitable for their purposes under local conditions. While there are a few poultry farmers who carry on the production of table birds or eggs as a separate business, the bulk of the produce of the colony comes from farmers, orchardists, vignerons, or gardeners who make poultry-keeping an adjunct to other branches of rural industry, and the poultry yard is generally a profitable and reliable department. The Department of Agriculture has rendered great service by organizing the export trade. It gives directions as to suitable breeds of poultry, and the methods of management, while it also undertakes the proper shipment of eggs and birds through the Government Cool Storage Depôt. The industry is one requiring very little capital, and, as suitable land for the purpose can be readily obtained near railway stations and large towns, it offers promising opportunities to new settlers.

EXPORTS OF PERISHABLE PRODUCTS.

The modern system of preserving fresh perishable produce
by means of cool storage has raised Victorian agriculture,
and set it upon a new plane of prosperous development. Our
limited population provided only a restricted local market,
and our distance from the world's great centres of consumption confined agricultural development to the production of
such staple commodities as grain and wool that were suitable for exportation. All the valuable perishable products
of agriculture had to be kept strictly within the narrow
limits of local consumption. The introduction of the cool
storage system has produced a revolution. Artificially
cooled stores, refrigerated railway trucks, cold storage
depôts at the ports, and refrigerating chambers in ocean
steam-ships, have opened up the markets of the world to the
most perishable products of our farms, dairies, orchards,
and vineyards. A beginning only has been made in
exploiting this new field of agricultural wealth. Dairying
has certainly, with wonderful rapidity, demonstrated the
potency of the change, but the various other branches of
agriculture are only taking the first steps in this new
career of prosperity.

EXPORTS FOR 1897.

The exports for the year ending April, 1897, through the
depôt of, and under the inspection of the Department of
Agriculture, give an indication of the variety of products
which the colony is now beginning to place upon the British
markets :—

Produce.	Quantity.	Estimated Value.		
		£	s.	d.
Butter (tons)	9,895½	942,247	3	4
Mutton and Lamb (carcasses)	79,062	39,531	0	0
Rabbits (pairs) ...	932,203	77,683	11	8
Hares (,,)	5,533	1,383	5	0
Game (,,)	316½	31	13	0
Turkeys (,, ...	664½	664	10	0
Ducks, Fowls, and Geese (pairs)	10,219	3,832	2	6
Eggs (dozens)	12,338	616	18	0
Milk (tons)	11	123	4	0
Mutton (legs)	12,338	1,233	16	0
,, (haunches)	58	11	12	0
Beef (quarters) ...	400	1,000	0	0
Pork (carcasses) ...	434	868	0	0
Kidneys (crates)	54	54	0	0
Veal, Sausages, Ox Tails, Tongues, and Sundries (packages)	165	200	0	0
Totals	—	£1,069,480	15	6

IN THE COLD STORAGE DEPÒT.- MELBOURNE.

WHEAT AT COUNTRY RAILWAY STATION.

In the above the exports of some private companies who ship beef and mutton from other ports, such as Geelong and Portland, are not taken into account. So far, the exports of chilled meat from these ports have not reached large dimensions, but they may be expected to increase considerably in future years.

For further information apply to Mr. J. M. Sinclair, the Representative in London of the Victorian Department of Agriculture.

OTHER INDUSTRIES.

Some of the rural industries dealt with under this heading are sometimes called "novel" on account of being generally unrepresented among the avocations of ordinary farmers. Requiring special skill or unusual conditions for their development, they are not so common as grain-growing, dairying, stock-raising, and other branches of agriculture, but in many cases they are quite firmly established, and in as advanced a condition. In the old colonial days, circumstances prevented their extension beyond prescribed limits, but the conditions affecting them are rapidly changing under modern conditions.

BEE FARMING.

Bee-keeping is receiving increased attention in the colony, and owing to its profitableness it may be expected to extend to large dimensions. Under the old close hive system the expansion of the industry was held in check by the limited yields of the stocks and the ravages of disease. The new system of frame hives, however, enable the bee-keeper at once to prevent disease, and greatly increase the yield of honey. The natural forests which surround the various farming districts provide excellent bee pastures, and the sunny climate of the colony provides a long working season. Under these circumstances it is not surprising that bee-keeping is a profitable business. At times, the prices of honey have been discouraging, owing to the local and other colonial markets becoming temporarily over-supplied, but already something has been done in the way of finding markets for exports. In 1895, 204,435 lbs. of honey was exported, 180,055 lbs. having been sent to the United Kingdom. The bee business requires very little capital, and it is one presenting special inducements to settlers, either for their exclusive attention or as an adjunct to other branches of rural industry.

HOP-GROWING.

Hop-growing has had a long and checkered career in the colony, much money having been both made and lost during the various phases of the industry. The soil and climate in the hop-growing districts have been proved to be specially suitable, and much heavier crops of hops can be relied upon

A HOP GARDEN.

than in England, but as the industry is one involving much hand labour, there has been a difficulty, owing to our limited population, in keeping the cost of production down to the level required in the carrying on of an export trade. Our exports are principally confined to the neighbouring colonies, and the hop-growers, with all their natural advantages, have yet to accomplish the feat of producing cheaply enough to compete in the markets of the world. Upon the fertile river flats of Gippsland, in the east of the colony; along the rivers flowing into the Murray, in the north-east; as well as in the Otway Forest, in the west, successful hop gardens are carried on. The number of growers at present is 128, cultivating an area of 791 acres. Yields sometimes reach a ton of dried hops to the acre, and an average of 15 cwt. to the acre is frequently obtained. In the hop-growing districts the school holidays are given at the picking season in order to allow the children to assist in the work. With an increase in the population, and the adoption of more labour-saving methods, it may be expected that this industry, for which there is almost unlimited scope amid exceptionally favorable natural conditions, will be largely extended.

Flax and Linseed.

That flax would grow luxuriantly in the colony has been known from the earliest times, but owing to the labour involved in managing the fibre crops, very little attention was, until recently, given to the growing of flax or linseed. During the last few years, however, a stimulus has been given to the industry by the action of the Hon. J. W. Taverner in importing fibre working and oil making machinery, and employing experts to give instruction in the various manufacturing processes. In all but the very driest districts of the colony flax grows well, producing a good yield of both seed and fibre, and as a market is being found for the products, it may be expected that the area devoted to its culture will rapidly increase. Mr. Jos. Knight, the Government Expert, says—"The flax crop should find a place in the ordinary farm rotation; the industry is a payable one, suitable for all classes of our agriculturists, and requires only to be properly understood to receive that attention to which its merits entitle it." Farmers understanding flax culture in the old country would, no doubt, find in this industry profitable scope for their experience.

OLIVE CULTURE.

Olive culture is one of the most promising industries in the colony. Trees planted in various parts of Victoria grew so well and yielded so freely, that settlers were impelled some years ago to take note of a product of which they possessed little knowledge. An olive grove, also which was planted twenty years ago at the Dookie Experimental Farm, in the north-eastern district, began after the establishment of an Agricultural College at the farm to produce olive oil of excellent quality. Later on olive culture and the making of olive oil were established at the Longerenong Agricultural College, in the north-western district, and that was followed by the successful production of olive oil at Mildura, the irrigation settlement on the Murray River. As the result of these and some other local experiments, it has been demonstrated that the extensive inland areas of the colony are specially suitable for the growth of the olive. In Southern Europe the olive does not bear until ten years old, but in Northern Victoria trees begin to bear at three years old, and profitable crops are obtained after the fifth year. Very heavy yields are sometimes obtained, but 60 gallons to the acre is considered a fair average. The working expenses are reasonable, being not more than £7 per acre, including interest on cost of manufacturing machinery, so that there is a handsome margin of profit. The prices obtained for the locally-produced oil have ranged between 7s. and 10s. per gallon. Even at the lower price a profit is shown of £14 per acre, while it may be concluded that such a special product as pure olive oil will always command a good market.

OIL SEEDS AND SCENTS.

In addition to the growing of linseed, such plants as sunflowers, castor oil beans, and pea nuts are beginning to receive attention. That they grow well in different parts of the colony has been fully proved, for settlers from early times have been led to make trials of nearly every known kind of useful plants. While sunflowers and castor oil plants have been found to grow well and yield heavy returns the absence of a market for the produce has prevented their extensive cultivation. The Department of Agriculture, however, has done much to encourage these cultures by importing an oil mill, and thus assisting to create a market for the seeds. The results so far have been highly

ORCHARD WORK.—Mildura.

A GROUP OF HOP PICKERS.

encouraging, and there is no doubt that castor oil plants,
sunflowers, and other oil-producing crops will in a few years
be extensively cultivated. Flower farming for the production
of essential oils is another industry which has recently been
receiving attention, and which is likely to be developed under
the highly favorable climatic conditions of the colony. An
Experimental Farm for testing various scent plants was
established by the Government some years ago, and the
result has been to direct attention to an industry which is
likely when better understood to be highly profitable.

Silk Culture.

Natural conditions are exceptionally favorable to the silk-
growing industry, which is so great a source of wealth to
different countries; but as a dense population with an
abundance of cheap labour is necessary for its development,
only limited progress has been made. This interesting
industry, however, has received attention from sanguine
persons from early colonial times, and at present an active
society is pushing its interests with considerable success.
As silk culture is suitable for profitably employing the
members of a settler's family who cannot engage in the
heavier work of rural life, the industry is likely to make
gradual progress and ultimately assume considerable
importance.

THE SUGAR-BEET INDUSTRY.

The production of sugar-beet has received attention at various times during the last 25 years, but from different causes arising out of the peculiar nature of the business the several attempts to establish the industry have proved unsuccessful. The suitableness, however, of extensive areas in Victoria for the production of heavy crops of beet prevented the expectation of successfully introducing the sugar-beet industry from being entirely abandoned, and a company is now operating which is likely to establish this important branch of production upon a sound basis. The conditions of sugar-beet production are such that its inauguration stands specially in need of Government assistance. Farmers have no inducement to grow the beet crop until sugar factories exist which will provide a market, and capitalists have no inducement to erect factories until a supply of beet is assured.

GOVERNMENT ENCOURAGEMENT.

Recognising the peculiar nature of the case, the Turner Government resolved to render the necessary assistance. The Beet Sugar Works Act of 1896 was accordingly introduced and passed into law, under which liberal encouragement to the industry was provided. Under this Act advances are made to companies which carry out the sugar-beet business upon stated lines, and in a manner satisfactory to the Government. Any company establishing a factory in an approved district where there is an area of 10,000 acres of suitable land within a radius of 10 miles, and which has entered into contract with farmers for the cultivation of at least 2,000 acres of beet crop for three years, is entitled to claim advances which ultimately reach the value of £2 for every £1 expended by the company. These advances are to be repaid in 46 half-yearly instalments, the sum bearing interest at 4 per cent., and the property of the company being security under a first mortgage for the loan.

THE MAFFRA SUGAR BEET COMPANY.

The only company as yet established under the Act is the Maffra Sugar Beet Company Limited. The capital is £50,000, in 50,000 shares of £1 each. The first issue of 25,000 has been taken up, and the company, which is entitled

THE MAFFRA BEET-SUGAR FACTORY.—Front View.

THE MAFFRA BEET-SUGAR FACTORY.—Rear View.

CULTIVATING SUGAR-BEET - MAFFRA COMPANY.

to claim advances up to £50,000 from the Government, has up to date received the sum of £30,000. The factory, which has been erected and provided with all the most approved machinery, is in readiness to deal with the crop of the approaching season. Qualified judges who have recently visited the factory report that the company has shown commendable skill and enterprise, and nothing seems to have been omitted which is necessary to success. The situation is in a central portion of the Gippsland district, about 130 miles east from Melbourne, and no more suitable site could have been chosen, the surrounding soil being highly fertile, and the rainfall reliable and copious. The machinery has been imported from Germany, and an expert staff of skilled operators has been obtained from the same country. An area of 1,700 acres has been cultivated with beet crops by farmers, under arrangement with the company, and the roots now approaching maturity have yielded highly satisfactory results upon analysis.

The following are the analyses of thirteen samples made the second week in February, 1898:—

—	Average Weight of one root in grammes.	°/₀ Brix.	°/₀ Sugar.	°/₀ Non-sugar.	Purity.
Sample 1	546	21·5	19·58	1·92	91·7
„ 2	276	24·	19·74	4·26	82·3
„ 3	381	19·4	16·53	2·87	85·2
„ 4	157	24·3	19·76	4·54	81·3
„ 5	246	23·2	18·92	4·28	81·5
„ 6	440	23·6	18·97	4·63	80·3
„ 7	205	21·6	...	...	...
„ 8	543	19·2	17·26	1·94	90·
„ 9	226	20·	17·95	2·05	89·7
„ 10	202	20·7	17·89	2·81	86·4
„ 11	578	19·5	16·63	2·87	85·3
„ 12	455	18·2	16·85	1·35	92.5
„ 13	319	17·2	15·85	1·35	92.4

Encouraging Prospects.

Mr. J. M. Sinclair, now the London representative of the Victorian Department, who was employed by the Government to inquire into the sugar-beet industry of the United States, presented a report in 1895, which has been a powerful factor in bringing about the present movement. Mr. Sinclair's report brought under notice the success of some of the American companies, notably those of California, a state whose general conditions are in many respects similar to those of Victoria. The report also was highly favorable to the opinion that the industry could be successfully established in this colony. After visiting the scene of beet-sugar productions in Utah, under a system of irrigation, Mr. Sinclair, in his report, deals as follows with the advantages of the industry and its suitableness for the Australian colony of Victoria :—

"The successful establishment of a beet-sugar factory in a community means the placing of a cash market at fixed prices for the farmer's produce at his own doors; it enhances the value of land at least threefold, by giving it an income-paying value; it means the distribution in the community of many thousands of pounds annually, and profitable and healthy employment for hundreds of families, besides the saving to the country of the value of the sugar, which otherwise would have to be purchased abroad, being so much money gone out of the country that should be kept at home.

"The success attending sugar-beet culture with irrigation in Utah indicates what may also be accomplished in the same way at Mildura, in Victoria. The rich sandy loams at Mildura are capable of producing sugar-beets equal in quantity to Utah, and Mildura is in possession of a much more favorable climate. The higher percentage of sugar in the Chino beets over those at Lehi is simply the result of its warmer climate, and there is a similarity of climatic conditions existing between Chino and Mildura. Sugar-beet culture, under favorable conditions, is perhaps the most profitable use to which land suited to it can be put, and a trial should certainly be made of it at Mildura and other places along the Murray River where rich friable loamy soil exist.

"I omitted to mention that the agricultural superintendent at Lehi informed me that all land suitable for beet culture there had risen over 80 per cent. in value during the past eighteen months. He pointed out land on the lower plateau for which 150 dollars, or £30, per acre, could be obtained. On the upper plateau virgin sage brush land, of which I was afraid to name a value, had recently been purchased for 40 dollars, or £8, per acre.

BEET SUGAR-MAKING MACHINERY.—MAFFRA COMPANY

"In the foregoing reports I have endeavoured to give a concise statement of the methods of beet-root culture at two of the most successful factories in the United States. I think it will be recognised by the Victorian farmers that the two places—Chino and Lehi—from their similarity in soil, climate, and rainfall to a great portion of Victoria have enabled a study to be made of the sugar-beet industry which may prove of supplementary value to what information is already in their possession. There is not the slightest doubt of the fact that large areas of land in Victoria are as well suited for sugar-beet culture as either California or Utah. It is the most interesting, and at the same time profitable, agricultural industry I have seen in the United States. There is no reason why Victoria should send away annually thousands of pounds for the purchase of sugar when it can be grown and manufactured in the colony, furnishing at the same time a profitable occupation for a large number of its people."

As showing the profitableness of the industry to the farmer, Mr. Sinclair instances the Watsonville Factory, in California, in connexion with which the beet crop netted one year £13 11s. 4d. per acre :—

"The following year, the season being a bad one, results were not so good, a yield of only 13,500 tons of beets from 2,000 acres being obtained, for which the factory paid 5 dollars per ton. The sugar output was 1,650 tons, for a run of 47 days. The farmers, however, were satisfied, and increased their area of beets, and the company increased both its capital and plant. Both parties have since, from year to year, steadily extended their operations, the farmers getting an average of from 13 to 14 tons per acre, for which this season they were paid 3½ dollars (or 14s. 7d.) per ton. The Watsonville Factory is now one of the most successful in the United States, everything in connexion with it being carried on on a satisfactory basis."

In connexion with the Chino Beet Company, another Californian enterprise, Mr. Sinclair says :—

"In 1893 Mr. Gird and 170 farmers cultivated over 4,000 acres of land with sugar-beets, 2,500 acres of which were in good condition, and the remaining 1,500 acres were sod-land broken up for the first time, and from which the tonnage was necessarily light. There was distributed during 1893 (the last campaign) £60,000 for beets and labour, which would otherwise have gone out of the country to purchase foreign sugar.

"At the close of the campaign for 1893 the Chino Valley Beet Sugar Company decided to increase the capacity of their factory still further to 1,000 tons daily, to erect a complete Steffen's plant for the extraction of the small amount of sugar left in the molasses, all of which necessitated the expenditure of £50,000. The winter and spring saw these improvements completed, and the factory was opened to receive beets on the 27th July, 1894. The winter and spring previous to my visit to Chino were exceptionally light in rainfall, there being only 11 inches of rain instead of 18 inches, the usual average. (I may here state that California has absolutely no summer rainfall, thunder-storms, as mentioned in one of my previous reports, being almost unknown.) The surrounding country has consequently suffered for want of moisture, fully half the crops being a failure in the San Joaquin Valley and Southern California. In spite of these climatic disadvantages during 1894 the Chino Sugar Beet Plantation has produced a fair average crop, with regard to tonnage—about 12 tons to the acre—and a very high record as regards sugar, the percentage being this year an average of 16 per cent. This, Mr. Gird said, would give gross returns of £12 per acre, and net £8 per acre, most satisfactory results in any season, the high percentage of sugar making up the loss in tonnage."

Mr. Clement Van De Velde, C.E., a gentleman of experience in connexion with beet-sugar production in Belgium and Holland, and who has interested himself in advocating the adoption of the industry in the Australian colonies, says :—

"In Victoria it has already been proved beyond question that a large portion of the colony, especially Gippsland, the Port Fairy, Warrnambool, and Ballarat districts, and the valley of the Yarra, are eminently suitable for the cultivation of sugar beet. Experiments made, especially those under the direction of Mr. A. N. Pearson, Chemist of the Department of Agriculture, show that more than satisfactory crops can be obtained as regards both quantity and quality of roots.

"Owing to the genial climate of South-Eastern Australia, the season for sowing and harvesting sugar-beet will be much more extended (at least double) than in Europe or some of the American States. This is extremely favorable to both the farmer and the manufacturer. To the farmer it means less extra manual labour, and with his own family he will be

INTERNAL VIEW.—Beet-sugar Factory.

MACHINERY. Maffra Beet-sugar Factory.

able to look after a much larger area, the total amount of labour required being divided over a longer period. To the manufacturer it means a great saving, as instead of having to take delivery of the whole crop within four or five weeks (before the frost sets in) and protect a large portion of it in silos about the factory, where it loses part of the sugar contents for which he has paid, he will be able to take delivery of the beet in quantities almost equal to his daily requirements, and so save also a double manipulation of the roots."

It is evident, therefore, that the industry has been commenced under favorable prospects in Victoria, while it is satisfactory that practical results, so far as they have yet been obtained by the Maffra Company, have been highly encouraging.

TOBACCO-GROWING.

Tobacco-growing is carried on successfully in various districts for which the soil and climate have been found to be specially suitable. Progress, however, has been retarded by a variety of removable circumstances. Beyond growing a comparatively limited quantity of tobacco for local manufacture, the industry has not advanced, and it was recognised that the principal cause was a lack of knowledge on the part of growers as to the best methods of cultivating the plant and treating the leaf. The Minister of Agriculture, Mr. J. W. Taverner, in order to overcome this difficulty, some time ago engaged an American expert, Mr. A. J. Bondurant, of Virginia, who has already done much to place the industry on a satisfactory basis; and Mr. Bondurant, who is well pleased with the prospects of tobacco-growing in the colony, writes as follows :—

TOBACCO IN VICTORIA.

The cultivation of tobacco for commercial use was commenced in Victoria about thirty years ago. Its cultivation, as I am informed, was introduced owing to the difficulty of obtaining it from the Southern States, on account of the civil war that existed between the States of America.

It was found from the first cultivation of this plant in Victoria that it grew well, though the methods of cultivation, curing, and general management were of a primitive character—open thin-thatched sheds used for drying, on curing, thereby exposing the plants to the varied atmospheric changes that exist in this climate. Yet, notwithstanding this fact, the industry has continued steadily, though not rapidly, to increase, much of this home-grown tobacco being used by the Melbourne manufacturers for blending with the American tobacco in making plug for smoking purposes.

THE YIELDS.

The crop for the year 1896 exceeded 800 tons. The bulk of this was sold to the Melbourne buyers as soon as it was placed on the market last November.

The locality in Victoria where this plant is generally cultivated is known as the north-eastern part of this province. In this section there is an abundant rainfall, and the climate generally favorable for the growth of the tobacco plant. It is grown mostly on the rich alluvial bottom lands on the King, Ovens, Kiewa, Mitta Mitta rivers, and to some extent on the Murray—though there are parts, such as the Goulburn Valley and many others, where the cultivation has not been undertaken, in which it is thought the tobacco plant can be grown with success.

Under favorable conditions, the yield on these soils is large, much above the average soils in America. During the past season, from 2¼ acres, one grower produced 2 tons and 700 pounds, which was sold to a Melbourne manufacturer for 6d. per pound. Though this instance must not be misleading—it is only safe to say that from half to three-quarters of a ton per acre can be produced, and, should the supply be large, lower price than the above will be realized, the manufacturers here claiming that they have only a limited demand for the home-grown leaf.

An Export Trade.

However, this difficulty should be overcome by finding a demand in England, the best tobacco market in Europe. If this Victorian tobacco has been used for more than thirty years by the tobacco manufacturers here *alone*, and by blending with foreign tobacco, why can it not be successfully utilized by the Mother Country?

The Quality.

The tobacco hitherto grown here resembles much in general appearance, flavour, &c., that grown in some of the Western States of America, namely, Kentucky, Missouri, and Ohio, and the soils upon which it is grown are similar to those soils in America.

The Government of Victoria, through its Minister of Agriculture, is doing all that it can to encourage this industry.

Though having been in this colony during only one season's growth, I am encouraged with the improvement that is going on among the growers, as to adopting better methods as to growing, curing, and preparing this plant for market. The present season (1897) will show much tobacco of better colours, flavours, and general management than has hitherto been obtained here.

EXPERIMENTS.

The Minister of Agriculture, on my advice, has established a Tobacco Experimental Farm at Edi, on the King River, for the purpose of educational instruction to the tobacco-growers as to the best methods of management.

This experimental farm was not started in time last year (1896) for conducting this work as fully as desired. Nevertheless, a suitable curing house was constructed, a crop grown on the Experimental Farm, the curing by heat, and I am fairly well satisfied with this preliminary trial. Should the season of 1897 be favorable for growing, it is proposed to have placed in the curing house for this year's crop, a suitable heating appliance, whereby the temperature can be controlled, and still better results obtained. A brighter tobacco, now much sought after in the markets of the world, is likely to be secured by this improved process of curing.

Thus far, the soil, rainfall, conditions, &c., seem favorable for producing tobacco of good quality under improved methods of management; though we have to contend with the unexpected frost, liable to occur frequently, even in midsummer, and this is detrimental to this tender plant. This, however, is not so much to be dreaded as a fungus disease known as "blue mould."

This fungus is similar to rust in wheat, and it is believed that it is produced by the same atmospheric changes.

While this is a serious drawback to the successful cultivation of tobacco in Victoria, and every effort is being made to combat it, it is well to state that this fungus does not occur every year, and seldom does it attack the plants to such an extent as to utterly destroy them, and usually, even though the "blue mould" does make its appearance, a moderate, though not a full, crop can be secured annually.

FAVORABLE PROSPECTS.

Many thousand acres of suitable soil for tobacco-production are not yet under cultivation, and upon these a settler with small capital upon a few acres, by employing intelligent methods, should make a competent support for a family. Under the aid of this enlightened Government, that is doing what is necessary to aid this new industry, here is good reason to hope that before many years it will attain that prominence that the dairy, mine, fruit, &c., occupies.

As before stated, the work of the expert in the tobacco industry has not progressed to that extent that will at present justify him in drawing definite conclusions, though he is hopeful as to the success of this industry ultimately, specially if it is, as a home industry, protected with wholesome legislation.

here is good reason to hope that before many years it will attain that prominence that the dairy, mine, fruit, &c., occupies.

WHY I SETTLED IN VICTORIA.

WHAT AN ENGLISH FARMER SAYS.

The agricultural depression in England has lasted about twenty years, and no means has yet been discovered by which the British farmer can successfully compete with the cheap produce of the colonies and new foreign countries. A Yorkshire farmer, who gave up the struggle fifteen years ago, and emigrated to Victoria, has favoured the editor with the following views upon the subject :—

WHY I EMIGRATED.

I had been bred a farmer, and I knew my business, but I was rapidly losing money. My landlord was a reasonable man, and he made all the reductions in the rent that any one could expect : but it was all the same. My capital was disappearing, and I made up my mind to do something before it was all gone. The cause of my losses was the low markets brought about by the cheap produce coming in from Australia and America. I was making a little out of cattle, but I could see that would not last ; and as for butter, although it was not coming from Australia at that time, it was coming from somewhere cheaper than I could make it. As I was being ruined by cheap production, I reckoned I would go out and be a cheap producer myself. And very glad I am that I did it in time. I have not made a fortune, nor have I done quite as well as I expected, but I have done a lot better than stopping at home. Things have been getting no better with the farmers at home. Rents have been reduced from time to time, but markets have been getting lower and lower, and the farmers getting poorer and poorer. It is not only grain and meat that pours into London now from abroad, but butter, cheese, poultry, pork and bacon, fruits, and everything. My neighbours would have done well to have come away with me, for most of them have lost all they had. What little capital I had left bought me the freehold of a farm, so I am my own landlord at any rate. Those who have less than I had would do well to come out, for this is a better country for making a fresh beginning in than England.

SPLITTING SHINGLES IN THE FOREST.

Little Capital Required.

A man who has capital enough to be a tenant farmer even on a very moderate scale in the old country can buy a good farm right out in Victoria. The value of farms in settled districts close to railway stations is only about equal to from one to two rents in England. That is, the freehold prices range from 30s. to £3, and up to £4, £5, and £6 per acre. Farms at these prices consist of good average land, and they return a profit upon these prices. There are also limited areas of specially productive land, fetching up to £20, £30, and £40 per acre, but they are not more profitable than my own farm at £5 per acre. Not only is the freehold at the level of a rent or two in the old country, but the working capital required is also much less than that required by the English tenant farmer. The expenditure upon manures is insignificant, and although the system of farming would not be thought much of in England, it returns a profit, and that is more than can be said for the system under which I lost about £1 per acre per annum for some years in Yorkshire. An English tenant farmer can easily start as a freeholder in this country, and a labourer can become a tenant farmer. Many labourers have become freeholders here by settling on the lands which were granted on easy terms by the Government, and others have rented farms, some making money enough to buy out the land.

Making a Start.

It suited me better to buy a well-improved farm near one of the large towns than to go inland and settle as a "selector," but the selecting system offers good opportunities for those who have less capital, and who want to become land-owners at the beginning. As the Government undertakes the making of railways, the new settlers are soon followed by the lines, so that their produce is carried to the sea-board at low rates. There are plenty of opportunities for men of very small capital to get on to the land. Good farms near the large towns can be taken at low rents by men who have little more capital than their labour and that of their families; while by going to the more distant districts opened up by the railways, the selector can obtain land at 20s. per acre, being allowed twenty years to complete the purchase, or he can obtain perpetual leases from the Government at a few pence per acre. And then there is the "share system" of farming, under which a start can be made by men of no capital.

Under this system farms are taken for one, two, or three years, the tenant doing the best he can, and the landlord taking a share of the crop as rent. The landlord's share is from one-third to one-fourth of the crop, according to arrangement. The advantage to the tenant is that the rent is in proportion to the yield of the land. When it is remembered that in this country land is plentiful and the population small, it will be understood that there are many opportunities of entering into the business of farming. Things are cut very fine in England, but here most of the settlers were not bred to farming, so that carrying on under easy conditions, they could not be expected to have developed a high system of agriculture. Skilled farmers from older countries are not likely to fail where so many untrained settlers succeed.

NEITHER FROST NOR SNOW.

There is no doubt that cheap land was the principal cause of the great fall in the values of agricultural produce, but the cheapness of the fertile lands of Victoria is only one of the advantages which the colony possesses in competitive production. There are cheap lands in Canada and the United States, but it is only in Australia that a genial climate prevails. There is literally no winter here in the English sense of the term. Snow is a rarity seen only on the highest mountains, and all that is known of frost is an occasional hoar-frost, which does not injure ordinary crops. The climate is even milder than that of the Mediterranean coast, and growth continues all through the winter. There is no housing or feeding of live stock, but the flocks and herds remain in the fields throughout the year, growing and fattening upon the rich pastures provided by nature. This natural pasture, which is very abundant, is highly nutritious and fattening, and it produces the best butter in the world. It has only recently been proved that the butter made from the natural pastures of Victoria possesses qualities of firmness and flavour unequalled by the best in the London market.

AT THE ANTIPODES.

In speaking of the immense advantages possessed by Victoria in her wonderful climate, the Yorkshire farmer missed out a point of great importance, viz., the unique good fortune of the colony in being situated at the Antipodes. It is often referred to as an interesting fact that Victoria is on

ONE OF THE GIANT TREES.

GRAIN BOAT ON THE MURRAY.

BOATING ON THE MURRAY.

the opposite side of the globe to England—that it is day in Victoria when it is night in England; winter here when it is summer there, and so on: but the vast practical importance of this state of things is seldom recognised. It is evident, upon reflection, that our position at the Antipodes confers upon us a unique advantage as competitors in supplying the world with agricultural products. If, by some miracle, the rigorous winters of North America could be exchanged for the warm genial climate of Australia, the Great Southern Continent would still retain its unique advantage of an antipodean situation. While the severity of the winters would have been removed, its season of abundance would still occur at the same time as the spring and summer of Britain and Europe. Victoria has not only a mild winter, but its prolific spring and summer produce their abundance at the very time when Europe and North America are passing through their annual periods of suspended vegetation and destructive cold. Successful competition in agricultural production depends upon three dominating conditions, viz.:—1. Cheap productive land. 2. A favorable climate. 3. Seasons of maximum productiveness concurring with the annual periods of scarcity and maximum prices. The first is possessed in common by Victoria and North America; in regard to the second, the colony's frostless and snowless winter places her at an immense advantage; while the third, with all its incalculable potency, is the exclusive possession of the antipodean competitor.

Ports and Railways.

Victoria is fertile to the sea-shore, and, being narrow with a long coast line the ports are close to the scenes of production. A line drawn 100 miles from the coast would include more than half of the colony, and a similar line 150 miles from the sea-board would take in more than three-fourths of the colony, while the great grain fields of the United States, Canada, and India are from, 500 to 1,000, and as much as 1,500 miles, from the shipping ports. A network of Government railways is spread all over Victoria, reaching every district, and the railway charges are low. The railways have not been made by private companies for profit making, but by the Government, in order to benefit the inhabitants, so that freights are always as low as the working expenses and interest on cost of construction will allow. As a matter

of fact, the railway charges do not pay the whole interest on
their cost, the balance being paid out of the general revenue
of the colony. As the volume of traffic increases with the
increase of population, and the growth of production, freights
will be further reduced, and the transport facilities of the
inhabitants enlarged.

LOCAL GOVERNMENT.

The local government system of the colony is admirable.
There are cities, larger towns, and smaller boroughs, with
local councils managing all internal affairs, and the country
districts are divided into self-governing shires. The rating
in the shires is for purely local improvement, and instead of
having burdens laid upon them by the Central Government,
the local bodies are handsomely assisted by annual subsidies
out of the general revenue of the colony.

GENERAL ADVANTAGES.

While entirely self-governing, the colony enjoys the
inestimable advantage of being an integral part of the
British Empire. The inhabitants are a free people, intelligent, industrious, honest, law-abiding, and as loyal to the
British Crown as they are to the principles of individual,
political, and religious liberty. The Government, in the
constitution of which every adult male has a voice, carries
out a system for primary education, free, secular, and
compulsory, and State schools are established, not only in
every village, but in every distant corner of the colony where
ten or twenty children can be gathered together. A map in
this volume showing the positions of the State schools will
convey an idea of the wide-reaching character of the State
primary education system. The colony is also well provided
with secondary schools and colleges carried on by private
enterprise, while the education system is crowned by the
Melbourne University, an institution liberally assisted by
the State. The Melbourne Public Library and Art School
would be regarded with admiration in any city in the world,
and throughout the numerous towns of the colony popular
technical colleges and mechanics' institutes receiving
Government assistance have been plentifully established.
There is no State aid to religion, but churches of all denominations are voluntarily supported by the people, and various
places of worship have been erected in even the smallest
and most distant villages. The same widespread and

HOSPITAL IN A COUNTRY TOWN.

minute distribution is characteristic of the various popular amusements, which differ little from those of England, and no critic would accuse the colonists of taking life too seriously. At one time emigration to the colony meant the sacrifice of many social advantages, and the new-comer's idea was to make a fortune and "go home." All this has now been altered, and those who make fortunes as a rule take a trip to the old land, but soon "come home" again, drawn by the social attractions of their adopted country.

CHEAP MONEY.

One of the principal difficulties in the way of successful farming in the colony has been a defective system of obtaining financial accommodation. Agriculture is an industry which is not adequately served by the banking system that meets the case of other lines of business. Accommodation for a short term serves the purposes of the merchant or speculator, but the improvement of land, whether it be fencing, clearing, building, or draining, does not pay for itself in a few months, or even in a few years. Investment in land improvement may be wise and profitable, but the capital cannot be returned for a term of years. For want of some means of obtaining capital on terms suitable for their industry farmers and settlers have, in the past, been seriously handicapped, but recently Sir George Turner's Government introduced a Crédit Foncier scheme for the purpose of removing this difficulty. Through the Commissioners of the Government Savings Bank local loans are raised from time to time as required. The capital thus obtained is advanced to farmers on the security of their land. Advances are made to the extent of 75 per cent. of the land valuation. At present the rate is 6 per cent., and the amount includes interest, working expenses, and 1 per cent. to a sinking fund, which extinguishes the debt by the end of the term. The system has been in operation three years, and an amount of £176,695 has been advanced to 425 farmers, averaging £415 15s. each. As the system is working satisfactorily, it will no doubt be largely extended.

HORTICULTURE.

Horticulture has received a good deal of attention from the early days of the colony, but during the last 30 years there has been a more widely-diffused interest in the subject. Gardening in all its branches has been greatly extended, while such departments as wine-growing and the production of fruits and vegetables for market have developed into important industries. The acreage under gardens and orchards in 1857 was estimated at less than 2,000 acres : it had reached 20,000 acres by 1884, while for 1896 the estimate is 35,000 acres. The late Mr. William Elliott, for many years the horticultural editor of the *Leader*, contributed to a former *Handbook of Victoria* a valuable essay upon the Horticulture of the colony. The following revised extracts from that essay deal comprehensively with the subject :—

BOTANY.

Victoria can boast that her Department of Botany has been presided over by one of the most eminent botanists of the present age, in the person of the late Baron Ferdinand von Mueller, K.C.M.G., F.R.S., M.D., who worked uninterruptedly in Australia from 1847 to the end of his brilliant career in 1896. By his assiduous labours on the flora of this and adjacent countries, his explorations of a large portion of the Continent of Australia, his extensive herbarium, his chemical and phytographical researches, his large and valuable contributions to the flora of Australia, and his numerous other publications, he has extended the bounds and enriched the science of Botany to a large and much-appreciated extent. With his name must be honorably associated that of Mr. Joseph Bosisto, C.M.G., one of the pioneers of botanic research in Victoria. Mr. Bosisto, singularly enough, was a fellow labourer in the paths of science with Baron von Mueller in South Australia as far back as 1849, and afterwards both were closely identified with the important discoveries connected with the Eucalyptus vegetation. In all matters connected with *materia medica* Mr Bosisto occupies a high position, and the College of Pharmacy in Melbourne now stands as a monument of his efforts as a legislator to advance the cause of science.

Public Parks and Gardens.

Land for Public Parks, Gardens, and Recreation Grounds has been reserved in connexion with all the most important cities and towns in the colony ; the land being placed under the management of the respective town and borough councils. The grounds are supported by rates, subsidized by annual grants from the general revenue. During the year 1884-5, the sum of £7,233 7s. 6d. was granted to 67 councils, in sums varying from £2 5s. to £957, independent of those in the neighbourhood of the metropolis. The latter comprise an area of 4,766 acres, including 604 acres under the joint control of the Government and the Melbourne City Council ; the Botanic Garden, 84 acres ; Government House Domain, 152 acres ; University Grounds, 109½ acres ; and the Burnley Experimental Garden and School of Horticulture, 28 acres. The grant for Horticultural Societies amounts to £300 per annum.

Botanic Gardens.

Public Gardens, generally termed Botanic Gardens, are common throughout the colony, ground for the purpose having been set apart in connexion with all the principal towns. The gardens of Ballarat, Bendigo, Castlemaine, and other inland cities are very handsome. The Melbourne Botanic Garden, situated on the banks of the River Yarra Yarra, about a mile from the city of Melbourne, is 84 acres in extent. It adjoins the grounds of Government House and the public Domain, of which it forms a part. It was formerly under the direction of the Government Botanist, the late Baron von Mueller, but some years ago the garden was placed in charge of a landscape gardener, under whose curatorship the grounds have been extended, altered, and greatly improved. The newer portions, as well as some of the old ground, have been laid out in broad gravel walks, and extensive lawns with clumps and single specimens of trees and shrubs, which have rendered the garden highly attractive to the public, who frequent it in large numbers on Sundays and holidays.

The garden contains two large conservatories, one devoted to the cultivation of ferns and some plants of industrial value ; the other is filled with a miscellaneous collection of stove plants in pots. A smaller house is occupied by succulent plants. There are also several other small houses for propagating and other purposes, besides frames, and a large shelter shed for the hardier plants. The older portions of the gardens contain numerous fine specimens of palms, araucarias, and other conifers, various oaks, elms, and other deciduous trees, besides Grevilleas, of which G. robusta forms a splendid picture when in flower, and numerous other native trees and shrubs.

Among other recent improvements, an extensive "fern gully" has been formed ; large collections of palms and cycads have been planted, as well as groups of the more hardy of the Queensland plants.

In the lower portion of the grounds, near the river, is a large and beautiful lake, spanned in places by rustic bridges, and dotted with charming little islands, which, planted with ornamental trees and shrubs picturesquely arranged, produce a splendid effect. A portion of the native vegetation, having been allowed to remain, adds to the interest of the scene.

Upwards of £100,000 has been spent on the gardens and Domain during the ten years between 1876 and 1886, and the sums annually granted by Parliament for the purchase of plants have enabled such an increase in the collections to be made that the total number of plants catalogued exceeds 7,000 species, exclusive of varieties. The whole of the species are distinctly labelled with name, native country, and natural order. The condition of the gardens is in every way creditable to the city of Melbourne, and especially to its present Director, Mr W. R. Guilfoyle, F.L.S.

Adjoining the Botanic Garden is the Domain, 305 acres in extent, including the grounds of Government House of 157 acres in gardens, pleasure grounds, and extensive lawns, the whole in charge of the Director of the Botanic Garden. The Domain is intersected by walks and drives leading to the city and various parts of the southern suburbs. A small part remains in its natural condition, but the greater portion has been planted with an immense number and variety of trees. These have attained a considerable size, and produce a fine effect on the landscape, the Domain extending within close proximity to and commanding one of the best views to be obtained of the city.

Horticultural Societies.

Societies for the advancement of horticulture have been established in every city and town of any importance in the colony, while half-a-score exist in Melbourne and its immediate neighbourhood. They are supported by the subscriptions of members, supplemented by annual grants from Government: the Royal Horticultural Society of Victoria, located in Melbourne, the oldest and most important, for many years conducting an experimental garden.

The garden, now carried on by the Government, is situated in Richmond Park, about 3 miles from the city. It comprises an area of 28 acres, one-half of which is under cultivation as orchard, shrubbery, flower, and vegetable grounds, the remainder being planted with specimens of ornamental trees.

The collection of fruit is very large, the varieties numbering—700 apples, 7 almonds, 48 apricots, 5 brambles, 18 crabs, 90 cherries, 4 chestnuts, 2 citrons, 28 currants, 56 figs, 120 gooseberries, 5 guavas, 2 limes, 5 lemons, 5 medlars, 7 mulberries, 27 nectarines, 24 filberts, 24 oranges, 10 olives, 400 pears, 102 peaches, 17 Japanese persimmons (Diospyros Kaki), 148 plums, 7 quinces, 18 raspberries, 4 shaddocks, 50 strawberries, 170 grapes, 2 walnuts. Of these, scions are available to members and Government institutions, and the number distributed has averaged 20,000 annually during the past ten years. Seeds and roots are also distributed to members.

The fruit produced is exhibited at the monthly meetings of the society; at the great exhibitions, of which two or more are held annually; collections are also sent to country societies; and the surplus, amounting to about 3 tons a year, is distributed among the charitable institutions.

New varieties of fruit are annually imported from Europe, America, Japan and other centres of production. Communications and exchange of scions, &c., are maintained with the neighbouring colonies, India, Japan, and other countries.

The gardens were for many years in charge of the late Mr. George Neilson, a gentleman who devoted many years of his life to practical horticulture, and to whose unremitting care the present high state of perfection attained in the gardens is mainly due. The present Principal is Mr. C. Boyne Luffmann, and pupils are received for instruction in horticulture.

MARKET GARDENING.

The business of growing vegetables for market has attained a high degree of proficiency in the colony, more especially in the neighbourhood of the metropolis, where a large area of land is devoted to it, and whence supplies are sent to up-country towns, as well as to the neighbouring colonies, nearly 2,000 tons being yearly exported. In the country the principal supply of vegetables is grown by Chinese, who are located in the neighbourhood of the principal towns, and also in the suburbs of Melbourne. They are the chief hawkers of vegetables, and, besides growing a supply for that purpose, purchase largely from European cultivators. The Chinese cultivate their gardens in small patches by hand labour, but the Europeans employ horse labour wherever it can be applied. The bulk of the gardens are situated to the east and south-east of Melbourne, where the soil is almost pure sand, and easy to work. Some of the yields of vegetables obtained are simply marvellous. Cabbages averaging 26 lbs. weight, and parsnips 36 inches in length, are common; while mangel-wurzel are grown turning the scale at 56 lbs. The land is highly manured, and heavy yields are obtained. The produce is also of excellent quality. Two crops a year, or three crops in two years, are generally grown. The produce not exported is disposed of in the metropolitan markets, chiefly the Victoria Market, where an average of 300 carts attend twice a week during the summer season, each grower selling his own produce.

Plant Nurseries.

These have become numerous of late years, one or more being established in the neighbourhood of every large town, and several in country places, where the propagation of fruit trees constitutes the principal business; the demand for these being very large both in Victoria, the neighbouring colonies, and New Zealand. In the neighbourhood of Melbourne, nurseries are numerous, some being of considerable extent, and kept in a style that would be creditable to similar establishments in any part of the world. The collections of plants are now very extensive and are being annually increased by importations. Owing to the mildness of the climate in winter, a large number of species that require to be housed in Europe thrive out of doors the year round, stove plants alone requiring the protection of glass and artificial heat; but they are not much grown in nurseries, owing to the smallness of the demand. Fuchsias, pelargoniums, cinerarias, cyclamens, and Chinese primroses are grown in unheated houses. In these nurseries the plants are mostly grown in pots, and, except when being propagated, are located in shelter sheds constructed of frames, covered with lattice-work or brushwood. There are also a large number of smaller nurseries, in which flowers and market plants are grown. A large business is done in bouquets both in the markets and in shops in town, where excellent taste is displayed in their make-up. Flowers are plentiful both summer and winter. Nurserymen's catalogues have attained a size which, with the exception of orchids and other stove plants, will bear comparison with those of Britain.

Numerous seed shops exist in the principal towns, some of them managed in conjunction with plant nurseries. The bulk of the seeds consumed is raised in the colonies and New Zealand, whence a large proportion of the grasses and clovers are obtained. Several improved varieties of vegetables have originated in Victoria, obtained by means of crossing and selection. The newer varieties of flowers and vegetables are annually imported from Europe and America by the principal seedsmen. Some business is also done in the exportation of cauliflower and other vegetable seeds to Britain.

Private Gardens.

These are rapidly increasing in number, especially in the neighbourhood of the cities and towns. Villa gardens generally contain one or more glazed structures for the culture of greenhouse and stove plants, including orchids, of which some collections are being formed. Among the estate owners in the country districts are some who have gardens of a few acres in extent, but in general they are no larger than is necessary to meet household requirements, though some have planted trees rather largely for shelter and ornament. Cottage gardens are numerous and generally well kept, the climate admitting of their being gay with flowers throughout the year. Scientific gardeners are not in great demand, but there are a few in the colony whose productions would pass with credit in any part of the world. Flower gardening is chiefly of the old-fashioned style, massing or any other form of bedding being rarely attempted.

In shrubberies and other ornamental grounds a great variety of trees and shrubs are to be found, most of the best species and varieties procurable in Europe, America, and other parts of the world having been imported, the enterprise of nurserymen and some amateurs being great in that direction. Coniferae are in great request, nearly all the pines and cypresses procurable in California, besides many others, being cultivated. Of these, Pinus insignis and Cupressus macrocarpa are in the greatest demand, many thousands being planted annually for shelter or ornament. Both of these grow with great rapidity in almost any kind of soil, and in a few years form large timber trees. European pines are also grown, as well as those of the Abies and the Picea sections, which, however, succeed best in the cooler districts. Of cedars, the Deodar is the favorite, being the quickest grower and the most graceful. The Wellingtonia (Sequoea) gigantea thrives fairly, handsome specimens of 30 feet or more in height being not uncommon. Of Araucarias, some six species are grown, forming specimens of perfect symmetry and great beauty. A. imbricata is the most suitable for the cooler districts, the others preferring a more genial climate. The bunya bunya, of Queensland (A. Bidwilli), grows very rapidly, and forms a handsome specimen, well furnished with a mass of polished green foliage. The golden arbor vitæ (Biota aurea) is in great request. The native pines—Frenella—form handsome dwarf trees. The larch thrives in the cooler districts, where it competes for pre-eminence with Abies Douglasii.

Taking a few of the more ornamental shrubs in alphabetical order, the acacias are amongst the most beautiful when in flower. The tree myrtles—Acmena—form very handsome finely-shaped bushes, beautiful both in flower and fruit. The American aloe, agave, grows luxuriantly, and flowers at from twelve to twenty years of age. The species of arbutus succeed fairly well in the drier parts, and much better where the temperature is lower. Brugmansias stand exposed the year round, and flower magnificently. Cacti of numerous kinds thrive admirably out of doors. Camellias require shade when grown in the open air, and then flower magnificently. The common and Portugal laurels thrive and attain the size of trees in the cooler districts. Eucalyptus ficifolia, which produces crimson flowers in abundance while quite young and small, forms an object of exceeding beauty. The laburnum prefers the cooler climates, and flowers freely. The native and New Zealand species of Dracæna form noble objects. Ficus australis and F. macrophylla form large dense bushes or low trees. Magnolias of all species form large bushes, and flower magnificently. Neriums thrive well, and flower freely. The plane—platanus

—attains a large size in the cooler districts. Pittosporums are, of all evergreens, the best adapted to the climate, forming handsome specimens and fine ornamental hedges. Rhododendrons require shade in the warmer parts of the colony, but flourish exposed in the cooler districts. Schinus molle is of great value as a shade tree. Besides those already mentioned, there are an immense number of dwarf shrubs that attain great perfection, such as the Indian azalea, daphne, indica boronia, bouvardia, chorizema, deutzia, eriostemon, erica, erythrina, escallonia, fuchsia, hydrangea, lantana, lasiandra, pomegranate, pelargonium, petunia, salvia, veronica, and weigela. Of roses, about 400 varieties are grown. Among climbers are bignonia, bougainvillea, clematis, lapageria, passion flowers, including Tacsonia and Glycine sinensis.

Among herbaceous plants, dahlias, chrysanthemums, phloxes, pentstemons, carnations, columbines, cyclamens, iris, mesembryanthemum—numerous species—and verbenas. Bulbous and similar plants flourish exceedingly, including amaryllis, anemone, gladiolus—grown in every garden—hyacinth, ixia, lilium—magnificent, narcissus, ranunculus, tulip, sparaxis, Guernsey lilies, tuberoses, tritoma, tritonia, and several others.

Fruit.

Fruit culture is practised throughout nearly the whole of the colony. In some of the more densely-populated districts orchards of 100 to 150 acres have been planted, and their numbers are rapidly increasing. They are very numerous in the neighbourhood of the metropolis, where they generally exist in conjunction with market gardening; these range from 8 to 20 acres in extent. Owing to the variety of climatic conditions, all the fruits of temperate regions can be cultivated. A large number of varieties are grown, all the best to be obtained in Europe and America having been imported and propagated. Numerous varieties of fruit have been raised from seed, the parent blossoms being, in most cases, carefully intercrossed. In apples, varieties of great excellence, both dessert and cooking, some of the former almost equalling the best of the imported sorts. While in pears, some colonial varieties are unsurpassed by the best European sorts. Peaches, plums, cherries, and strawberries of excellent quality have been also raised.

Apple.

This fruit is, of all others, the most esteemed; it thrives in all parts of the colony, succeeding best where the summer temperature is moderate. The trees grow with great luxuriance, come early into bearing, and yield a crop every year, unless the blossoms happen to be injured by insects or frosts, which, however, rarely occurs. They thrive in all kinds of soil, from a nearly pure sand to a strong loam. The fruit is large in size, fine in colour, and excellent in flavour. Canker in apple-trees is unknown in the colony.

Apricot.

The apricot is highly esteemed, and is in great demand for dessert, cooking, and preserving. It thrives everywhere, but prefers the warmer regions, where its produce is both large and fine. The trees attain a large size, and rarely miss yielding a heavy crop.

Almond.

The almond thrives everywhere: it is specially adapted to dry stony soil, and requires very little attention. It is frequently used for shelter on the exposed sides of orchards, and bears abundantly. In the shrubbery it forms a splendid object when closed with a mass of blossoms in early spring. Seedling almonds are frequently used as stocks for peaches.

Cherry.

This fruit is very largely grown, the trees almost invariably bearing a heavy crop. It thrives in all climates, and is the best adapted of all fruit trees to the strong volcanic loams that exist in various parts of the colony. The fruit attains a large size, and is of excellent quality. The trees commence to bear at an early age, and occasion very little trouble in pruning; they are very rarely attacked by either disease or insects.

Currant.

The different kinds of currants succeed well in the cooler districts, where they yield heavy crops of fine fruit. The black currant is in great request for jam-making and other culinary purposes.

Fig.

The fig thrives in all, except the coldest, parts of the colony, and exceptionally well in the warmer northern districts, where it grows with great luxuriance, the trees attaining a large size, and fruiting heavily every year, the fruit being of large size and good quality. Fig-drying has been successfully practised, but has not yet become established as a business.

Filbert.

Trees of the filbert and other nuts grow with remarkable luxuriance in the rich soil of valleys in the more temperate regions, where they bear enormously. Nuts are in great demand, and bring high prices in the market.

Gooseberry.

This well-known fruit thrives in all parts of the colony except the warmest, but grows best where the summer temperature is low. In such situations the bushes attain a large size, and bear enormous crops. The fruit is much used for cooking and jam-making.

Grape.

The grape and wine-making have been treated elsewhere : it is only necessary to remark that, as a dessert fruit, it thrives and ripens its fruit in all but the coldest climates, and in all varieties of soil or situation. It grows as a bush in gardens, or trained to a fence or trellis; it rambles over the cottage verandah, and even in the heart of a city or town it continues to thrive, its roots extending dozens of yards beneath the pavement. It, however, brings its fruit to the greatest perfection in the zones of highest temperature, where bunches and berries of enormous size, fine colour, and excellent flavour are produced.

Melon.

The melon thrives in the open ground in all the warmer and more temperate parts of the colony ; the seed being sown in ordinary garden soil: little or no attention is required by the plants until the fruit is ready to gather. Both rock melons and water melons are in great demand in the markets, and also a cross-bred variety of sugar melon, which attains a large size and is much used for jam.

Mulberry.

This is well adapted to the more moderate zones, where it rapidly forms a tree and produces abundance of fruit. The silk-worm mulberry also grows well, but is rarely utilized.

Peach.

This fruit, one of the most delicious grown in the colony, ripens its fruit nearly everywhere. The trees require much attention in warding off the attacks of aphides in spring, and they are not long-lived. When in good soil the fruit attains a large size, and acquires an excellent flavour. A number of colonial seedlings have been raised; these prove more robust than some of the imported varieties and are generally preferred by growers for market.

Pear.

The pear is highly esteemed as a dessert fruit, many of the imported, as well as several seedling varieties being unsurpassed for flavour. The trees quickly attain a large size, and rarely fail to produce a full crop, the fruit attaining a large size. They thrive in nearly all parts of the colony.

Persimmon (Diospyros Kaki).

This fruit, introduced only a few years ago, is becoming popular on account of the rich flavour and fine colour of its fruit, which renders the trees highly ornamental; these are very precocious, trees of 3 or 4 feet in height producing several dozens of fruit. Young trees are annually imported from Japan.

Plums.

Plums are in great request, and are largely grown in all districts. The trees are very prolific, rarely failing to produce a full crop, and when not overloaded the fruit is very large; it is much used for jam and other culinary purposes. On account of its abundance, the fruit can be obtained in the markets at a low rate.

Quince.

This fruit is grown, though in small numbers, in nearly every garden. The trees crop well, and produce fruit of large size.

Raspberry.

This fruit succeeds well in the moderately cool districts, where it bears abundantly, rarely missing a crop. The fruit is highly esteemed, and in great request by jam manufacturers as well as private persons. It is grown in several parts of the colony, chiefly for local supply. The metropolis obtains its principal supply from the rich valleys of the upper portions of the Yarra, and it is estimated that the value of this fruit forwarded to Melbourne exceeds £150,000 per annum; the average price in the market being 3d. to 6d. per pound.

Strawberry.

The strawberry is very prolific, and the plants continue to bear for a great number of years; two crops invariably, and sometimes a third, being borne in succession every year. The fruit attains a large size on properly-enriched soil.

Walnut.

This tree thrives in all districts except the hottest, and produces abundance of fruit at an early stage, but is not extensively grown.

VEGETABLES.

Vegetables of all the kinds commonly grown in temperate climates, and some that cannot be successfully grown in Britain, succeed well, and are extensively cultivated, hardly a family in the longer-settled districts being without a daily supply, either purchased or grown by themselves, all the year round. A large quantity can be grown with a moderate amount of labour, where the soil is properly tilled and manured.

Asparagus.

This esteemed vegetable grows luxuriantly in all parts of the colony, and attains a large size under liberal culture. It is in great request during a long season, and can be purchased at reasonable rates.

Bean.

Broad beans can be grown in all climates, as the seed is sown in autumn, and the crop gathered in spring before the heats of summer arrive. Kidney beans, both dwarf and runner, are grown extensively; they bear abundantly, and are in season from the beginning of summer to the end of autumn. They are sold at such rates as bring them within the reach of all classes.

Beet.

This root succeeds in all soils and all climates. It is in great request, being used in a fresh or pickled state. The roots, like others of similar nature, are allowed to remain in the ground until wanted for use, a supply being obtainable at all seasons.

Brocoli.

This is rarely grown, as the plants require too great a length of time to attain maturity, and its place is filled by the cauliflower.

Cabbage.

The cabbage is the most largely grown of all green vegetables. The plants come quickly into use, and attain a large size : cabbages can be had every day in the year, and with very little labour.

Cauliflower.

The cauliflower is one of the most esteemed of vegetables ; it may be obtained throughout the year in the cooler districts, and in others except during two or three of the hottest months. It grows luxuriantly, becomes rapidly fit for use, and attains a large size. Plants, including leaves, stem, and roots, have been grown to 42 lbs. weight, the head, dressed for market, weighing 36 lbs.

Carrot.

This root, which thrives everywhere, is in great request, and very extensively grown. The roots are rarely troubled with any kind of insect.

Celery.

Celery prefers the cooler districts, but may be had everywhere during winter and spring. Its culture has greatly increased of recent years.

Cucumber.

A few growers cultivate the cucumber in heated houses during the winter season, but the demand is not great at that time. Large quantities are grown in the open ground in summer. They are in considerable demand for pickling.

Leek.

This attains an immense size under liberal culture ; it is in use for nine months in the year.

Lettuce.

This grows well, with little trouble, throughout the year. The summer crops are sown where they are to remain. Only the cabbage lettuce is used.

Onion.

Onions are grown in large quantities both in the garden and the field, many tons being exported. In gardens the early crops are sown in autumn and transplanted ; field crops are sown in spring.

Pea.

Peas can be gathered throughout the year, except occasionally in summer, should the drought be severe ; they are, of course, finest in spring and early summer. The plants are rarely supported in any way, as they do not attain a great length.

Potato.

Potatoes are very largely grown in gardens and fields, a large proportion being exported. Young potatoes may be obtained in gardens at all seasons.

Pumpkin.

This fruit attains a large size ; it is grown to some extent for use in winter.

Rhubarb.

This is in great request, and is largely grown by market gardeners, who are able to pull three or four crops a year from each plant. It is in use during eleven months out of the twelve.

Tomato.

The demand for this fruit has largely increased within recent years, and immense quantities are now grown and sold very cheaply. For early crops the plants are raised in heat and planted against fences or walls, where they sometimes remain till the following season. fruiting all the while. Later crop plants are supported by stakes or trellises. The markets are supplied for about nine months in the year.

Turnip.

Turnips are in season every day in the year. They become quickly fit for use. but do not succeed well in the drier districts. except during the winter season.

Vegetable Marrow.

There is a large consumption of this vegetable. The seed is sown in the open ground in spring. and where the soil is good heavy crops are yielded ; very little attention beyond gathering the fruit being required.

THE FRUIT-GROWING INDUSTRY.

(By D. M. Dow, of The Leader.)

Fruit-growing is one of the most promising industries in Victoria. Settlers who have been engaged in the orchard business for many years are generally among the most prosperous members of the community, while there are few colonial industries that can compare with fruit-growing in offering encouraging prospects of future development. The past history of the industry has served to prove its profitableness. The scope for expansion is practically unlimited.

WILL IT PAY?

Some few years ago, when fruit-growing as a business was receiving a large share of attention, the most contradictory statements were made in regard to the prospects of the industry. Persons interested in promoting the growing of fruit pointed to the wonderful results obtained in California and elsewhere, while others, posing as practical men on the strength of having produced wheat or potatoes, pronounced strongly upon the impossibility of a family being able to live upon a holding of 10 or 20 acres. The owners of established orchards not being desirous of calling too many competitors into the field had very little to say on the matter. The yields of their orchards, however, gave encouragement to the advocates of progress, and as the objectors had nothing but prejudice to contribute to the controversy, the victory was with the progressive party. As the result, an important movement in the direction of tree-planting was made in nearly all parts of the colony, and under the stimulus of Government bonuses the area of land under orchards was greatly increased. Most of the new orchards have now come into bearing, and from a variety of causes the financial returns have fallen somewhat short of expectations. Many new planters are disappointed with the results, and their complaints, added to the statements of the original objectors, constitute a charge of failure against the fruit-growing industry. Those who always opposed progress are saying, "I told you so," and disappointed planters are aiding by misrepresenting the position and prospects of an important and promising industry.

EXPECTING TOO MUCH.

In seeking to arrive at the actual position of the case, the views of those may be disregarded who say—"I always told you fruit-growing would not pay," for they have learned nothing from recent experiences; but the men who have invested in fruit-growing, and are disappointed, have a right to be heard. Their complaint is that the business is not what it was represented to be; and this is a fact. There is no doubt that many were induced to plant orchards upon exaggerated estimates of the returns to be obtained. Maximum yields and high prices were quoted as an encouragement to planters, and persons who were induced to invest in what was too often represented as a fortune-making enterprise have naturally been disappointed. In regard to the quality of the fruit there is no complaint, for in this respect the most sanguine expectations have been realized; but the yields have in some cases come short of anticipations. In the matter of yields, the disappointment has arisen in most cases through planters having been led to expect full returns too soon. Trees from seven to ten years old have seldom failed to yield heavy crops; but, as growers expected maximum returns two or three years earlier, grounds have been furnished for discontent. This objection, it is evident, time will be able to remove, and the industry must be judged by its actual results rather than by its relation to the exaggerated anticipations of investors.

GOOD LOCAL MARKETS.

The markets, too, have been a cause of some disappointment. The expectation of higher prices for fruit has perhaps caused more discontent than having to wait an extra year or two for maximum yields. In the matter of prices, however, growers cannot plead that they were encouraged to expect a local fresh fruit market at payable rates for the produce of their orchards. An export trade in fresh fruits and a resort to canning and drying were always insisted upon as necessary to place the industry on a sound basis. In all the circumstances of the case, the growers could not have expected better prices in the fresh fruit market than have been obtained. Instead of resorting to canning and drying, the whole of the colony's fruit has practically been thrown upon the local market. Not only has the local consumer been expected to take the produce of our orchards, but he has been required to make use of it within a few months, and then he has been allowed to supply himself with imported preserved fruit for the rest of the year. When the surroundings of the case are taken into account the wonder is that the fresh fruit market has stood this process of glutting as well as it has done. At a time when the large area of new orchards brought into existence by the planting bonuses were coming into bearing, the colony was passing through a period of extraordinary depression. With a greatly restricted purchasing power, the colony's demand for fresh fruit has absorbed the produce of our enlarged orchard area, a highly encouraging result that is nothing short of surprising.

Room for Expansion.

A common saying is that "there are too many in the industry"; but this does not fit in consistently with the fact that Victoria imports £59,000 worth of fruit per annum. Going into details, it is found that the quantity and value of fruits and jams imported into Victoria during the year 1897 were:—

Fruits, Jams, &c.			Quantity.		Value.
			Dozen packets.		£
Bottled fruits...	...	...	59,581	...	4,277
			Lbs.		
Dried fruits (unenumerated)		...	839,327	...	11,307
Currants	...	...	3,215,476	...	25,882
Raisins	...	...	1,116,579	...	15,461
Jams and jellies	...	...	89,383	...	2,239
Totals	...	...	5,260,765	...	59,166

And 59,581 doz. pks.

The Tariff rates are:—

Fruit, dried, boiled or partly boiled, or
    pulp ...   . 3d. per lb.

Fruits, preserved in bottles, &c.—

Quarts and over a pint	6s. per doz.
Pints and over half-pint	3s. per doz.
Half-pints and smaller	1s. 6d. per doz.
Over a quart and not exceeding a gallon	18s. per doz.
Fruits, green, being oranges and lemons	9d. per bush.
Fruits not otherwise enumerated ...	1s. 6d. per bush.

If the question is asked—"Why, in spite of these protective duties, Victorian growers do not supply the market?" the reply seems to be "Because foreign competitors give their attention to the selection of high-class fruit, and adopt up-to-date methods in their general management."

Fruit-Preserving.

Canning and drying have not been resorted to, except to a small extent, because prices are believed to have not yet reached a preserving level. The most sanguine advocates of fruit-growing anticipated that preserving would have been necessary before this, and they formed their conclusions without supposing that a check was to be put upon the increase of the colony's population. To account for the circumstance that, in spite of the depression, fruit-preserving has not required to be resorted to, it must be concluded that the lower prices have led to a greatly increased consumption of fresh fruit. The manner in which prices have stood the strain of the present crisis gives rise to hopeful anticipation as to the future of the industry. In the first place, there is a prospect of an enlarged fresh fruit market from an increase of population. It is not to be supposed that the colony is going to stand still. Progress is again taking place, and fruit-growing will advance with the colony in general. There is not likely to be another planting boom for a considerable time, so that even the local fresh fruit market is not to be despaired of. But this is apart from the prospect opened up by the export trade in the various branches of fruit-preserving. It is well known that a very small surplus is capable of bringing about a very serious fall in a market. In view of this fact, it is evident that a comparatively small preserving trade would serve to give a considerable relief to the market for fresh fruits. The fact that our total output of fruit has not yet been able to force prices down to a preserving basis shows that the canning or drying of only a small proportion of future crops will suffice to secure fair values for the general bulk.

An Export Trade.

When, by means of co-operative preserving factories, we are catering for the colony's requirements throughout the year, instead of for only a few months, the demand will be so increased that there is likely to be little cause for complaints of glutted markets. It will be said by those who oppose progress that we cannot compete with Californian preserved fruits; but, as we are not handicapped by any natural disadvantages, the statement amounts to a serious reflection upon our intelligence as a people. We are to-day competing successfully for an export trade with the most advanced dairying countries in the world, and yet our natural conditions are quite as favorable for fruit-growing as for dairying. If dairy farmers can do this, surely fruit-growers can supply the local markets all the year round. Nothing has, so far, been said of the export of fresh fruit to the London market. Another season's experience has demonstrated that there is a demand in London for all the good fruit that we can send, and that a successful method of getting the fruit to the market is in a fair way of being discovered. From a view of local markets and the prospects of an export trade, there are no grounds for any but hopeful anticipations concerning the future of the fruit-growing industry.

For further information apply to Mr. J. M. Sinclair, the Representative in London of the Victorian Department of Agriculture.

VICTORIAN VINEYARDS.

The production of wine is unquestionably destined to become one of Victoria's greatest industries. Receiving attention from the earliest days of the colony, the progress of wine-growing has been slow but sure. Measured by the volume of production, development has been only moderate; estimated by the extent to which the colony's resources have been successfully tested, and the manner in which the superiority of the wines has been demonstrated, it has been immense. It was from the first recognised that with a limited population wine production could not become a great industry without depending upon an export trade, and consequently improving the quality of the wine has always received more attention than the extension of the vineyards. The result has been that Victoria, with a comparatively small area under vines, has since 1851 been represented at all the great exhibitions of the world. Having proved by the honours won at the various exhibitions that wines of the highest quality could be produced, the extension of the vineyards was commenced about twenty years ago. The area under vines now reaches 30,000 acres, yielding annually about 2,500,000 gallons of wine. As wine is not the ordinary beverage of the local population, a surplus of from 200,000 gallons to 400,000 gallons is annually exported, and as our wines become better known to the consumers of the old world the demand for them will gradually increase. The consumption of such superior wines as our vineyards produce is upon such a large scale that, with the footing already secured in the world's markets, our vintages will rapidly take their places among the most valuable productions of the colony.

EARLY HISTORY.

In dealing with the early history of the industry, as well as the other branches of the subject which follow, extensive use is made of the writings of Mr. Hubert de Castella, one of the pioneers of wine-growing in Victoria, and author of the interesting book, *John Bull's Vineyard*. In 1860, says this authority, the number of acres under vines had not reached 2,000. Some of the wines made, however, had already found their way abroad, and obtained favorable

A VINTAGE SCENE.

notice. About that time a rush for establishing vineyards took place ; the Victorian Government offered, in various localities. lands considered as best adapted to that cultivation, under especially favorable conditions : the newspapers issued periodical encouragements in shape of reports on the plantations going on. and on the successes obtained or expected ; the *Argus* gave a large gold cup to the best-appointed vineyard : lawyers, doctors, and men of means, taking land under the wine industry clause, planted by proxy ; various companies were formed to work large areas of vines. In four years over 2,000 acres were planted. All, in fact, seemed to indicate great and immediate prosperity.

Unfortunately, however, the colonial taste was for strong drinks. Port and sherry advocates had taken up the movement, the warmest districts were proclaimed as the best to settle in, and the men who planted in more temperate countries were pitied for their mistake.

But to those growers who took as types the strong wines of low commerce. it was not sufficient to obtain, by proper maturity, musts equal in richness to those of Spain and Portugal. Many of them left their grapes standing on the vines until they were turned into raisins ; and we recollect the case of an amateur vigneron who had his grapes placed on the zinc roofs of his house and cellars, previous to crushing them, in order to leave them for two days *improving*. as he called it, under a burning sun.

Wines made in this fashion. not from must. but from syrup, incapable of a complete fermentation, true compounds of sugar and alcohol, soon turned to vinegary sourness. The light wines of the cooler districts. mixed by inexperienced wine merchants with these strong ones. only developed their acidity. Day by day the name of colonial wine became more ignominious, the trade died out, and neglected vineyards were gradually rooted out. The statistics of 1880 showed a diminution of 553 acres of vines. as compared with those of 1875.

The Turning Point.

All the while. however, a few persevering men. both in the northern districts and around Melbourne and other towns. careful of their plantations and diligent in study. were every year improving their vintages. and the Melbourne Intercolonial Exhibition of 1881. displaying a real and solid advance, again brought the wine industry to the fore.

A grand *prix*, a trophy of solid silver, of the value of £800, was offered by the Emperor of Germany to be awarded "to an exhibitor in one of the Australasian Colonies as an acknowledgment of the efforts in promoting art and industry as shown by the high qualities of the goods manufactured by such exhibitor."

The fact that, after a keen competition, this prize was awarded to the most successful exhibitor of Australian wine, as fulfilling best the conditions specified by the Imperial donor, caused a stir which is remembered to this day; and not only in the colonies, but in England and in foreign countries was the announcement received with marked interest.

From that day colonial wine was no longer thrown promiscuously under general condemnation. People who had never tasted it before condescended to have it on their tables. Clubs and hotels, full of visitors, could no longer refuse it admission, since it had obtained such high recognition. It was a benefit to all. A few months afterwards the growers of Victoria could count the value of their produce, even of their properties, substantially advanced.

Yet another benefit, still more important, was conferred by that eminent distinction upon the wine-growers at large. It opened their eyes to the requirements of the public taste—at least, of educated taste—and it educated their own.

Many vignerons, some of them possessors of smaller extent of vines than the lucky winners of the Emperor's prize, had run closely with them in the race. Their wines had been of equal value, but were exhibited on a lesser scale. The result was that the other growers—those who, to that day, had desired to obtain strength, and what they mistook for body— began to ponder over the list of awards. When they found these awards given to delicacy and bouquet, to light wines principally, and to those only amongst the heavy ones which were free from alcoholic taste and non-converted sugar, faith in alcohol was shaken in their hearts, and the value of proper fermentation dawned upon them. From that time dates a general improvement in the manufacture.

At Other Exhibitions.

Australia's best chance of making her wines known was by sending them to the World's Great Exhibitions. Her first display was at Paris, in 1851, and since then those of London, Vienna, Paris again, Philadelphia, Amsterdam, and Bordeaux have received her samples, and she may well be grateful for

A WINE CELLAR.

CARTING GRAPES TO CELLAR.

RECEIVING GRAPES AT CELLAR.

the reception they met with at the hands of her elders. It may have been kindness of heart toward a new-comer, or perhaps, as was said in a French report we are about to quote from, "kind curiosity"; but the prizes given, although perhaps only to encourage the young scholar, were numerous and highly esteemed. Three years ago, Bordeaux, the queen city of wine, invited the world to exhibit samples of its vintages within her walls, and, amongst others, 70 appeared from Australian vignerons. A book was published reviewing impartially the produce of the exhibiting nations, and our beginnings were given full consideration to.

Mr. R. Sempé, the writer of the review in question, begins by showing the admirable adaptability of our soil and climate for the cultivation of the vine; and by exposing, we quote him now, "the unique spectacle of development and greatness of the colonies, which, born yesterday, have arrived by their courage and energy, coupled with liberty, to a degree of richness and civilization which rivals even the largest towns of old Europe." The results of other later exhibitions have fully confirmed the high character of the Australian wines from Victorian vineyards.

VINE-GROWING DISTRICTS.

The Rutherglen district, situated in the Murray Valley, is the most extensive wine-producing section of the colony, and there are in the same division millions of acres equally suitable for viticulture. Mr. Hubert de Castella speaks thus of other centres of the vine-growing industry :—

"The whole of the northern slopes of the ranges in the centre of Victoria, from Stawell to Bendigo, a zigzag line of 200 miles of mountains and gullies more or less auriferous, and all producing, or capable of producing, fine wines, is dotted about by townships which are only awaiting a signal to increase their plantations. The Shire of Stawell, for example, includes, with a rural population of 3,500 people, many vineyards. At Ararat several growers cultivate an average of 10 acres each. Strathfieldsaye, near Bendigo, contains several vineyards of old repute on the Emu Creek. Castlemaine counts also some valuable vineyards, and there are a good many on the River Goulburn in the same latitude.

"Up to the present time, with the exception of the vineyards around Melbourne and those of the Yarra, the whole of the southern coast of Victoria, the most temperate parts of all of Australia, and perhaps the most fertile, a stretch of

land 500 miles long by 60 miles broad, extending from Cape
Otway to the River Glenelg, has scarcely been tried for
viticulture. Should, as we may anticipate, experience prove
the value of wines grown in mild latitudes, there are
16,000,000 acres on that southern coast hitherto held as
a region too cold for growing vines, which may yet become
one of the most valuable parts of the Australian continent
for that purpose."

THE CHARACTER OF THE WINES.

All the wines of the northern region of Victoria are full-
bodied and generous, of magnificent colour; the red can be
similar to the fine wines of Roussillon and Asti, and we
have met on the Emu Creek, at Stawell, and sometimes in
smaller vineyards, where wines had been fermented in
smaller quantities—brilliant ruby wines like the côte-rôtie
of the Hermitage, and sprightly ones like the best of the
Valteline. If the wines of the Murray can be compared to
those of Spain and Portugal; the wines of Bendigo, Stawell,
and the Goulburn to those of the Rhone and Pyrenees;
the grapes near Melbourne, growing in a cooler latitude, one
or two degrees more south, and often visited by the coast
rains, produce wines more similar to those of the Rhine and
Bordeaux. The fine wines of Sunbury, of Essendon, and
the Yarra district have gained colonial reputations.

At the time of the Melbourne Exhibition in 1881, the
proprietor of one of the Yarra vineyards requested M.
Eigenshenck, the representative of the well-known house
of Arles-Dufour, of Paris, &c., to take back with him some
samples of his wines and have them valued in Bordeaux.
The result of this inquiry is so important, by the high
position of the judge it was submitted to in Bordeaux, that
it is only right for us to give the full particulars.

In December, 1881, Messrs. Arles-Dufour communicated
the following, written to them by Mr. A. Lalande, of
Bordeaux, to whom the wines had been submitted :—

"We have found the Nos. 1 and 2 (red wine 1879, made
from Cabernet-Sauvignon) *very good,* and we have given
them a value of frs. 1,000 per tonneau of 900 litres.

"We have found the No. 4 good (white Hermitage 1879),
and we have given it a value of frs. 600 to 700 per tonneau."

The name of Mr. Armand Lalande, the president of the
Chamber of Commerce of Bordeaux, is a household word in
England as well as in France. He is the first authority on

WINE MAKING.

wine. He was told that these wines were Australian, and his opinion was asked, as compared with Bordeaux value. The price he fixed for the two red wines, 1,000 frs. per tonneau, was the price of the crus *bourgeois* superior of Margaux and St. Julien at two years old, the age the Australian wines were, also the price of the third classified crus St. Emilion. As to the price of 700 frs. for the white, E. Ferret, in his recent book on Bordeaux wines, speaking of the white wines of the canton of Ste. Foix, which he classes amongst the fine white wines of the Gironde, says— " These wines, in the first crus, have a handsome pale-yellow colour, much finesse, sometimes mellowness, and a very agreeable bouquet ; they are worth, young, from 450 to 600 frs. ; old they reach up to 700 frs. the tonneau." Pardon these lengthy details, they show in what company the Victorian wines were placed.

YIELDS AND PROFITS.

The question of profits depends upon the cost of production. All the operations required for the cultivation of the vine are reduced to a minimum in warm countries. A thousand plants to an acre, half the quantity which is planted in cooler districts, are sufficient to give normal returns. The heat develops the vines, and they bear more fruit with considerably less labour in winter pruning, in stalking and trellising, and in other works necessary in summer where the fruit must be exposed to the sun. As to the cleaning of the ground, without which there is nowhere a crop, in cool countries weeds require to be kept down, constant ploughing, scarifying, and hand-hoeing : in the warm districts, if weeds are only disturbed, the sun, the lover of the vine, destroys them. All through, and in every way, the expenses of a vineyard increase or decrease according to the mean temperature of the land. In the warm districts of Victoria, the total cost of the cultivation of a vineyard by hired labour can be set down at £3 per acre, exclusive of vintage expenses. A moderate extent of grapes, say 15 acres, can be cultivated by a farmer and his family at a trifling outlay. Time can be found to attend to them without interfering with the ordinary work of a farm. At Rutherglen, the district for us to judge by, there are five wine-growers cultivating an average of 200 acres each—not a bad beginning— and 147 farmers an average of 12 acres each. With these latter rest the future of the industry. "Their wines," says

Mr. de Castella in conclusion, "cost them 6d. per gallon, or about that, and if they can sell them at their farms, during the year following the vintage, for 1s. 6d. per gallon, there is, on an average crop of 250 gallons per acre, a profit of over £12 per acre, which no other crop can give. A cultivation based upon such returns cannot but increase."

AUSTRALIAN CHAMPAGNE.

The manufacture of champagne has engaged the attention of three or four growers in Victoria and New South Wales for many years, and much experience has been gained as to the requirements of the industry under local conditions. Colonial experimenters have had good natural wines to work with, and they have, with considerable enterprise, obtained the best expert assistance from France. Considerable difficulty was experienced in adopting the peculiar and delicate manufacturing process to the peculiarity of local climatic conditions, but within the last few years a large measure of success has been achieved. Mr. Hans W. Irvine, of Great Western Vineyard, 139 miles from Melbourne, having obtained highly satisfactory results. A great difficulty with other experimenters has been that of controlling the temperature in a naturally warm climate, and in overcoming this obstacle Mr. Irvine has been effectively assisted by the possession of a deep underground cellar, the features of which are unique in the Australian Colonies. The cellars are excavated out of decayed granite rock, 25 feet below the surface, and the temperature in its vaults remains at about 58 degrees, showing very little variation throughout the year. Although the cellars were originally constructed for the accommodation of the clarets and hocks for which the vineyard has been long celebrated, and which are still the basis of Mr. Irvine's extended business, their suitableness for the preparation of sparkling wines has, during recent years, led to an increasing use of them for that purpose. The making of champagne, sparkling hock, and sparkling burgundy was commenced at the Great Western Vineyard in 1890, and the results have been fairly successful. There are at present 150,000 bottles in the cellar, and an additional 48,000 bottles of the 1896 and 1897 vintages are being added. Considerable difficulty has been experienced in obtaining the necessary skilled labour, a drawback to which every new industry is subject. The Great Western sparkling

A CHAMPAGNE CELLAR.

wines have been successful at several important exhibitions, and have been well spoken of by many qualified experts. Having overcome many of the difficulties inevitable to a new industry, champagne-making is likely to prove an important branch of Australian wine-growing in Victoria.

Australian Brandy.

A considerable quantity of wine is made into brandy, this branch of production having increased during recent years owing to the low prices ruling for wines. On account of the exportable surplus of wine having increased beyond the capacity of the existing demand, local prices have fallen to a low level, and considerable quantities of new wines have been sold to distillers at about 6d. per gallon. There are eight distilleries in the colony, and the quantity of wine made into brandy in 1895 was 213,193 gallons. While the prices offered by distillers are unsatisfactory to growers who have produced wine for the proper wine market, growers who produce specially for distilling prices find the prices remunerative. It is probable, therefore, that an increase in the production of brandy will take place, along with the development of the wine-growing industry.

For further information apply to Mr. J. M. Sinclair, the Representatative in London of the Victorian Department of Agriculture.

IRRIGATION AND WATER SUPPLY.

About twenty years ago the highly satisfactory returns obtained by a few scattered settlers as the result of artificially watering their crops directed attention to the subject of irrigation. The representatives of the two leading Victorian newspapers, who visited America in 1883, reported that irrigation was being carried on with great success in that country, and soon afterwards the Hon. Alfred Deakin, a member of the Government, accompanied by Mr. Derry, an experienced engineer from India, proceeded to America for the purpose of investigating the subject. The results of this investigation were favorable, and public opinion having been thoroughly aroused upon the subject the Hon. Alfred Deakin, as Minister of Water Supply, introduced and successfully carried through a scheme providing for national irrigation.

A NATIONAL SCHEME.

Under the scheme the land-holders of suitable districts were allowed to constitute irrigation trusts for the purpose of carrying out water supply works, the Government lending the necessary capital at a low rate of interest upon the security of the land supplied with water. So confident were land-owners that they readily pledged their holdings as security, constituting trusts, and borrowing large sums of money from the Government. Nearly the whole of the occupied lands in the drier portions of the colony were placed under the control of local trusts and provided with more or less expensive water supply works. The national scheme was universally popular, and its immediate effect was to greatly improve in the drier districts the supply of water for domestic and stock purposes. When, however, the time arrived for the commencement of the payment of interest considerable difficulty arose. It was a feature of the scheme that the interest was to be provided out of funds received by the trusts for the sale of water used for irrigation purposes. From a variety of causes, however, very little irrigation had been carried out by land-owners, and consequently interest had to be met by the clauses of the Act providing for taxing the land. Two causes may be assigned for the failure of the land-owners to use the available water for irrigation. In the first place, a series of wet seasons had

MAIN IRRIGATION CHANNEL.—From Goulburn River.

prevailed rendering good crops available without recourse to irrigation; and, in the second place, the population occupying the land were not acquainted with the practical details of the various methods of using water artificially in agriculture, or the culture of the several crops suitable under such a system. The outcome of the whole matter has been the discovery that a slower rate of progress would have been better. All concerned—Government, officials, and land-owners—have been too sanguine, but in the long run, although not so quickly as anticipated, the national irrigation scheme will prove remunerative. The payment of interest to the Government has been postponed, but the land served has permanently improved, and the practice of irrigation to render the investments remunerative is being extended.

The Future of Irrigation.

Irrigation has not been disappointing. It is the lack of irrigation that has caused the temporary trouble. When water has been applied to the land the results have been equal to expectation. Recent dry seasons have given fresh evidence of the value of irrigation, and with the growth of knowledge the system is likely to increase until the irrigation trusts are placed upon a sound financial basis. The following account of the various irrigation schemes of the colony is condensed from a report of Mr. Stuart Murray, Chief Engineer of the Water Supply Department:—

The Goulburn Valley.

The Goulburn is the largest of Victorian rivers. It has the largest drainage area, the greatest mean volume, and the most permanent stream. The area of its basin, down to the weir recently constructed near Murchison, is little less than 4,000 square miles, and a considerable proportion of this area consists of high mountain ranges, whose melting snows maintain the volume of the river far into the summer. The term Goulburn Valley would, strictly applied, include this great basin. It is, however, by popular usage limited to the plain that extends from Murchison northward to the Murray, through which winds the Goulburn River after its debouchment from the ranges. Here it is to be understood in a still more restricted sense—it is to be taken as including only that portion of the plain commanded by the works.

actual or projected, of the Goulburn irrigation scheme. This comprises, east of the river, the projected East Goulburn Irrigation Trust district, with an area in round numbers of 225,000 acres; and west of the river, the district of the existing Rodney Irrigation Trust, with an area of 278,000 acres, and that of the Echuca and Waranga Waterworks Trust, with an area of 272,000 acres, or about 775,000 acres in all.

The district of the proposed East Goulburn Irrigation Trust—it has not been actually constituted—includes a great part of the Shires of Shepparton and Numurkah, and smaller portions of the Shires of Goulburn, Euroa, and Yarrawonga.

Irrigation Trusts.

The Rodney Irrigation Trust district is nearly coterminus with the Shire of Rodney. The Echuca and Waranga Waterworks Trust district, comprising part of the Shires of Echuca and Waranga, has also been constituted. Within the area referred to as the Goulburn Valley there are also included the Towns of Shepparton, Numurkah, and Wunghnu, Tatura, Kyabram, and Mooroopna. These, which have a joint population of 5,260, are not reckoned as part of the area commanded by the works. That area is 775,000 acres on both sides of the river, with a total rural population of 10,400 persons, an annual rateable value of £145,000, and an immediately dependent urban population of 5,260, settled in six towns that are within the borders, though excluded from the area, of the irrigation district. Each of these towns, excepting Wunghnu, has a separate water service of its own, some of them dependent on the irrigation works as their source of supply. The lands on the east side of the river are supplied with water for domestic and stock use only by the Goulburn River, the Broken River (which is one of its tributaries), and the Broken Creek (which is an affluent of the Broken River), also by some artificial channels supplied chiefly by pumping from these sources. The west side of the river has a much more efficient system—a very complete reticulation, comprising nearly 400 miles of channels, supplied by gravitation from the national works constructed by the Government. These are ample to provide fully for domestic and stock wants, with a surplus available for the irrigation of a limited area.

MURCHISON WEIR.—GOULBURN RIVER.

The Murchison Weir.

The national works, designed to provide water for the service of the Goulburn Valley, comprise a weir on the river, about 8 miles above Murchison; a channel on the east side from the weir, northward about 36 miles; a channel on the west side, about 26 miles north-westerly, to a large reservoir to be constructed at the Waranga Swamp; and a channel from the Waranga reservoir, about 40 miles further north-westerly, to the crossing of the Campaspe River. Of these there have been completed to date the weir, the off-take regulators at the heads of both the eastern and western main channels, and about 15 miles of the channel on the west side, with two regulating sluices and offtakes on it. The weir is a large and costly structure of solid masonry, with flood-gates of cast and wrought iron, manipulated by turbine gearing, and lowering into chambers provided for them in the body of the work. The constructed portion of the western main channel has a normal mean width of 124 feet, by a carrying depth of 7 feet, and is capable of conveying a volume of rather more than 100,000 cubic feet of water per minute. The sum expended on these national works to date—inclusive of the cost of lands taken, the large area submerged above the weir, the provision of roads and bridges in lieu of those interfered with or destroyed by the works, and the other charges incidental to such an undertaking— has been £418,000; and a further sum of £754,000, or a total of £1,172,000, will be required for their completion. Besides this, the trusts have expended on works, chiefly for the supply of water for domestic and stock use, a sum of about £140,000 advanced to them by the Government; and will have to expend a further £800,000 before water can be made fully available for irrigation throughout their districts.

It will be understood that as the Goulburn River must of necessity be the source of water supply for irrigation within this district, and as on the east side of the river there has not yet been constructed a single mile of channel from the weir, there can be no irrigation on that side of the river. On the west side the main channel has been carried 15 miles, and the construction of a further 4 or 5 miles will be proceeded with immediately. The reticulation channels of both the Rodney and the Echuca and Waranga Trusts are supplied from the national channel. The works of the former are already capable of giving a supply for irrigation to part of the trust area, and they are being enlarged and extended so as, in time, to be able to supply the whole. Those of the latter are on a smaller scale, adapted to provide an ample supply for ordinary use, but not for irrigation, except in a very limited way. To enable them to carry a full irrigation supply they must be enlarged in the same way as those of the Rodney Trust are being now. It is within the area of the Rodney Trust, therefore, that any irrigated lands are to be looked for in the Goulburn Valley.

Irrigated Holdings.

Within the district of the Rodney Trust about 2,000 acres have been prepared and planted with fruits intended for irrigation, and a similar area has been prepared and laid down under various kinds of fodder crops, also intended for irrigation. The fruits most largely planted are raisin vines, and, after them, wine grapes, apricots, apples, and mixed fruits. The irrigated green crops are chiefly lucerne : and there are some areas of maize, sorghum, amber cane, and broom corn. The lands irrigated or prepared for irrigation are not in compact areas, but are scattered over a comparatively wide area—a circumstance which adds materially to the cost of supplying them with water, and in various other ways handicaps the cultivators. Some attempt has been made, however, to establish settlements here on similar lines to those at Mildura and Renmark. The Ardmona Estate, Mooroopna, containing 1,000 acres, was purchased by a syndicate, cut up, and sold in blocks varying from 10 to 100 acres to intending cultivators. The whole of the estate is commanded by the channels of the trust, and most of it has been planted with vines and fruit trees, and are now under irrigation. One of the blocks is devoted to the growth of nursery stock. The experience of the proprietor is that, with the climate and soil of the Goulburn Valley, irrigation is highly beneficial, improving both the quantity and quality of every description of fruit, the olive only excepted. Without water the raising of nursery stock would be impossible. The same parties who negotiated the subdivision and sale of the Ardmona property similarly operated on an area of land near Toolamba, also commanded by the trust's channel.

It is in this locality (the neighbourhood of Mooroopna) that there is to be found the greater part of the irrigated land within the district of the Rodney Trust. About 2 miles from Ardmona is the Lake Erie farm of Mr. Michael Kavanagh. On this property there are 60 acres laid down in lucerne, divided into paddocks and kept under irrigation. This land has maintained eight sheep to the acre throughout the summer. Mr. Kavanagh has also 16 acres under mixed fruits and 20 acres under raisin vines irrigated, the whole in excellent condition and bearing annually a heavy crop of fruit of unexceptionable quality. Several of Mr. Kavanagh's neighbours have areas under lucerne, chiefly used for beeves and dairy cattle, and plantations of vines and fruit trees. Wherever there is water available the lucerne paddocks and the plantations are under irrigation, and the area is continually being extended.

Population Wanted.

On the east side of the river, though there is no irrigation and no water yet available for the purpose, there is a considerable area of planted land. There are, in fact, more than 450 acres of plantations, two-thirds of which, or about 300 acres, are in close proximity to the Town of Shepparton. These plantations comprise apples, apricots, peaches, table grapes, and mixed fruits. There are no grapes grown specially for raisin-making nor for the production of wine, but the possibility of having to dispose of surplus produce, and eventually probably of the bulk of the crop, by drying, seems to be kept in view in all planting. Besides the fruit plantations there are a good many small areas of lucerne, maize, sorghum, and broom corn. The plantations generally are kept in a high state of cultivation, and it is surprising what crops of fruit are obtained, both as to quantity and quality, under dry tillage.

The devotion of the soil to intense culture (for which it is so well adapted), the utilization of the water of the magnificent river that nature has provided, and its application to the land as solvent for the stores of plant food it contains, can only be the work of time. The land is there far beyond the possibility of utilization by its present handful of occupants. It is of unexceptional quality ; the water is available, or is rapidly being made available, to stimulate its productiveness and develop its resources. It is not possible to doubt that time will solve the problem of how this development can be best accomplished.

The Lower Loddon and Gunbower Districts.

The Lower Loddon and Gunbower districts may be briefly described as including the alluvial plain that stretches from

Bridgewater, on the Loddon River, northward to theMurray, and embracing the lands adjacent to the latter river from the head of the Gunbower in the east to Swan Hill in the west. It is distinctly of deltaic formation. With the exception of some isolated tracks of hill country of comparatively small extent—such as the granitic outcrops of the Terricks Range, Mount Hope, and the Pyramid—it consists of an almost absolute level, built up of the water-borne silt carried down by the rivers from the high lands of the Dividing Range. The southern portion has been so built up by the agency of the Loddon: the northern by that of the Murray, of which the Loddon is a tributary. Its deltaic character is attested by the numerous old river channels that furrow its surface, and by the network of effluents and anabranches that constitute one of the most striking features, especially of the portion adjacent to the confluence of the rivers. That portion of the district bordering the Murray River and its anabranches—the Gunbower, Barr Creek, and Marrabit—is subject to inundation by the overflow of the river. Over some portions these floodings occur every winter: over a larger extent, some miles in width at some points, inundations occur only in winters when there is a high river: but no means has been yet suggested whereby one can foresee or foretell when these seasons of high flood will occur. For the protection of the river bank lands, earthen leveés have been built along portions of the frontage, and these have proved of service in saving the farmers' crops from destruction by the overflows. There are about 5 miles in length of levée so constructed by the Benjeroop and Murrabit Trust, and about 8 miles by the Swan Hill Irrigation Trust. There is also a further length of 2 or 3 miles constructed by the Water Supply Department for the special purpose of protecting the head of the Kow Swamp supply channel. This likewise affords protection to a limited portion of the area.

The gross area of the district treated of in this report is about 1,250,000 acres, whereof about four-fifths are irrigable, either by gravitation or by means of a lift of a few feet only. The rural population of the district is, in round numbers, about 11,000, and there is an urban population of 2,400 in the towns and villages of Swan Hill, Kerang, Boort, Durham Ox, Pyramid, Mincha, Macorna, and Cohuna. It is watered by the Loddon River and by the Murray and its effluents. The works for the distribution of the water supply are under the control of the Loddon United and Swan Hill Shire Waterworks Trusts, their function being limited, however, to providing for ordinary domestic and stock requirements. But a great part of the area, aggregating a total of 523,000 acres, is under the control of irrigation trusts that have been carved out of and excised from the old water trusts. Of these seven in the southern part of the district take their supply from the Loddon, namely, Tragowel Plains, East Boort, North Boort, Leaghur-and-Meering, Wandella, Twelve-mile, and Dry Lake. The Loddon itself is regulated and controlled by a national work—that is, a work under the direct control of the Water Supply Department—the Laanecoorie weir and dam, situate upon the river at a point about 16 miles in a direct line above Bridgewater. It has a storage capacity of 610,000,000 cubic feet, or 3,812,000,000 gallons—that is, one-sixth greater than the Malmsbury reservoir, as recently improved and enlarged. Its purpose is to regulate the river by storing water during flood, so as to maintain the flow during the dry seasons. The middle portion of the district has three existing irrigation trusts (Marquis Hill, Kerang East, and Macorna North). These will take their supply from a national work that is now approaching completion. A canal, consisting in part of an artificial cutting and in part following the line of natural creeks, will convey water from the Murray when in flood into a large reservoir, formed by embanking and otherwise improving the Kow Swamp. From the reservoir a channel will carry the supply for delivery to the trusts. The northern part of the district has five trusts adjacent to the Murray frontage and supplied from that river. These are the Cohuna, Koondrook, Myall, Benjeroop and Murrabit, and Swan Hill Irrigation. The areas of the trust districts are exceedingly various. The Tragowel Plains has nearly 250,000 acres, the Cohuna 100,000, while the Dry Lake has but a little over 1,500. The trust works are all in a condition to deliver water over the greater part of their areas, while most of the trusts have their schemes practically completed. The middle and northern portions of the district are supplied from the Murray—the former by means of the Kow Swamp scheme of works, the latter from the river direct ; or it would be more accurate to say that they will be so supplied when the projects in hand have been completed.

A present feature of the Lower Loddon and Gunbower country is the popularity of dairying among the smaller holders and the increasing output of dairy produce, chiefly separated cream to be sent to Melbourne for conversion into butter at the factories. To this industry irrigation is a priceless boon, and a sufficient supply of water for ordinary use a prime necessity. There must be good drinking water for the cattle, and a proper supply for the dairy. Winter-irrigated straw crops for conversion into ensilage would prove of immense value ; watered paddocks of lucerne and sorghum promote the health of the beasts, and augment the milk-giving faculty of the cows through the summer.

The necessity for an artificial water supply was here more obvious. The demand for a supply for irrigation is more urgent than in the Goulburn Valley. At the same time, the natural facilities for providing them are far less. This is especially true of the southern part of this district— that commanded by the water of the Loddon River. Still the available volume is such as, with a proper system of conservation and distribution, carefully supervised and wisely administered, to be capable of rendering immense service to the farmers.

The Castlemaine and Bendigo Districts.

The Coliban system of works, the principal portions of which were carried out during the years 1865-70, but which have since been much extended and improved, form, as is pretty generally known, the basis of the water supply to Castlemaine and Bendigo. The principal storage basin of the scheme is that on the Coliban River, at Malmsbury. Its original capacity, measured from the sill of the outlet to the level of the waste weirs, was 2,908,000,000 gallons : but, in consequence of the supposed insufficiency of the flood escapes, the whole of the storage was never fully availed of, and the practical capacity was thus no more than 2,400,000,000 gallons. Improvements carried out some four or five years ago have increased the available contents to 3,255,000,000 gallons. The catchment area of the reservoir includes 72,000 acres of country, with a mean annual rainfall varying from 28 inches in the lower to 45 inches in the upper portion, and the whole of which is of a character favorable for the discharge of the rain precipitated on its surface. Besides the principal reservoir, there are eleven minor storages scattered throughout the supply district, all of them except three— the Harcourt and the Upper and Lower Grassy Flat reservoirs—being connected to Malmsbury, and chiefly fed from it. From the Malmsbury reservoir the supply is carried in an open channel to the area served by the works. The distribution is by branch channels and by reticulations of iron piping. There are in all 187 miles of main and branch channels, and pipes are laid for the service of the tenements in the whole of the towns. The distribution area embraces the towns and villages of Castlemaine, Chewton, Fryers, Maldon, Elphinstone, and Taradale, Bendigo, Eaglehawk, Huntly, Lockwood, Marong, Raywood, and Sebastian, and some smaller hamlets, with the mining districts and part of the agricultural and horticultural lands adjacent thereto. There are also two small trusts supplied from the works of the Coliban system—the Harcourt and the Emu Valley Irrigation Trusts.

The original purpose of the Coliban system of works was to supply water for the mines of the Castlemaine and Bendigo districts ; and no doubt was entertained, at the time of their initiation, that they would bring in a revenue amply sufficient to warrant the outlay incurred for their construction. The service of the gold-fields towns was a secondary matter. The supply to the mines themselves—for sluice-washing auriferous earth, for engine boilers, and for the stamper boxes and ripple tables of the quartz batteries—was relied on as the main source of revenue.

The major portion of the irrigation from the Coliban system is of orchards and vineyards : a little water is used for raising green forage crops, but its total is quite insignificant. In the Harcourt and Barker's Creek portion of the Castlemaine district, there are over 500 acres of fruit planted. Almost the whole of this area is irrigated, in a greater or less degree, from the Coliban works ; and such plantations as are not now commanded by the channels have been laid out in anticipation of extensions.

The orchards are chiefly on the granitic soil formed from the detritus of the Mount Alexander Range. An idea of the success of the fruit-growing industry here will best be conveyed by describing one of the orchards. That of Mr. Lang is fairly typical of the better class of these properties. He has 25 acres planted in fruit (apples and pears predominating), other kinds being peaches, plums, cherries, table grapes, oranges, and lemons. The trees (apples and pears especially) bear heavily, and the fruit is of excellent quality. One tree during the past season yielded twenty cases of fruit ; a good many of them yielded fifteen to sixteen cases ;

but these are exceptional, a fair crop being six cases from each full-grown mature tree. Mr. Lang thinks that command of water is a condition essential to successful fruit-growing in the Castlemaine district. The bulk of the crop is disposed of in Melbourne, Bendigo, and Castlemaine, but a portion has during each of the past four years been exported to London. In the present season 600 cases of apples have been despatched to England, all packed in the modern American manner—that is, each separate apple rolled in a sheet of tissue paper. The cost of transit to London, in the cool chambers of the mail boats, is about 4s. 6d. per case, which, at recent prices, leaves a fair profit to the grower. The trade is enlarging. Besides fruit-growing there is a little dairying in the Barker's Creek district, and the two industries seem to run well together, the refuse from the cow-yards forming excellent manure for the trees. In the Campbell's Creek district, lying south-east from Castlemaine, there are about 350 acres planted with fruit, the bulk of which is cultivated dry, though some of the orchards get a partial supply from the pipe reticulations.

A few miles south-east from the City of Bendigo, in the valleys of the Sheepwash, Emu, and Axe Creeks, there are about 1,000 acres under plantations of various kinds. About 600 acres are under vines, and 400 acres are under other descriptions of fruit. None of this area is irrigated, but the necessity for watering during the past season has been painfully obvious : indeed, of late years, it has suffered a great deal from drought. The works of the Emu Valley Trust command the greater part of this area, and could be extended so as to command almost the whole. The vines are nearly all of wine varieties. Many of the vignerons—all the larger growers—are wine-makers, working up their own crops and purchasing those of their smaller neighbours. The wines command good—some high—prices, and are well in request. To the north of Bendigo, along the Huntly-road, and the valley of the Bendigo Creek, about 600 acres of old diggings have been taken up, under the provisions of a law recently passed, for fruit-growing, and about 250 acres have been reclaimed and planted with trees and vines. A good example in this way has been set by Mr. Carolin, late mayor of the city, who has invested a large sum in the business. About 400 acres are commanded by the Huntly race, and the balance by one of the pipes of the reticulation. Lower down the Huntly-road there are about 240 acres of orchards and vineyards, all commanded by the Huntly channel, and occasionally getting a supply from it. Along the Specimen Gully race, between Crusoe Gully reservoir and Eaglehawk, there are 150 acres under fruit and vines supplied in dry seasons, and in some measure in all seasons, from the channel. On this line, owing to the character of the soil, fruit cannot be successfully grown without command of water; while in the neighbourhood of the Huntly race it can.

The Wimmera District.

The country watered by the Wimmera River, its tributaries and effluents—or rather that portion of it that is commanded by the work of irrigation schemes existent, or that have been actually projected—may be described as lying within the following boundaries:—From the Town of Stawell, by a line about 18 degrees north of east to Clear Lake, 8 miles south-west of Noradjuha, a distance of 50 miles; thence by a line northerly, passing by Mount Arapiles to the inlet of Lake Hindmarsh, about 55 miles; thence by a line south-easterly to the debouchment of the Richardson, at Lake Buloke, 58 miles; thence by an irregular line southerly, following nearly the course of the Richardson River, the Swede's Creek, and the Melbourne to Adelaide railway line, about 60 miles to the commencing point. It includes an area of nearly 2,000,000 acres, about 170,000 of which in the north-west portion have been settled under the provisions of the mallee sections of the *Land Act* 1896. Excluding Stawell (which is strictly a mining town) it contains the following towns and villages, namely, Glenorchy, Lubeck, Murtoa, Minyip, Sheephills, Warracknabeal, Jung Jung, Horsham, Dimboola, Noradjuha, Natimuk, Donald, and Rupanyup, and several small hamlets. The entire urban population numbers 8,000. Of the towns mentioned Murtoa, Warracknabeal, Jung Jung, Horsham, Dimboola, Natimuk, and Donald have pipe systems of water supply administered by water trusts. A supply to Glenorchy is administered by the shire council. The rural population of the area numbers 16,000; and the annual rateable value of property in the rural district—that is, exclusive of the towns and villages—is in round numbers £246,000, an amount that appears high as compared with the valuation of other rural areas in the northern districts. Its affairs in the matter of water supply are administered—in the east by the Wimmera

United Waterworks Trust, and in the west by the Western Wimmera Irrigation Trust, and, as to a small portion, by the Lowan Shire Water Trust. The water supply to the Borough of Horsham is administered by a separate urban trust.

The whole of the area, if we except a small portion of the Grampians Range that intrudes on the southern boundary, is of alluvial formation, though generally much more irregular in profile than the eastern portion of the riverine plains in Victoria. The soil is generally of good quality, or from fair to good, of loam, varying from sandy to clayey; the subsoil more retentive than the surface soil, and with a varying infiltration of lime.

Excluding the portion held under the mallee settlement provisions about one-third of the area is held as originally selected in blocks not exceeding 320 acres; the remainder chiefly in blocks of from 640 upwards to 3,000 or 4,000 acres, but for the most part not exceeding 1,000 acres. There are also some half-dozen properties of larger dimensions, and about 20,000 acres of land are let in farms of from 100 to 300 acres each.

The farmers of the Wimmera district were among the first to avail themselves of the facilities offered by the Government for the provision of efficient systems of water supply in the rural districts. The leading features of their scheme are a succession of weirs on the Wimmera River at points favorable for diversion, and the construction of lines of channel, with distributaries for the service of every part of the area. The river weirs are the Glenorchy, the Ashens, the Longerenong, and the Dooen weirs, the main purpose of which is the diversion of water from the river, though they act to some extent as storages. There is also a weir at Horsham, whose sole purpose is to impound water for the supply of the town. From the Glenorchy weir a short artificial channel leads into the head of the Swede's Creek, an affluent of the Richardson River, which in turn empties itself into Lake Buloke. But for the supply thus artificially diverted from the Wimmera the Lower Richardson would in most years have no flow whatever, and when it ceases to flow it soon becomes so salt as to be unfit for ordinary use. Another short cut from the weir carries a supply into the head of the Dunmunkle Creek, from which diverge the Laen, Lallat and Minyip channels, and their numerous branches, and lower down the Carron channel and its branches. Like the Swede's Creek, the Dunmunkle Creek would have no flowing water in the greater part of its length in most years but for the water artificially diverted into it. From the Ashens weir is supplied the Ashens and Murtoa channel, with its numerous branches. The Longerenong weir diverts a supply into the Yarriambiac Creek—a natural effluent of the Wimmera, the supply to which would, however, be both scanty and precarious but for the influence of the weir in raising the surface level of the river and regulating the diversion. The Yarriambiac supplies the Bangerang channel and branches on the east and the Cat's Swamp channel and branches on the west; the surplus it carries to Lake Corong. From the Dooen weir a cutting of about a mile and a quarter leads to a pumping station. Here the water is pumped through an iron main a further distance of a mile and a quarter, with a rise of 54 feet, into a basin, whence is led the Dooen-Kalkee channel, with its numerous branches. A noteworthy feature of this portion of the works is that in seasons of drought, when the Wimmera at Dooen ceases to run, water can be delivered at the weir from the Wartook storage reservoir. The Wartook reservoir, in a valley of the Grampians near the head of the Mackenzie, is the only storage of any magnitude yet constructed for the service of the Wimmera country. It has a drainage area of nearly 30 square miles, and a capacity of 1,037,000,000 cubic feet, equal to rather more than that of the Yan Yean reservoir. From this storage the water flows down the natural course to the head of the plain at a point about 22 miles south from Horsham, thence a branch is diverted into the Burnt Creek, and thence again into the Wimmera at Dooen and at Horsham. From the same point is diverted the Natimuk channel, the Lower Mackenzie itself also, of course, getting a supply. At a distance of 7 miles down the Natimuk channel there is a diversion into the Norton Creek, which is crossed here; and 17 miles further down the channel bifurcates, the Natimuk branch being 19 and the Arapiles branch 25 miles in length. The Wimmera country has thus a good water supply for domestic and stock use—good, that is, as compared with the state of affairs before the days of water trusts and Government assistance in the form of loans. Doubtless it is susceptible of great improvement, by the provision of additional storages and by the extension and multiplication of the channels; that is a mere matter of time and cost. But neither the towns nor the country can now be said to be in any sense badly off for water. Besides the domestic supply the works are capable of affording something to be employed in irrigation, especially from the channels dependent on the Wartook storage.

The colony system of settlement has been attempted here with some show of success, the colonies being generally the result of the action of syndicates, who sell land to settlers at prices ranging from £10 to £20 per acre. Burnlea is close to the Wimmera River, and within the Borough of Horsham : it derives a supply of water from a branch of the channel from Wartook storage. It contains a total of 550 acres, all of which is reticulated with channelling. A considerable portion has been sold, chiefly to business people in Horsham, and of these 50 acres are planted with mixed fruits. Young Brothers' colony has also been all reticulated. The purchasers in the Young Brothers' colony are chiefly tradesmen and workmen settled in and about Horsham. £300 worth of produce — grapes, apricots, and peaches— were sold from the settlement in 1893, and the returns have since largely increased. Riverside is on the south bank of the Wimmera, a few miles above Horsham. It contains 430 acres, all reticulated, and all sold to actual or intending settlers, the bulk of whom are business people or mechanics from Melbourne and other towns. Of the latter a few have entered into possession, are settled, and working in the district. The holdings have been planted with vines and fruit trees. At Dooen there is an area of land subdivided for sale and settlement, reticulated, and supplied by a branch from the Dooen pumping main. About two-thirds of it have been planted with vines and fruit trees. Quantong is a co-operative settlement, on the right bank of the Wimmera River, about 12 miles west from Horsham. It contains 2,253 acres of sandy loam, whereof 500 acres have been disposed of, chiefly to mechanics and others from the towns. Some ten or twelve substantial wooden houses are built or in course of building by settlers, and several blocks of land have been planted. The Arapiles colony is near Mount Arapiles, 20 miles west from Horsham and 5 miles from the township of Natimuk. It contains 640 acres, whereof 200 have been sold in blocks of 10 acres and upwards, most of the purchasers being trades people in Natimuk and Horsham, though a few are of the agricultural class. Besides these colonies there are a number of individual holders who have patches of irrigation, either fruit trees, vines, or lands permanently laid down in fodder plants. Some are supplied from the channels, some by pumping from the river. These settlers cultivate fruit trees, lucerne, sorghum, and pastures. The fruits, other than grapes, comprise apricots, peaches, almonds, oranges, lemons, apples, and mixed fruits. The vines are chiefly of raisin varieties, though no raisins are yet made on any commercial scale, and there is no wine-making in the district.

CONCLUDING REMARKS.

These embrace by far the greater portion of the areas within Victoria where irrigation is now practised as an aid to agriculture. There are others, certainly. At Bacchus Marsh there are two small trusts, one of which has its scheme of works practically completed and in operation, the area operated upon, however, being exceedingly small. Then there are several trusts whose works are in process of construction, but have not yet proceeded so far as to be able to supply any water to irrigators. Among these are the Campaspe Trust, the scene of whose operations is the land on both sides of the Campaspe River, in the neighbourhood of Rochester; the Bairnsdale Irrigation Trust, formed with the view of irrigating the extensive and fertile area bordering the Mitchell River above Bairnsdale, known as the Lindenow Flats, and the country adjacent; and some others of less note.

As to the probable eventual outcome of irrigation in Victoria, it may be briefly summarized thus:—Many of us have been too sanguine: men are prone to be so in view of any novelty that promises increase of wealth. But, this admission being unreservedly made, there remains the solid fact that a large section of the land of this colony cannot be turned to its most profitable account without the aid of irrigation, the necessary water supply for which is likewise available; and that prominent among the accelerating or retarding causes in the realization of this profit must be the action of the State in guiding, promoting, or discouraging the movement.

THE MILDURA IRRIGATION COLONY.

In introducing a system of irrigation into Victoria, the Government not only passed the Irrigation Act, under which the various water supply trusts have been formed, but made special arrangements with a firm of Californian experts for the establishment of an irrigation colony—Mildura, on the Murray River, being the result. An extensive grant of land with liberal water privileges was given on easy terms to the Messrs. Chaffey Brothers, of Ontario, California, on condition that they would establish such an irrigation colony as would not only prove the suitableness of the mallee country for such purposes, but also serve as an object-lesson on irrigation to settlers in other parts of Victoria. The Mildura colony, which has now been ten years in existence, has proved the suitableness of the mallee for irrigation purposes, and has served as a valuable object-lesson in various branches of fruit-growing under irrigation, and the preservation and marketing of several varieties of fruit, although the colony itself, from a number of causes to be herein explained, has not been so successful as was at one time expected. It is sufficient for the present to say that the causes of such disappointment as has been met with in connexion with Mildura are in no way connected with the profitableness of irrigation as a system, or any natural unsuitableness of the soil or climate for the purposes originally intended.

FOUNDING THE COLONY.

Five years after the agreement was made with the promoters, Mr. Stuart Murray, the Chief Engineer of Water Supply, wrote as follows :—

"Any account of the progress of irrigation in Victoria that did not take note of Mildura would be incomplete. The Mildura settlement is the scene of the greatest experiment in irrigation yet undertaken here, and the success or failure of irrigation at Mildura would have largely influenced its success or failure throughout the colony. The Government has not invested money in the Chaffey enterprise as it has invested money in the form of loans advanced to trusts, and in the construction of costly national works in the Goulburn Valley, in the Loddon Valley, and throughout the settled portions of the dry northern districts : yet it has a distinct

CULTIVATING AN ORCHARD.—Mildura.

GATHERING FRUIT.—Mildura.

right of property in Mildura in virtue of the concessions it has made to its founders. They have been given, subject to the fulfilment of certain conditions on their part, a block of 50,000 acres of land as a free gift, with a further area of 200,000 acres on very favorable terms. But, more than all, they have had handed over to them a large share of the colony's inheritance in the waters of the Murray River—a concession, practically in perpetuity, of so much water as may be required for the complete irrigation of this enormous block of 250,000 acres, and for the service of the community of, it may be, 500,000 or more of people that will eventually dwell there.

"The agreement between the Victorian Government and the Messrs. Chaffey was signed in May, 1887, and possession of the property was entered upon on the 4th of August following. The progress may be briefly summarized as follows :—The present population numbers 4,000, of whom nearly one-half are actually engaged in the clearing, preparation, and cultivation of the soil, either as land-owners or as workmen. The area of land sold by the Messrs. Chaffey is, in round numbers, 17,000 acres, whereof 10,000 have been planted, 500 are under various kinds of annual or green crops, and an additional 3,000 are cleared and ready for cultivation or planting. The remainder are held for future improvement. Of the plantations about two-thirds consist of raisin vines. The others, in the order of their importance, comprise wine grapes, apricots, oranges and lemons, peaches, olives, and other fruits. The expenditure by the Messrs. Chaffey on works for the service of the settlement has been far in excess of that provided for by their agreement. These comprise eleven pumping plants (ranging from 200 to 1,000 horse-power each), 150 miles of main and 300 miles of secondary and distributing channels (whereof about 3 miles are lined with concrete, made from the local lime), together with syphons, flumes, bridges, and other secondary works.

"So much for the extent and character of the settlement and the work done. Now for the results of the work, in its financial and commercial aspects. So far the settlement has been maintained chiefly by the capital brought into it by the settlers themselves and by the expenditure of the firm of Chaffey Brothers and Co. Little of what it has produced has been sold to the outside world. No doubt a material contribution to the support of the settlers has been derived from their own produce. Some of them have earned a few pounds by growing fodder for the horses employed by the firm and in other similar ways, and one or two of the more energetic and enterprising have made a living by supplying fruit and vegetables to their neighbours. But all this contributes nothing to the solution of the main problem. Even the few tons of raisins and dried apricots purchased from the settlers by the firm last year, or the larger quantity purchased this year, go but a little way towards solving it. The price the firm will pay for these small lots of first produce is hardly any criterion of what the world will give for the general bulk of the crop, when the whole of the land is under cultivation and the limit of the local market has been reached. It is a fact that, at the present moment, as much as 5d. per lb. may be obtained in Melbourne for first-class samples of colonial-grown cooking raisins, and good currants fetch a price but slighly lower. In the London market, however, good currants are worth no more than 1½d. per lb., cooking raisins 2¼d., and the best table raisins 7d. The difference between the Melbourne and London prices is due to the import duty of 2d. per lb., the cost of freight, insurance, &c., and the addition of the charges of the merchant and shipper.

" The wine industry at Mildura is on a somewhat different footing from the dried-fruit business. Victorian wine may be fairly said to have already found its place among the beverages of the world. Rutherglen and Great Western are not so well or widely known as Bordeaux and Dijon, but they are undoubtedly in a fair way of becoming so. People who drink good wine, and who can afford to pay for what they drink, consume the wines of these localities, not because they can get no other, but of choice. They are drunk under their proper titles in England, and to some extent on the continent of Europe : and there is good reason to believe that they are used for blending purposes, or, in other words, for the production of high-priced French clarets. Victorian wine, therefore, may be said to have passed the ordeal. Its price, in competition with other wines of a like class, is established : and the grower who can live by his vineyard now may assume that he is in possession of a property that will maintain its value, and that will provide a living for himself and his descendants in perpetuity. But Mildura will not produce good wines of the claret and Burgundy class. Any attempt to produce these, in its soil and climate, would result in failure. But it will produce good

A RAISIN VINEYARD.- MILDURA.

wines of another class—heavy-bodied, rich, or fruity red wines, suitable for the manufacture of port or for blending with the thinner but more delicately-flavoured dry wines, will do well here. So also probably will the heavier class of sherries. The results thus far obtained from the vineyard of Messrs. Murray and Seal, in Deakin-avenue, point to this conclusion : and there is every reason to think that the crops will be heavy. The deep soil, strongly impregnated with lime, the hot sun, and the ever-available water, will insure a large production of must. For high-class brandy Mildura will, in all probability, attain a reputation that will be worth money to vignerons.

"It would be hardly possible to speak too highly of the manner in which the Messrs. Chaffey's firm has given effect to their part of the agreement relating to the Mildura settlement, or the pains they have taken to instruct, guide, and assist the settlers there. It has been such as to entitle them to all the assistance and support the Government can fairly and lawfully give. The position and prospects of the cultivating land-owners is as hopeful and promising as reasonable men will expect. By the outlay of a little capital and a good deal of hard work, the industrious may be assured a present livelihood, under conditions that to most will prove agreeable. The future promises competence, independence, fortune, to those who are willing to labour and wait."

Progress Suspended.

Soon after this date trouble arose at Mildura. The long period of prosperity in Victoria began to give place to commercial depression. Many banks and other financial institutions failed, and the promoting company—Chaffey Brothers Limited—which had been lavish in its expenditure began to get into serious difficulties. The income of the company depended largely upon the selling of land in the irrigation colony, and land sales almost entirely ceased, partly on account of the general depression, and partly owing to serious disputes which arose between the promoters and the settlers. These disputes were continued for a lengthened period, and finally the promoting company was compelled by adverse circumstances to go into liquidation. As the promoters were no longer able to perform their functions under the contract the Government was obliged to step in and make arrangements for the proper carrying on of the colony.

Careful inquiry was made, the various interests concerned were considered, and an arrangement, which it is expected will be satisfactory, was made under an Act of Parliament passed into law during the year 1897.

The New Arrangement.

Under the Act of 1897 the affairs of Mildura are carried on by the irrigation trust which is elected by the settlers, and possesses the necessary rating powers. The Government of Victoria assists the trust with a sum of £40,700, and if necessary, with an additional £2,000 per annum for five years. Settlers had, in many instances, mortgaged their holdings, and the promoting company had issued debentures. Under this arrangement mortgagees have been required to reduce the rate of interest, and advance to the trust the sum of £1,500, while the debenture-holders are required to advance £2,500, and expend upon planting and improving property a further sum of £7,500 within five years. The various sums provided are for putting the channels in proper repair, keeping the pumps going, and generally securing the successful carrying out of the original scheme. The financial troubles of the promoters, the necessity of making these arrangements, and the delays which have necessarily taken place have seriously interfered with the progress of the settlement, and caused great loss and disappointment to settlers, but under the new arrangements it is hoped and expected that Mildura will soon enter upon another era of prosperity.

The Future of Mildura.

If Mildura's progress had been checked by any disappointing results of irrigation or fruit-growing there would be less hope of a successful future for the settlement. As it is those who are best acquainted with the resources of the settlement are the most hopeful of its future. The returns from the irrigated orchards and vineyards have exceeded expectations both as to quantity and quality. One source of local disappointment must be mentioned, and that is the discovery that there are limited patches of alkaline soil which has proved to be unsuitable for various fruits, especially fruits of the citrus family. It was not until irrigation had been carried on for some time and the application of water had brought the silt from an underground stratum that this defect was discovered. The area of such soil, however, is comparatively limited, and the indications of alkaline

A YOUNG OLIVE GROVE.—MILDURA.

deposits are now well known, so that further loss is not likely to be sustained from this cause. Such lands will in future be avoided by planters: they will be devoted to the growing of cereal and fodder crops, and there is a very large area available for extending the orchards and vineyards. The yields of fruit as has been said have exceeded expectations, and all qualified judges who have seen the fruit have spoken of them in the highest terms.

A railway connecting Mildura with Melbourne, Ballarat, Bendigo, and other large towns is necessary to insure the success of the settlement. It was expected by the first settlers that a railway would soon be constructed, but soon after the period of colonial depression the proposal to make this line was indefinitely postponed. Recently, however, the matter has been again receiving public attention, and the Government are now seriously inquiring into the prospects of such a line proving remunerative. There is a growing opinion among public men that a railway to Mildura cannot be much longer delayed, and there is no doubt that railway communication would give a great impetus to the settlement. New-comers to Victoria, who may intend entering upon fruit-growing, would do well to see Mildura before settling down. Owing to the check which this settlement has met with, planted orchards and vineyards in full bearing can be purchased much cheaper than they are ever likely to be again, and investors who avoid the small patches of alkaline land already described have good prospects of doing well.

FLOCKS AND HERDS.

The keeping of live stock may be considered the pioneering branch of Victorian agriculture, for it was as pastures for flocks and herds that the fertile lands of the colony were first occupied. The rich natural pastures, and the genial climate of the Port Phillip district, attracted pastoralists from the adjacent island of Tasmania and the more northern portion of New South Wales, and the occupation of the country for grazing purposes led to the discovery of gold with its influx of population, and the introduction of the various branches of agriculture. At first stock-raising was carried on upon large divisions of country called "runs," which were leased from the Crown, and afterwards when a great portion of the land was alienated large estates were acquired, upon which the grazing of sheep, cattle, and horses were carried on, while the keeping of live stock also became an important feature of the farming system adopted by settlers who acquired smaller holdings. In the colony, therefore, we have the breeding of sheep and cattle as a separate industry, as well as a department of general farming. Owing to the excellence of the natural pastures and the mild climate, grazing has from the beginning continued to be highly profitable, the small amount of labour involved having been a favorable condition where wages have always been high.

SHEEP.

The merino wools of Victoria (first known as Port Phillip) are the finest in the world. Mr. G. A. Brown, author of *The Merino Sheep in Australia*, writes as follows upon the introduction of the merino into the colony:—"Victoria, under the old name of Port Phillip, was the first of the Australian Colonies to demonstrate to the world that merino wool of the exceptional fineness, length of staple, softness, and lustre could be grown in large quantities on the wide pasture lands. For nearly half-a-century the wool produced by the famous flocks of Victoria has held a foremost place in the estimation of European manufacturers, and has always realized the highest prices in the markets of Europe. Though great strides have been made by the flock-masters in the other Australasian Colonies, Victoria still holds her pride of place in the front rank. The advantage that Victoria possesses over other pastoral lands in the production of merino wool, of the highest quality, is in a measure due to

MUSTERING CATTLE FOR MARKET.

the skill of her flock-masters ; but it must be admitted that the beauty of Victorian wool is mainly owing to the climate and pastures of the country. In summer the heat as measured by the thermometer is very great, but such is the character of the atmosphere that Europeans can work under the blazing sun, and in the greatest heat, without injury to their health. In winter the cold is never excessive ; snow is seldom seen save on the highest mountains. Frosts are frequent, but not so severe as to injure the stock, and the sharpest frost is dissipated before the sun is a couple of hours high. The climate much resembles that in which the merino flocks were reared in their old home in the Spanish Peninsula, when they passed the summer in the mountains of Montanat, the winter on the plains of Estremadura. By some people it has been thought that in this peculiarity of climate lies the secret of the beauty of Victorian merino wool."

THE LAND OF THE GOLDEN FLEECE.

"Victoria," says the same authority, "has been justly called the land of the golden fleece, for it is her golden fleeces that have brought wealth to the country more than any other industry. This colony is another illustration of the truth of the old Spanish proverb—'Sheep have golden feet, and whenever the print of their footstep is seen the land is turned to gold.' The originals of the Victorian merino flocks were obtained from the mother colony of New South Wales and from the adjacent island of Tasmania. The country was fortunate in having for its first inhabitants men having sufficient skill, backed up by a fair amount of capital, to secure the finest sheep in both colonies. It is, however, to Tasmanian flocks that the best Victorian studs trace their origin, and even now rams from the island flocks are highly prized, and realize very high prices at the annual ram fairs held in Melbourne. The first to introduce sheep into Victoria were the Messrs. Henty, who sailed from Launceston in 1834, and settled down near Portland, now a small town on the coast of Victoria. These gentlemen were not only the first to introduce sheep in Victoria, but they were the first colonists who set foot in the land. To Mr. T. Henty and his sons Australia is greatly indebted for the introduction of merino sheep of the highest class. The flock was formed in England, towards the end of the last century, with pure merinos obtained from the flock kept by H.M. George III. The following notice of this flock appears in Thos. W. Horsefield's

History of Sussex:—'In the year 1796, Thomas Henty, Esq., purchased the demesne lands in this parish (West Tarring), consisting of 281 acres. . . . . The breed of merino sheep has been brought by Mr. Henty to great perfection, and from his flock many have been sent to New South Wales.' Mr. Henty took first prizes wherever he exhibited his sheep in England, till at last he became an exhibitor merely for honour, being barred from taking prizes on account of the immense superiority of his sheep over those of any other flock in Great Britain. This flock wandered a long distance before it rested in its final home in the west of Victoria. A portion was shipped to Western Australia in 1829 in charge of two of Mr. Henty's sons; but, finding the sheep did not thrive, they shipped them on board the *Cornwallis* and sailed for Tasmania, where they were joined by their father with the rest of the flock. Being unable to obtain the grant of land he was led to expect on leaving England, Mr. Henty sailed for the mainland of Australia, and took up his residence at Portland Bay, in what was then an unknown land. Sheep from Mr. Henty's flock have been used in many of the old and most famous studs of Victoria; but the flock itself, owing to bad management and neglect, has been entirely lost.

"Another source whence early Victorian colonists obtained merino sheep was at the annual sales held by the Van Diemen's Land Company. This company was formed in 1827 with the patriotic object of relieving England from dependence upon foreign countries for a supply of fine wool. The company imported all descriptions of stock into Tasmania, and in one year expended £30,000 in the purchase of merino sheep from the best flocks in Germany. Many private individuals in those days imported Saxon merinos, and of their produce a fair share of the finest specimens found their way across the straits to the rising young colony of Port Phillip. From New South Wales some good sheep were obtained, but almost the only flock of any note was the celebrated Camden flock, established by Captain Macarthur in 1797 with a few pure merinos imported from the Cape of Good Hope. These were the first merinos ever brought to Australia. The only sheep added to this flock were a few purchased by Captain Macarthur from George III.'s stud. Since that time the flock has been bred without the addition of any foreign blood. The Macarthur family lost their old flock, but it has been preserved in Victoria, and is now in

the possession of the Hon. William Campbell. The Camden sheep did much good to the Victorian flocks, there being scarcely a leading stud flock which does not owe some of its excellence to an infusion of Camden blood. In a few studs, French sheep, from the Rambouillet flock, have been used, and in one or two others American merinos, from Vermont, have been introduced ; but the finest sheep in Victoria are descended from Saxon merinos, and those are most esteemed that have no other blood."

The Most Valuable Wool in the World.

Mr. G. A. Brown, quoted above, pronounces as follows upon the character of Victorian wool :—

" With a wide extent of the finest pasture land, and a climate so genial that it was named by the first settlers 'Australia Felix,' it is not surprising that Victoria soon outstripped her neighbours in the production of merino wool of the highest quality. It was noticed by the first colonists that the sheep bred in Victoria grew wool of quite a different character to that produced by Tasmanian or New South Wales flocks. The staple was longer, the wool was softer and had a brighter lustre than had ever before been seen on merino sheep. Beside it other wools looked mean and dull. In its brilliancy and softness it seemed to reflect the sunny skies under which it was growing. The Port Phillip wool became the favorite with European manufacturers, and ever since it has maintained its place as the most valuable merino wool in the world."

Farmers' Sheep.

The keeping of sheep on farms has increased with the development of Victorian agriculture. With the first extension of agricultural settlement over the various districts of the colony a system of continuous grain-growing was introduced, which was followed after a few years by a combination of cultivation and grazing. For the purposes of this improved system sheep offered many advantages, and consequently the farmers' flocks became an interest of increasing importance. Although sheep-keeping has been greatly extended among farmers, and increased attention has been given of late years to the improvement of the stock, there is still ample room for development in both particulars. Owing to the special character of the fine wools produced under the exceptionally favorable climatic conditions, the merino breeds have received the largest share of attention, but during recent years the smaller difference between the relative values of fine and long wools, together with the prospects of an increasing export trade in frozen mutton and lamb has brought several of the English breeds into increasing favour. The Lincoln breed which has long had its supporters not only among farmers, but also among some of the large estate-owners, is being more extensively used, and recently flocks of Downs sheep, as well as of Leicester, Romney Marsh, and Cotswold, have been established by farmers. The suitableness of these breeds to the requirements of farming under modern conditions is likely to lead to their extensive adoption.

Wool Exports.

In 1836 the number of sheep in the colony was 41,332, and the quantity of wool exported in 1837 was 175,081 lbs. In ten years afterwards the colony possessed about 3,400,000 sheep, and exported 6,406,950 lbs. of wool. Progress after this date was steady, reaching in 1896, a total of 13,180,943 sheep with exports of wool amounting to 116,902,509 lbs. The value of wool exported, the produce of Victoria, in 1896 was £4,011,962. Owing to the reduced price of wool in the markets of the world, increased production has not been able to maintain the total export value of this staple at the standard of some twenty years ago, but production is now upon such a scale that a small rise in the market would soon swell the volume of value beyond previous limits. The extensive wool stores of Melbourne are amongst the prominent features of the city, and during recent years large quantities of this wool have been sold in the colony, buyers from all parts of the world attending the local sales in order to obtain supplies at first hand. From 60 per cent. to 70 per cent. of the colony's wool product is now disposed of at the local sales. The possibilities of increasing production being considerable, it is likely that exports of wool will increase and that this staple will maintain its place among the leading contributors to the sum of the colony's wealth.

Light Horses.

The first need of the pastoral settlers who occupied the extensive grazing lands of the colony was for riding horses, and this need was supplied by the importation of thorough-bred stock from England. In the earlier times of the

colony racing was established as the most popular amusement, and the hacks used in doing the pioneering work of the colony soon became remarkable for speed and endurance. A liking for good horses thus easily established has been maintained through all subsequent changes. The meetings of the Victoria Racing Club, at the Flemington course, near Melbourne, have become national events, and racing is a popular sport in all the country districts, while the importation and breeding of thoroughbred horses receive a large share of attention in all parts of the colony. Light driving horses are much used in colonial life, and their breeding is an important branch of rural industry. During recent years the American trotting horse has been introduced, while ponies of all kinds, which have long been represented, are becoming more numerous. The principal outside market is the Indian army, and to this Victoria sends large numbers of remounts and artillery horses.

Draught Horses.

The discovery of gold and the introduction of agriculture caused a demand for draught horses, and colonists from the first showed a preference for good animals. Importations of high-class stallions and mares from Scotland and England were at once introduced, and systematic breeding was introduced, the standard having been continuously raised by fresh importations. Local conditions proving highly favorable, the early breeders were successful, and they have been followed by increasing numbers of imitators, so that Victoria has not only been able to supply its own requirements, but has sent large numbers of draught horses to the neighbouring colonies. English bred horses are represented in the colony, but the more popular breed is the Clydesdale. There have been fluctuations in the values of good draught horses, but on the whole the business of the breeder has been a profitable one, while owing largely to the demand created by the mining development in Western Australia the prospects at the present time are highly encouraging. The number of horses of all kinds in the colony increased from 180,342 in 1873 to 431,547 in 1894.

Cattle.

In the pioneer days of the colony cattle increased so rapidly, and the consumption of the limited population was so small, that large numbers of the stock had to be boiled down for the tallow. which. with hides. constituted an exportable product. This state of things was changed by the influx of population which followed the discovery of gold. and cattle-raising became a profitable industry. Settlers from the first believed in keeping good stock. so that the Shorthorn and Herefords were introduced at an early date. The Shorthorn herd retained the most permanent hold of public favour. and in the 70's there was a " Shorthorn boom " in Victoria. during which as high as 4.000 guineas was given for an imported " Duchess " bull and 2.000 guineas for a locally bred heifer. A period of low prices followed, and several of the best herds were broken up. resulting in stock animals of the first quality being widely distributed over the colony. A number of first-class stud herds have been retained. and the general stock of the country has been more graded up, while Victoria continues to do a good business in stud animals with some of the other colonies. There are pure herds of Herefords and Polled Angus cattle. with a few Devons; but the Shorthorn is the most popular of the beef-producing breeds. In 1873 the cattle of the colony numbered 883.763, and there was from that date a gradual increase. reaching 1.833,900 in 1894.

Dairy Cattle.

The popular milking breeds of cattle. viz.. Ayrshires and Jerseys. were introduced at an early date by the importation of pure stud animals, and since the recent extension of dairying the numbers have greatly increased while Holsteins and Kerries have been added. By the use of these herds the ordinary cross-bred dairy herds of the colony are being improved. but it cannot be claimed that the average milking qualities of the dairying cattle are satisfactory. Dairying has increased too rapidly for the breeding of the best kind of cows to keep pace with the demand. Breeding. however. is receiving some attention, and the use of the milk tester will enable our dairymen in a few years to produce a more profitable class of stock. That dairying should have proved highly remunerative by the use of the ordinary stock of the country before breeding for the special purpose could be carried out, gives an indication of the liberal margin of profit possessed by the industry. The returns for 1896 show a total of 462,578 cows on dairy farms, and 217,930 calves.

A GROUP OF CALVES.